The Good The Bad
and Everything Inbetween

Phoenix Saige Whytock

AuthorHouse™
1663 Liberty Drive
Bloomington, IN 47403
www.authorhouse.com
Phone: 1-800-839-8640

© 2011 Phoenix Saige Whytock. All rights reserved.

No part of this book may be reproduced, stored in a retrieval system, or transmitted by any means without the written permission of the author.

First published by AuthorHouse 8/22/2011

ISBN: 978-1-4634-4426-6 (e)
ISBN: 978-1-4634-4427-3 (hc)
ISBN: 978-1-4634-4428-0 (sc)

Library of Congress Control Number: 2011914200

Printed in the United States of America

Any people depicted in stock imagery provided by Thinkstock are models, and such images are being used for illustrative purposes only. Certain stock imagery © Thinkstock.

This book is printed on acid-free paper.

Because of the dynamic nature of the Internet, any web addresses or links contained in this book may have changed since publication and may no longer be valid. The views expressed in this work are solely those of the author and do not necessarily reflect the views of the publisher, and the publisher hereby disclaims any responsibility for them.

This Book… is dedicated to more people than I know what to do with… no not really.

I have a list, just bare with me here for a moment.

My dear daddy who, instead of telling me fairytales at night of cute little woodland creatures, always told me stories of his adventures at sea that always happened to start with, "Fairytale starts with: Once upon a time, a sea story starts off with: Now this ain't no shit," no I'm not shiting you. I love him 10x more for it.

My mum for getting me started and helping me the whole way through (EVEN IF YOU WERE BRUTLY HONEST! …nawh it wasn't that bad. Ha-ha)

And then there's God. All I have to say is, thank you for giving me the joy to write.

Now, can someone shoot me? I feel like I'm rambling.

Contents

1. Loving Wildflowers — 1
2. Never Let Me Go — 89
3. Bury Me in the Frozen Ground; Bury Me in a Blanket of Rose Petals — 127
4. Snow — 139
5. Finding Balance — 153
6. Crash — 193
7. Wake Up — 205
8. Welcome to My Silly Life — 217
9. The Perfect Match — 231
10. Goodbye — 243
11. I Will Follow You Into The Dark — 253
12. We Are Born Again — 285
13. Goodbye — 286
14. Hello — 287
15. Surrender — 289
16. For You — 290
17. Naked — 292
18. If I Die Today — 293
19. White — 294

Loving Wildflowers

Chapter One

In a white cottage surrounded by a field of flowers far from the city, lives' a girl with light blonde hair, one blue eye and one green. Her name is Marie and she loves to pick the wildflowers that grow in the fields....

"Marie can you set the table for two more?"

Marie looked up from the table she was setting and stared at her mother who was standing behind her, with confusion, "Why? Is it not just the two of us?" She asked sliding a piece of her lightly curled blonde hair behind her ear.

Her mother smiled at her, "We are having guests over to stay for a few days, Mr. Balvien and his stepson Alex have just flown over from Germany and I want them to feel at home when they stay with us." She said patting her daughter's soft cheek lightly before walking across the old hardwood floors into the kitchen.

The sun was low in the sky as Maria set the table grabbing two more plates from the cream colored cupboard. The light from the sun set the room in a glow of warm yellow and orange. The cottage wasn't fancy and new but rather old, it was located in the country of southern France set on fifty acres of land and fields. The cottage itself was well cared for, it had been passed down from her father's family for over a hundred and twenty years. The Dumas family had been, and still are, farmers. Though Maria and her mother are not, Dumas's are spread around the country sides of France like the flowers that surround their quaint home.

After the table was set and after Marie made sure everything was set in its place around the house, she went up to the second floor and walked down the hallway, her bare feet creaking on the hard flooring; the house was over a hundred years old so you couldn't blame it for its moans. Maria thought it gave her home character and life which suited her fine.

Stepping into her room, she shut the door behind her quietly, padded over to her closet, and pulled from it a light white halter dress and a pair of white laced ballet flats. Walking over to her bed she laid the items on the quilt, stripping her loose fitting jeans off and pulling her white embroider peasant top off she stepped into the dress pulling it up and over her somewhat small chest, tying it at the back of her neck in a knot. Slipping her shoes on she went to stand in front of her full length mirror.

Marie stared at herself curiously her reflection staring curiously back. Marie wouldn't consider herself ugly, but she wasn't some rare beauty either, she was just Marie. With light wavy blond hair, she never wore makeup and she stood at 5'5 her figure was small in the bust and backend, and trim every place else with little curves. The part she liked most about herself though were her eyes, the left was bright blue while the right was a leafy green, she loved her eyes as they were the only thing about her that stood out and made her different.

Marie looked away from the mirror and took her father's picture from her nightstand, going over to her bed, she lay back against her pillows, legs crossed in front of her, "Hi papa, it's Marie." She laughed at herself for a second knowing she didn't have to say who it was.

Her father had died of a heart attack six years ago when she was eleven, the doctors didn't know what had caused it; they said it could have been caused by stress on his body and of little rest. They had had a small funeral with just family that lived close by and buried him in a small patch in the field a bit away from the house.

"Mamma invited guests over; she said they are from Germany. I wonder what they'll be like. Mamma says they're going to be staying with us for a few days. I don't know the father's name but his son's name is Alex, though just between us, I don't get why mamma invited them in the first place. Does she know the dad or something and why did they fly all the way out to the middle of France instead of staying in Germany?" Marie sighed, pursing her lips in thought, why had mother decided to tell her at last minute? It's not as if she would have objected. It would be nice to have someone else around the house for a few days, "I'll probably find out at dinner, right papa?" She heard the front door open, voices could be heard talking and then the door shut, "well it sounds like they're here, I'll tell you how it goes." Marie gave a small kiss to the top of the silver frame and placed it back down on the night table.

Getting up from the bed, she straightened her dress smoothing out any creases, brushing her fingers through her hair one more time she took a deep breath and walked out of her room ready to meet their visitors.

★★★★

Marie walked down the stairs and turned into the living room. A middle aged man with graying hair at the temples stood by her mother chatting with her; Marie stared at the back of who she presumed was Alex. All she could see was his tight black clothes and a mass of black hair reaching passed his shoulders slightly, clearing her throat to announce that she was there all eyes turned to look at her as she took the last stair.

She approached the two males and her mother with a small, but pleasant, smile. "Hello."

"David, Alex, this is my daughter Marie." Marie's mother introduced.

David smiled at Marie his eyes crinkling at the ends, "Hallo Marie," he said, his accent was thick as the words rolled off his tongue, "it's very nice to meet you, and Anaïs has told me so much about you. You look so much like your father has anyone ever told you that?"

Marie shook her head no, "you knew my father?"

"We where friends in university, you have his smile."

Marie grinned at David, she liked this man, he was very kind, "Will you tell me about him when he was younger?" She asked, her eyes lighting up with the thought.

"If we have time, your mother here tells me that she intends to keep you busier than a bee." He teased with a chuckle.

His laugh reminded her greatly of her papa, she smiled at the man before turning to Alex now, and she noticed he was looking her up and down as if trying to find flaws in her bodily appearance, she didn't like it. "Hello?" She said hesitatingly.

The boys brown eyes flew up to meet her blue and green ones, "your eyes are different colors." He said bluntly, his accent, Marie noticed, was lighter that his father's but still distinct.

Marie raised an eyebrow at him, "yes. They are, you're very observant."

"It's weird."

She turned to her mother, "Il n'est pas très gentil." *He's not very nice.* Anaïs tsk-ed and gestured for her to go on. Swallowing, she tried again, "Are you hungry?" He hummed a reply. "Dinner is ready; if you want, I can show you to the table?" He hummed again. Marie sighed, it seemed he didn't want to speak. "Come." Taking his hand in hers, she tried to lead him in the direction of the dining room, but he pulled his hand from hers.

"I can follow just fine." He snapped at her, glaring while he did.

"Alex be good, she is just trying to be nice to you, so stop being so rude." David scolded, giving his stepson a look.

Grunting in turn, he stomped passed her without a word. Marie ran quickly to follow him, leaving the two adults to themselves.

David sighed, rubbing the bridge of his nose, his eyes pulled shut tight, "Anaïs, I am so sorry."

Anaïs gave him a sad smile, "Don't worry so much. Alex will get used to it here, and he will get used to Marie and me, don't worry. Have you told him about your plans to move out here?"

The older man groaned, "No I haven't, and I won't tell him now. Did you see the way he acted to Marie? No, I'll tell him tonight when we're alone." He stated, nodding his head in a manner.

"If you think it's best, then that is what you must do." She said before clapping her hands together, "Now we must go eat because I prepared a meal and I don't want for it to get cold."

★★★★

The four sat around the white table passing around brightly colored bowls. Nothing was heard except for the clatter of utensils touching the dishware. The salad was placed back in the center along with the pasta; everyone started to eat quietly, concentrating on their food, a tense silence falling over the room.

Anaïs cleared her throat, wiping her mouth on her napkin; she looked at Alex, "How is the food? Is it alright?"

Alex nodded his hair falling over his shoulders in the process, "It's good."

"And you, David?" She asked, turning to the older man. "Have you tried anything like it before?"

David laughed, "Nothing like it before, Anaïs, it's wonderful." He said.

Anaïs grinned, pleased at the compliment, and turned to her daughter, trying to catch her eye. Marie's head was bent as she picked at her food, "Marie?" She watched as her daughter's head shot up, looking in her direction with question in her eyes. She looked towards Alex and then back again to Marie. She got the idea.

Marie set her fork down silently and turned to look at the boy who was looking down at his plate, not touching it. "Are you all right? You're not eating." He picked up his fork, took a bite of the pasta, and set the fork down again as he chewed, "How do you like France so far?" He shrugged. Looking at her mother for help, she noticed she was talking to Alex's father. She was at a loss for words trying to find something to say to the boy. "Do you like flowers?" She tried.

Alex turned to the girl who kept questioning him, why couldn't she just stop talking and leave him alone? "No I don't like flowers...not anymore." He muttered before looking away.

"Why not? I love flowers, don't they make you happy?" Marie asked, ecstatic he had answered.

Alex sighed, annoyed that the girl had not left him alone. "No they do not make me happy and it's none of your business why I don't like them." He snapped.

Anaïs and David turned to the two in question, watching them.

"I'm sorry, I didn't mean anything by it, I was just curious." She breathed in a small voice.

Alex stood up from the table with a jerk. "It's better not to stick your nose into other people's business when you don't belong there," he said so low that it was almost not heard. He scooted his chair back and left the table; moments later, they heard the front door swing open and slam shut.

Marie looked worriedly at her mother, "Est-ce que je devrais le suivre et lui demander pardon?" *Should I go after him and apologize?*

Anaïs looked at David, "Do you want Marie to go after him?"

David shook his head, "Leave him, and let him cool down. When he gets back I'll talk to him, tell him everything," He glanced at Marie, "Marie, could you try and befriend him, he needs a friend right now. I know he hasn't been the most pleasant to you but really, he's a nice boy, give him time. He's gone through a lot in the past months."

Marie thought for a moment before answering. "Oui, s'il le faut, je le ferai." *Yes if I must, I must.* With that, she got up from the table and began to clear away the dishes.

Chapter Two

Marie made her way to her room silently, closing her door behind her quietly. Leaning her back against the wood, she took a deep breath and let it out. Things could have gone a lot smoother, she thought closing her eyes briefly before reopening them. Walking over to her closet, she stripped out of her dress and hung it back up, and stepping out of her shoes in the process, she placed them neatly inside the smaller room closing the closet door after.

Walking over to her dresser, she opened the second drawer and pulled out a thin, soft, cream colored night gown. Letting the fabric fall over her body, it came to just below her knees. Shutting the drawer, she grabbed a small hair tie from on top of the dresser and pulled her hair into a loose pony-tail to the side.

Marie took her father's picture off her nightstand as she sat on her bed crossing her legs and leaning back into her pillows. "Hello papa, dinner was, well it could have gone better but it could have also gone a lot worse, David your friend from college is the father. He reminds me of you, you know it's as if a part of you is in him or something, the way he talks and acts, it's wonderful really. Alex though, is another case. He does not seem to like it here or me for that matter. David said that he isn't like that, so I'm guessing something happened. He wears a lot of black and dark makeup, I was going to ask him if he had anything lighter to wear since it will get hot wearing all the darker clothing, but he ran out before dinner was finished. Maybe papa, I can help him."

She thought for a moment, "I wonder what he looks like, without all the makeup on I mean. I bet he looks beautiful, not that he's not now it's just…" She paused shaking her head a bit, "Hmmm, never mind, papa. Bonne nuit." *Good night.* She set her father's photo on her nightstand again and opened the drawer that was attached; pulling out a book, she shut the drawer and settled comfortably on her bed. Flipping to the beginning of the story, Marie began to re-read the story of *Orgueil et Préjugés*.

★★★★

Little over an hour had passed since she had started to read, the sun that had started to set during dinner had finally gone down, leaving the moon to take its place.

Marie was well into the seventh chapter when she heard a door close from somewhere down stairs. Shutting her book, she looked curiously to her door getting up from her bed she walked over to it, opening it just a crack she peeked into the hallway. Alex had just reached the top stair by that time, Marie thought he looked tired. Just as she was about to open the door further to ask if he was ok, David stepped out of his own room and looked at his stepson.

"We need to talk." He said seriously before reentering his room.

Alex stood there for a second looking down at the floor. He sighed and turned into his father's room shutting the door behind him silently but still a sound echoed through the silent hallway.

Marie looked away and closed her door, walking over to her window she looked up to the sky. The stars left no black to be seen, the light from the many balls of gas creating a twinkling light, the moon a crescent in the middle. She placed a hand lightly over her mouth in thought, she wondered what Alex and his father where talking about.

★★★★

Alex walked over the bed that was pushed against the wall, and sat down. Looking at David, he watched as his stepfather paced quietly, his eyebrows knitted together in concentration.

"I need to tell you something and I don't want you to get upset." David said when stopping his pacing and turned to his stepson, "You need to know this is for the good of all of us."

Alex rolled his eyes, "what David?"

David took a deep breath, "well, we're moving here, to France. Very soon actually, that's why where here; Anaïs is going to help me find a place out here in the country. Also this will be a good chance for you to… get use to life, I guess I would say." He shook his head turning to face the wall, "You've been so dead to us lately, and I just wish you would come back to being yourself. I don't like seeing you this way."

All was quiet after that, Gordon didn't know what else to say and Alex didn't know what *to* say. His nostril's flared as he clenched his jaw together.

"When, did you decide this?" He asked through clenched teeth.

David turned to look at his stepson, knowing the subject was about to change, "A couple of months after the accident. I contacted Anaïs explaining the situation, she agreed."

"It wasn't an accident," He said breathing out a laugh, he got up from the bed not wanting to sit a second longer he walked over to the dresser and leaned against the old wood. "My mother tried to kill herself in front of me, anyone who does that could not, is not, considered an *accident*."

"She's sick Alex! She can't help herself for what she does!" David exclaimed going to stand in front of the boy, he grabbed hold of his shoulders holding them tight. "You know that, so why can't you just let it be? We all have to deal with it, just as much as you do we all have to suffer through this, your mother, though, is the one suffering the most!"

"All of you!" Alex's voice rising to match David's, "Did any of you have to watch as she tried to shoot herself? Did you have to watch as the person you love most, who when you where little read you stories and kissed your head at night, the person who told you not to be afraid of the dark because she would always be there to scare away the monsters, try to kill herself?" By then tears started to trickle down his face, "No you didn't have to experience that! You didn't have to see her try and take her own life, I-I tried to stop her, I did, but she pushed me away, it was, she was, she wouldn't let me, and I tried so hard to try and stop her! That day, that day, when the monsters really came, they came and they never went away, because she brought them… *she brought them!* And *she* wasn't the one who could get rid of them because it was she who was the monster, and I wasn't able to coddle her and say everything would be OK, I couldn't." He finished with a sob, his body shaking from the tears that ran down his face.

David released his grip from Alex's shoulders, shocked by the words that had spilled from the boy's lips. "It's not your fault Alex it's not." He said simply feeling a pain deep in his heart for the boy in front of him. Alex may be nineteen but he was still as fragile as a small child was when it came to this matter, and try as he may Alex always seemed to push him to a distance.

"I know it's not David," He said in a whisper after finally creasing his tears. "But when you see the person who use to hum to you every night to get you to sleep when you had bad dreams, try and kill herself and also watch day by day as she falls apart you can't help but want to block everything out." He whispered with a finish, closing his eyes briefly he walked around David and opened the room door closing it behind him.

★★★★

Marie heard a door open again and someone walk out shutting it behind them. Shuffling quickly over to her door, she opened it fully, watching as Alex's head disappeared from view a second later. Raising her eyebrows she waited a second, waiting for the sound of the front door, it came a minute later. Marie walked over to the stairs trotting down them at a fast pace and made her way to the front door, opening it she was met with a warm breeze.

She walked out of the house shutting the door behind her; Marie scanned the area in front of her, not knowing which way to go. Deciding the back would be her best guess she veered to the right and walked down the scattered multi-tiled path towards the solid honey colored wood gate that lead to the garden. The gate had ivy crawling over it covering the wood and making a vibrant green cover in its place.

When she reached the gate, she pushed it open with easy, the well oiled hinges not making a sound. The garden was something she and her mother, along with the help of her father, had done one summer when she was seven. Moss crawled along the ground while a large weeping willow stood high letting its branches drop low, the willow had been planted long before Marie had been born. Along the rim of the wall where different colored flowers, lavender and butterfly bushes, baby's breath and tea roses where scattered throughout it, a stone bench was placed alongside the path with dew on the side. The path though continued through the tangles of the willows branches winding away from view.

Marie pushed the long weeping branches from her path coming to a stop when it ended wrapping around the base of the tree. Light grass grew behind the willow for the rest of the garden, though this part was hidden from everyone who did not continue along the stones.

A white woven hanging basket seat was hanging from a branch on the tree facing away from Marie. Walking over to it she turned it around, there sitting in the middle was Alex his legs up to his chest, arms wrapped around his knees his face buried in them.

"Are you alright?"

Alex's head shot up he looked at her and then away. "Go away," he muttered, his words muffled.

"Can I sit down?" She asked ignoring his demand.

Alex grunted and moved to the left making room for her. "What do you want?"

Marie shrugged, "I saw you walk into your father's room and then I saw you walk out, so I decided to follow you to see if you were alright…. Are you alright?" She asked sitting down beside him bringing her legs to fold under her.

"Peachy."

"You know," she said sighing. "I am just trying to be nice and you're not really helping by being an ass about it."

He turned to look at her, eyebrows raised, "I'm being an ass? You're the one who is bugging me; I wouldn't have to be an ass if you didn't just leave me alone."

"That's just it, for some reason I don't want to leave you alone."

Alex shook his head, "whatever and what are you wearing?" He asked in a slight bemused tone while looking at her nightgown.

Marie looked down at her nightgown, "Pajamas?"

"Oh, I haven't seen those in a long time, last time I think was when my grandmother came to stay with us. Though yours are much nicer and not as old looking of course."

"Um, thank you?"

"Can I ask why you wear it and not, well, pants or something?" The topic was odd to him, but he felt that it was something to talk about.

"I'm comfortable in this," she said nonchalantly, "why do you wear so much make up? Your clothes look like they would be heavy to wear in this weather also."

"You're really nosey, you know that?"

Marie smiled, "you brought it upon yourself." She said with a small laugh.

He just rolled his eyes before asking her, "Why do you talk like that? You don't cut your words off as much as others do."

"Like I said, I'm comfortable. I've grown up talking like this, I've been taught to speak my words with proper pronunciation and to not stutter out an answer." She said with a laugh. "It's what I do and how I do it I guess. I wouldn't change the way I do things even if you paid me. Besides I do cut off some of my words, just as I have demonstrated a moment ago."

"Fine, ok, I'll stop asking questions then, since they tend to be pointless."

"Asking questions is fine Alex, so long as you ask the right ones." She said with a chuckle, and then added: "Questions are never pointless."

Alex raised an eyebrow, "fine then, how old are you?"

"Eighteen, I am turning nineteen in July, what about you?"

"Nineteen, my birthday is in September,; along with my brother's."

Marie turned to him confused, "you have a brother? Why is he not here with you and your father?"

"He's my twin his name is Daniel, and the reason he's not here is because he's back in Germany watching over our mum." He said brushing bits of his hair away from his face while looking away. "And David is my stepdad though he is more of my real father then my blood father.

Marie was silent for a moment watching the boy next to her, "do you want to talk about it?" She questioned sensing something was troubling him. He shook his head. "Ok," was all she said.

They didn't speak anymore after that; they just sat there in silence, a mild contentment surrounding them.

Chapter Three

The sun was at its lowest in the sky as it rose the next morning. The house cast in the brightest shade of yellow as the sun rose to set on it, letting the occupants of the cottage know that it was time to awake.

Anaïs was the first, like every morning and the ones before it, to awake. She took a deep breath before pulling her thin summer quilt back, sliding her feet over the bed letting her skin come in contact with the wood floors, she stretched for a moment letting her arms reach above her before she stood up.

Walking over to her window, she pulled back the light green drapes that hung to the floor, little white flowers embroidered into them. She opened the latch that kept the two glass paned, shutter like windows together and let them swing open gently, letting a mellow wind blow into the room. Anaïs smiled, she always liked the morning. It was always so calm and refreshing the way the night left at dawn, leaving a new day in its wake, everything becoming whole again.

Watching the fields from her window, she finally turned away from the scene. Taking her silk robe from the cushioned chair in the corner, she pulled it on, tying it lightly at her waist letting it fall open in front of her night gown.

Her husband Élie had given it to her right after Marie had been born, presenting it to her in a small purple box. Anaïs smiled at her husband's picture on her dresser wishing he could be here to see how much their daughter had grown up.

Like David had said the night before, Marie did look so much like Élie. Her mouth always seemed to turn up as if she were about to laugh or yet stilled into an everlasting smile that made her shine inside and out. The way her eyes twinkled whenever she spoke, just as his did. Though Marie did have her blonde hair, she took after her father in everything else.

Anaïs strode over to her door and opened it walking out of her room. Everything was quiet in the house, except for the occasional creak from the hardwood as she walked down the stairs to the kitchen. Anaïs walked over to the fridge and opened it, peering inside; she looked for something to make for breakfast.

Deciding eggs and crepes would do just fine, she grabbed some green onions from the shelf along with milk, four eggs and cheese. She searched for more eggs realizing they didn't have any more, shaking her head she shut the fridge placing the items in her hands on the wood cutting board like counter.

Strolling over to the back door Anaïs slipped on the shoes that waited by it, opening the door she was met with the sound of chickens clucking away while they pecked at the ground.

Grinning at the sight, she stepped over the wide stone path that leads away from the chickens. The chicken coop wasn't placed right beside the house, it was more tucked in the corner away from the path and everything else, though the chickens only went into the coop at night, staying the rest of the day outside to eat and enjoy the sun. The chickens were all white minus the light brown going down their backs, they had six in all. Though Anaïs hated to admit it, the females were the ones in charge, leaving their poor rooster Roger to do their bidding, it was quite funny to watch she had to admit, when he would try to take charge by chasing them all into the coop but failing utterly when he would slip and fall off the step leading up to it.

Anaïs slipped into the chicken coop ducking under the roofs support beam that ran across from one side to the other. She knelt down in front of the five nesting boxes and reached into each of them one at a time. After a minute of searching, she pulled out six eggs in total, three in each hand.

Standing up she walked out of the chicken coop, bending once again under the support beam before she stepped out of the coop and walked back to the house.

Once inside, she took her shoes off, nudging them back to where they were before with her foot, bumping the door shut with her back she walked across the room and into the kitchen placing the eggs gently on the counter near the stove top. After a moment of getting everything she needed she set to work of preparing the meal.

✯✯✯✯

Sighing she took a deep breath and stared at her handy work, four plates where set around the table, eggs and crepes set on each one, powdered sugar sat in a bowl set in the middle of the table. Smiling, she walked over to the stairs and walked up, knocking slowly on David's door, she waited a minute ready to knock again before she heard the sound of feet and the door opening.

"Breakfast is ready David whenever you're ready, I know you must have jetlag but if you get accustomed to waking up at this time, it will pass." She said with a smile not giving the man time to speak.

The man looked very tired as he yawned covering his mouth, "alright Anaïs, I'll be down in a few minutes just let me wake up. Maybe brush my teeth in the process," He said with a small chuckle.

Anaïs nodded and left walking over to her daughter's room, she opened the door slowly pushing it open when she noticed Marie wasn't in her bed. Curiously, she walked further into her room strolling over to the window; Marie's window looked out onto the garden, a place she liked to visit occasionally when she wasn't in the fields.

Peering out, she looked over the grounds passing the flowers and the stone bench, the path and the willow tree coming to stop at the hanging seat that her husband had hung there a year after they had made the garden.

Normally she wouldn't think anything of the seat but something stopped her when she saw a pair of feet hanging from it. Raising her brows she left her daughter's room walking down the stairs and over to the back door, pulling it open she walked the stone path that lead a quicker rout to the willow.

Once there she stopped at the sight that met her. There sitting in the basket was none other than Marie and Alex both asleep comfortably, Marie's head rested on Alex's shoulder her body curled into his while his head rested over hers. His arms wrapped around her in ease, Anaïs assumed they had fallen asleep there accidently because Marie hates sleeping outside ever since she fell asleep in the garden one night a few years back, having woken up covered in bites from the bugs.

Smiling gently at the site, glad that Alex had opened up enough to let her daughter in, she walked over placing her hand on her daughter's shoulder lightly she shook it trying to be as quiet as possible.

"Marie love, breakfast is ready." She whispered.

Marie groaned, her eyes squeezing shut before she let them flutter open she took a deep breath staring at her mother for a moment then looked at Alex who still had this arms around her. A small blush crept up to her cheeks lighting them with a small shade of pink.

"This is not what it looks like mother." She said, also whispering.

Anaïs smiled her eyes twinkling, "I know Marie, now wake Alex and come inside, breakfast is ready."

Marie nodded gently unhooking Alex's arms from around her, the movement causing Alex to wake up his brown eyes coming to stare at Marie.

Grinning lightly, Anaïs walked away leaving the two of them.

"Hey." Alex said his voice coming out ruff from sleep.

"Hello, did you sleep well?" Marie questioned as she stood up stretching her back out hearing little pops sound from it.

Alex hummed as he too stretch the kinks out of his neck and upper body, "not the best place to fall asleep though." Marie nodded in agreement, "did your mum say breakfast was ready?"

Marie nodded again. "I'm kind of hungry," as he said that, his stomach growled in protest, he laughed, "So could we go in?"

Marie smiled, "I was wondering when you were going to ask." She said while laughing. Turning on her heels she skipped down the path leading to the back of the house, the cool morning, before the hot sun took over, left her feeling refreshed and happy. Alex followed silently, but hurriedly behind her.

Chapter Four

When Alex and Marie walked in, they were met with the smell of pancakes and eggs, Alex's stomach growling in hunger. Marie shook her head laughing as she heard its protests.

"It's not funny." He scowled as they walked over to the kitchen table taking their seats.

"Oh, but it is Alex. Besides, you clearly need to eat more." She said, gesturing to his body.

David overheard their conversation topic and cut in, "don't be fooled by what you saw last night pet, Alex could out eat an army in only a few short hours. I don't know where he puts it all."

The comment made Marie laugh, "Really?" She questioned to Alex her eyebrows rising in amusement.

Alex scowled again, stabbing a pancake with his fork and putting it on his plate, "Don't listen to David, he thinks it's his job in life to embarrass me."

"But it's true!" David exclaimed, "I remember the time when you were, what, around fifteen? Your mum and I took you and your brother to the Eastern Buffet. Boy, I don't think I've ever seen a stack of dishes grow so high before."

"Now you're exaggerating."Alex said, with a roll of his eyes.

David grinned secretly, "Yes, alright, but it was still a pretty big pile of dishes."

Anaïs watched as the three conversed, Alex having changed the subject, much to his satisfaction, to the topic of music. Anaïs began to eat pieces of her egg slowly as she listened to the conversation.

"How can the *Beatles* win over *Bee Gees*? That's like saying your better than Daniel!" David said bewildered.

Alex gave an exasperated sigh, "Uh- hello? I am better than Daniel…at drawing," He added with a chuckle, "Oh, and the *Beatles* are better than the *Bee Gees* .I mean really, the *Bee Gees* actually sound like something got stuck in their throats and that's why they sound like chipmunks or some other odd furry creatures."

David gasped, "They do not!"

"I have to agree with Alex, David; the *Beatles* are really good but then again *Black Sabbath* and *Guns 'N Roses* are much better." Marie stated.

Alex and David turned simultaneously and stared at her.

Marie stared back confused, "What? My papa taught me to appreciate all genres of music."

"Yeah, but *Guns 'N Roses!*" Alex exclaimed.

"Hey, they had some great music."

David shook his head, "your both insane." He muttered.

And so it went on from *Elvis Costello* to *Elvis Presley* and then a rather heated debate on whether the group *KISS* were in fact aliens, or the aftermath of a rather bad makeover. After awhile of the three debating who where the best in the business and Anaïs just sitting there watching them with a smile on her lips, she finally had to call a stop to it all.

"I'm sorry to stop this but I need Marie to clear the table for me and I'll meet you in the kitchen, I would also like to speak with you David."

The three turned and nodded to Anaïs. Marie got up stacking the plates on one another and brought them into the kitchen placing them in the sink then going back for the others.

David walked into the kitchen leaning against the counter just as Marie brought the last of the plates in.

"David, don't you have to speak with my mother?" Marie questioned setting the dishes down, turning to David.

David took a deep breath waiting a moment before speaking, "I just want to say thank you." Marie gave him a confused look, "For Alex I mean, you've done more in half a day than I've been able to do in five months. So thank you. Even though there are things that are still painful and hard to heal, I have a feeling that you will help to make them alright."

Marie smiled, placing a hand on his forearm she said, "Your welcome. Alex is well, he is Alex, and for me, helping him comes naturally, so do not worry so much, everything will be better soon."

Just then, Anaïs came in walking over to her daughter and David, "Marie," She said turning to look at her daughter first, "I'll do the dishes, but I need you to go and pick me some *Chamomile,* the ones by the cluster of poppies. Take that basket and don't forget to wear the gloves that are in it." She said pointing to the small basket the rested on the counter.

Nodding her head, Marie walked over, grabbed it, and walked out of the room.

Anaïs now turned to David, "If you can wait ten minutes I will have these dishes done and then we will be able to talk in the living room."

David nodded and walked out going to go wait for her to finish.

★★★★

Marie, basket in hand, set outside. Her feet where bare and the light wind pressed her nightgown to her body lightly as she walked, she took a deep breath smiling to herself as she walked loving the feel of the sun on her skin. The long grass brushed against her bare skin, also making a soft cushion on her feet.

Upon arriving, Marie knelt down on her knees and stared to pick the tiny daisy like flowers, laying them gently into the basket as she plucked them from their stems.

★★★★

David watched from his position on the couch as Alex walk down the stairs, his freshly washed hair was hanging loosely around his shoulders, his clothes and make up though where what took David by surprise.

Alex's usual heavy all black attire was down to a bare minimum, with just a pair of black, loose fitting, jeans and a slightly large red shirt with a small v-neckline. And only a small amount of eyeliner encircled his eyes.

"Well, look at you," David said smiling.

Alex rolled his eyes upward as he walked into the room, "Marie said that I would be to hot in my usual get up, so I thought I would bring it down a notch." He said nonchalantly.

"A little, Alex this is a big improvement! You're actually wearing *color*!" He said emphasizing on 'color'.

"Yeah, ok if you're done. Is there anything I can do? Staying in this house without a computer or any sort of cell service is very boring."

David nodded, "yeah actually you can. You can go help Marie in the field; she's picking some *Chamomile* for Anaïs. I don't think she walked too far, you can use the front door."

Alex took a deep breath and walked away, his black shoes squeaking slightly as the rubber soles rubbed against the bare floors.

David shook his head as he watched his stepson leave, bringing Alex to France had to be the best thing he has ever done.

★★★★

Alex ever so quietly came to crouch beside Marie, like David had said she hadn't been hard to spot, only having been about a quarter of the way past the edge of the field. "Hi" He said, hands on his knees as he watched her pick the small flowers.

"Hello Alex." Marie said, shortly looking at the teen.

"Uh, so… what are you doing?" He asked after a pause.

Marie smiled a bit, "what does it look like I'm doing?" She asked picking the last of the *Chamomile*. Sitting fully on the soft ground now, she crossed her legs setting the basket on her lap.

Alex sighed and got up walking over to the red poppies that resided by the smaller daises. Bending down he picked one, bring it close to his face he inhaled deeply, not aware of Marie watching him.

"I knew you were lying. How can anyone truly hate flowers?"

Alex turned around to look at her, a small scowl on his face, a frown tugging on his lips as he came to sit across from her, the flower still in his hands.

"I have a reason to dislike them."

"But you don't hate them."

He shook his head, "no, I guess I don't hate them. See, my mum loves— loved, flowers. And she use to take me to these green houses when I was younger, even last year we had gone to The Floral House, where she would ask me which ones where my favourite, which ones I would want in the garden. We would always pick so many that year and then the next year we would get twice as many, our front and backyard where always so vibrant with color."

"What happen?"

"She tried to kill herself a year later, a day before we were supposed to go look at flowers." He paused, "After that I just sort of lost it... this is really stupid but every time I saw a flower I felt like crying, I guess that's why I stayed in my room all the time."

"It's not stupid Alex. When my papa passed away I didn't talk to anyone for months, I couldn't let it process into my mind that he was never going to walk into my room again and tuck me in at night. It was hard, and I didn't want to move on I wanted time to stand still for as long as possible, frozen." Marie sighed, "It didn't work though, after almost a year I finally had to realize that he was never coming back, but I also realized that I could still talk to him when I'm alone."

Alex looked at her with confusion, "what do you mean?"

"I have a picture of him in my nightstand, every night I pick the picture up, set it in my lap and I talk. I tell him everything that happen that day, any new people I met, what my mother did at the market... anything really. It's just a moment, but it's a moment that I cherish every day."

After a long pause Alex spoke up, "I envy you; I can't even talk to my mum right now. She's in some ward in some hospital; I don't know which because I never bothered to find out."

"Do ever plan on seeing her again?"

"I don't know."

"Do you know how it started? You mother I mean, how she found out about her sickness?"

"It's not a sickness, it's a small mass in a deep section of her brain, and it's about the size of my nail. The doctor said that it was digging on a very sensitive part of the tissue, causing it to bleed slowly, making it clot and causing her to see things. They preformed a surgery, causing the clotting to stop but she could still see the hallucinations.

A few months had passed after that, only a few minor things had gone on but that was it. The day she shot herself she came into my room, I was on the phone talking to Daniel. I remember when she opened my door and I noticed a gun in her hand, it was small, very small, but it was still a gun…."

★★★★

Alex slowly got off his bed as his mother entered his room, telling Daniel he would call him back later, and approached his mum all the while noticing the small gun in her hand, "When did you buy a gun?" He asked cautiously, he had never been one for firearms, being fonder of knives and baseball bats.

"Today," her voice sounded like that of a little girl, as if she had gone back to being five years old and not forty-five.

He soon realized by the change of her voice that she was having an attack, "Why?"

Simone tilted her head smiling, a far off look in her eyes, "they told me to." She said giggling like a child.

"They?" Alex asked he was getting a bad feeling about this. I should call Daniel and David, he thought to himself moving slowly back over to his phone. "Who are they, mum?"

"Oh no, I can't do that," she said giggling still, "I'll get in trouble." She said to empty space, her attention on Alex was lost.

Alex watched as his mother talked to the air, taking that time to slip quietly over to his cell phone that lay on his bed, dialing David's number quickly he waited as it rang.

"Hello?"

"David, its Alex, You need to get home."

"What? Alex is everything all right?"

"No it's mum, she's having an attack and she has a gun."

"Who are you talking to?"

Alex turned quickly to see his mother standing a foot away from him. His phone dropped from his hands without notice. The gun that had been hanging by her side before was now pointed in front of Alex.

Hurrying over, he stepped to the side lowering the hand that held the automatic slowly, "I'm talking to you aren't I."

"Hmm," She thought, "yes you are."

"Mum."

"Why do you call me mum? My name is Simone." She said with a laugh.

Clearing his throat Alex watched as she waved the gun around, "Right Simone, can I have that?" He asked pointing to the weapon.

"No!"

Surprised by her hard reply he tried again, "Why can't I have it, I just want to see it."

"You can't! They said if I gave it to you, I would get hurt."

"You won't get hurt, I promise. I would never hurt you and I'm the only one in the room. See," He held up his hands showing them to her, "their empty. Please Simone, can I have the gun?"

Her eyes were wide with thought as she sucked in her bottom lip. "Alright," She turned to the space next to Alex, "but he said he wouldn't hurt me, but he promised!" Alex was in front of her, his hand hovering over the gun in his mum's hand. "No!" She said yanking the weapon away, which caused her to push Alex back causing him to stumble, Simone in the process, pulled the trigger the shot ringing through the house and through Alex's ears.

A sharp pain erupted on the side of Alex's leg, looking down, he saw a darkening spot start to appear on his pant leg, and he could feel the sticky wrath spread down the side of his skin. He could feel tears prick at his eyes, the pain was intense.

"They said you where bad," Her voice had changed; Alex looked up startled by the sudden noise, his ears still ringing from the gun shot. She didn't sound like the little girl anymore, she sounded dead, as if all the life had been sucked from her.

"Simone? Mum?" He asked worried, his breathing labored from the pain.

"They said not to trust you; they said all I had to do to get away from here..." She stopped in midsentence.

"What? Mum what are you doing?" He watched as she brought the gun up to her chest. "No, mum, no! You don't want to do this." He tried to get up, using the side of his bed as support as he tried to hobble over to her only ending in his leg caving under him in his attempt.

"Pull the trigger."

And she did, Alex's scream's going unheard over the shot that seemed to go on forever, as if in slow motion. Alex could see as his mother's face changed from dead to shocked to nothing in a matter of seconds, as she fell backwards into a heap, the gun falling out of her hands landing a few feet away. A dark red sprouting on her light peach colored blouse as she lost consciousness.

"Alex?! Alex, Hello! I'm almost home!"

★★★★

"I couldn't do anything that day; I think that's what hurt the most. Not the shot, or the fact that she tried to kill herself... but the feeling I had of being useless. I tried to help but I was just not able, I wasn't fast enough, I wasn't strong enough to ignore the pain and just pull the gun out of her hands."

Marie looked at the boy across from her, tears misting her eyes. "You... are one of the strongest people I know." She said after clearing her throat. "I never want to hear you say you're not strong enough ever again. What happened is not your fault; it never was and never will be. Yes, you where there, but there was nothing you could have done than what you already had done."

Alex looked at Marie, "you think so?"

"I never think Alex, it takes too much time, I just know."

"Promise?"

She nodded leaning over to hug him, she whispered, "I promise."

Chapter Five

Both Marie and Alex entered the house, Marie with the basket tucked in the crook of her right arm and with Bill on her other, the poppy still held lightly in his hands as not to crush it. The sound of their footsteps echoed through the house as they entered the kitchen.

Marie set the basket on the wood counter, carefully dumping the contents out and spreading them delicately in a small section of the counter.

"What are we going to do now?"

Marie turned to Alex who was leaning against the island watching her, his arms folded over his chest. "We?"

He shrugged, "Yeah, I mean, if you don't want me around I'll just find something else to do. It's fine." He said pushing himself away from the island and walking toward the kitchens entryway.

"Alex, really don't be so dramatic. Of course I want you around, and you know that." Marie said coming around, going to stand in front of the teen, leaving the basket on the counter, "Why don't we take a walk, after I'm done getting ready of course. There's a place I want to show you."

"Are you sure? You're not just doing it for my sake are you? I mean I can always go…." He said gesturing behind him towards the door.

Marie raised a blonde brow giving him a look, "If you don't stop, I will smack you."

Alex laughed his eyes crinkling at the ends, "I'm joking Marie. A walk sounds nice."

"There you guys are. Oh wonderful Marie, thank you." Marie and Alex turned to look at her mother as she entered with David. Anaïs looked at the tiny flowers, running her hands over them lightly before turning to the two in turn. "I have been talking to David about a house I found just fifteen minutes from here. The owners apparently have a family crisis and have to sell their home. Now, while he and I are gone, I was thinking that the two of you could go see Marie's Cousin Evelyn and her family. I heard Evelyn is back from school, and her mother very much wishes to see Marie."

"Alex?" Marie asked, "What do you want to do? It's up to you."

Alex thought for a moment looking to the ground as he did so. Making up his mind he answered, a bit hesitant, "If it's alright, I would like to go meet some more of your family."

David smiled stepping in, "I think that's alright. Marie?"

Everyone turned to the girl who stood before them. Marie gave a slight smile, "I think that would be fine."

Anaïs grinned clapping her hands together, "Alright well then we'll leave now, Marie take the truck, I parked it at the end of the road."

Marie nodded and watched as her mother and David left, leaving them alone. "Well, why don't you go sit on the couch while I go take a shower and get ready? We have some books… I don't exactly know what you would like to do while you wait."

He shrugged as he heard a door slam shut, "I could draw. Do you have some paper and a pencil?"

Marie gave a small gasp, "Oh that's right! You draw don't you?" Alex nodded, "There's paper in the desk drawer by the window in the living room, and pencils should be in the one next to it. You will have to show me one of your drawings someday Alex, I would like to see one." Marie said walking out of the kitchen and towards the stairs.

Alex gave her a smile following suit, "one of these days you will."

"I hope it's soon then." She said as she made her way up the stairs and out of sight.

Alex, now left alone, walked into the living room finding the desk exactly where she had said it would be. The desk was old and made of dark, carved wood that complemented the room greatly. It had designs chiseled into the two drawers, and on the outer edge the same patters intertwined, the handles on the drawers where of a tarnished brass.

Opening the first drawer on the right he found calligraphy pens and ink to go with them, a large, old gold ring, and a few letters tuck underneath it all. Though, in the back of the drawer was a single pencil, Alex smiled, taking it out, noticing the sharp tip, he moved onto the next one coming upon thick cream stationary. "Perfect." He muttered pulling a piece out.

Paper and pencil in hand, Alex walked over to the dark red couch sitting down on the floor in front of it as he set the paper down on the brown whicker coffee table that was paced in the middle.

It wasn't long before he knew what to draw, putting the pencil to the paper, he began.

★★★★

Marie came down the stairs, her light embroidered green dress swaying lightly as she walked, her hair hanging in a mass of curls at her shoulders. She walked into the living space only to find Alex hunched over, his hair making a cover for his face though Marie could see as his hand moving rapidly over something, his other moving occasionally. "Alex, are you ready to go?" She questioned going over to the boy.

Alex's head shot up; startled by the intrusion, eyes wide he looked at Marie.

"I'm, sorry; I didn't mean to frighten you." She said kneeling down beside him.

"Hmm? Oh no, you didn't frighten me only a little startled" He looked down at his drawing, hiding it from Marie's view as she tried to peek.

"Why can't I see it?"

"Because this isn't the one you're going to see."

"Can you at least *tell me* what the drawing is of?"

Alex thought for a moment, "no." He said giving her a teasing grin.

"Alex... *please*? Just tell me what you drew."

Sighing he gave up, "Fine, though it's nothing spectacular just the desk." He said pointing to the desk by the window.

"You drew the desk?" He hummed a reply. "Ok, well I guess that makes sense since there's little to draw in this room."

"I don't know about that...." He said looking at Marie with a small smile, "Anyways, I think we should go now." He got up turning his paper over in the process and setting his pencil down. "You look nice by the way." He said looking her over.

"Not odd?" Marie asked walking out of the room.

Alex sighed, following her out, "I'm sorry about that Marie, I was very moody yesterday and I also didn't know you... could you forgive me?" He asked, turning her to him.

Marie stared at the boy in front of her. Shaking her head she sighed in turn, "I wasn't mad at you Alex, I thought you were a bit impolite, but that was before I knew what you had gone through. It's fine now, and thanks for the compliment."

"Are you sure?"

"Positive, now come on. I already called ahead to Evelyn letting her know where coming."

Alex rolled his eyes, "Ok if you're sure, you know we could always just take that walk like you said." He suggested.

Marie walked away calling over her shoulder, "I'm leaving Alex."

Chapter Six

The car ride there was an overall noisy one with Alex and Marie singing loudly, and very much out of tune, to the cassette that was in the player.

When they reached Evelyn's house, Marie pulled the car to a stop putting the brakes on and got out, the gravel on the ground crunching under the thin bottoms of her soles.

"MARIE!"

Marie whipped around to see her cousin running through a row of trimmed Cypress trees towards her, her dark brown hair flying behind her in a wild mess. "Evelyn!" Marie cried, meeting her half way. As she got there, she threw her arms around her hugging her tightly. "I'm so happy to see you!"

"And I you! School is so boring, not at all like here. It's so great to be back home, I've missed you so much, I miss the trouble we get into, stupid teachers don't let me do anything!" Marie rolled her eyes at that but couldn't help but grin, "How is your mother?" She asked, looping her arm through her cousin's, walking her towards the house.

"She's fine, papa's friend from college is staying for awhile, and his name is David Balvien." They reached the truck coming to a stop, "He brought his son with him—"

"Oh, can I meet him? Is he at the cottage?" Evelyn asked, her eyes lighting up.

Marie laughed, "He's here, though…" She looked around, "…I don't exactly know where he went. Alex!" She called out looking around their surroundings for the missing boy. "He's around here-"

"Hey, sorry, some little kid took me to see something he had made, cute kid though." Alex said as he walked over to the pair.

"Oh my gosh, he's gorgeous!" Evelyn squealed.

Alex rubbed his neck, feeling awkward all of a sudden, "Huh?"

Marie walked over to Alex's side grabbing his hand and tugging him closer to them, "Alex, this is my cousin Evelyn, Evelyn; this is Alex, David's son. Please don't scare him." She said giving Evelyn a look.

Evelyn smirked, "Moi? Effrayer un si beau garçon ? Jamais. Par contre, tu penses qu'il sortirait avec moi si je le lui demandais ?" *Me? Scare such a beautiful boy? Never. Though do you think if I asked him, he would go out with me?* She asked looking at Alex then at Marie.

Marie sighed, looking at her cousin. Same old Evelyn, she thought to herself. Shaking her head, she shrugged. "S'il te plaît, modère tes ardeurs… essaie de faire sa connaissance d'abord, d'accord ? " *Please, though, don't do anything too spontaneous, just get to know him first okay?* She knew her cousin inside and out, and she knew she could come off as a bit wild at times; she tended to move too fast for her own sake, and the other's.

Looking over at Alex, she stared at the boy for a moment, not knowing what to say to him or what to do. Shrugging again, she walked off leaving the two of them to themselves.

Alex watched as Marie walked away leaving them behind. Curious, he turned back to Evelyn, "Where's she going?"

Evelyn raised a brow, "Hmm? Oh, elle est entrée - sorry, she's just going inside to say hello." She said nonchalantly.

"Shouldn't we go too then? This was the whole point of us coming over, well, besides Marie seeing you that is." He said, turning back to the house.

"You can meet my family later. Now, come, I want to know all about you."

Uncertain, Alex followed as Evelyn led the way.

★★★★

Marie walked through the light-filled house, looking at the paintings on the walls. She hadn't been here for almost six months, and now she felt as at home as she did in her own home. "Hello?" she called out through the hall. Barking suddenly filled the silence and the sound of paws sliding on tiles could be heard from somewhere. "Princess? Here boy, here Princess!" She almost shouted as the barking got louder. Suddenly a long golden-haired shaggy dog appeared from around the corner, his tongue hanging out of his mouth as he ran, colliding with Marie.

"Oomph!" Marie fell backwards landing on her butt as Princess licked at her. "Princess down, down boy," She managed to push the happy dog back, and stood up straightening her dress. Laughing, she patted the dog's head while smiling. "Good boy."

"Marie?" Called a heavily accented female voice from the kitchen.

"I'm here," she called back, walking to the kitchen, following the delicious scent of grilled vegetables and marinated chicken. "This smells wonderful, Aunt," Marie said as she walked up behind her Aunt Melanie, wrapping her arms around her slightly rounding middle in a hug.

Mélanie turned away from the stove, enveloping her niece in a hug, "Comment ca va, chérie ?" *How have you been dear?, she* asked, pulling back to look her up and down, "Pourquoi tu n'es pas venue me voir ?? Evelyn n'est pas la seule qui t'aime, tu sais. Et tu as beaucoup manquée à tonton, mon lapin." *Why haven't you come visit me? Evelyn is not the only one who loves you, you know. You uncle has missed you greatly, love.*

Marie gave her an apologetic smile as she stepped back. Grabbing the wooden spoon on the counter, she began to stir the pasta that was cooking in the pot. "Vous m'avez beaucoup manqués aussi, et je suis désolée de ne pas être venue vous voir. J'ai été très occupée cet été : maman m'amène avec elle quand elle va en ville ces derniers temps, et nous avons repeint le salon. Il faut que tu le voies quand vous venez nous voir. Promets-moi que vous viendrez!" *I miss you and uncle too, and I'm sorry I haven't visited; I have been very busy this summer. Mother has been taking me into town with her lately. Also, we painted the living room walls, which you will have to see when you come over. Promise you will come over?* She said, as she tasted one of the noodles. Chewing slowly, she tested the firmness before deciding they were done and turned off the stove.

Mélanie nodded her head thoughtfully, "Et ta mère? Comment va-t-elle?" *And your mother? How is she?*

Marie walked across the Spanish tiles towards the sink, pouring the noodles into the yellow strainer draining the water from the pot, "Elle va bien, elle est heureuse. Elle a invité un ami de papa qu'il a connu à l'université, David Balvien, et son fils, Alex. Quelque chose leur est arrivé et ils ont besoin d'un hébergement pendant un certain temps." *She's good, happy. She invited a friend of papa's from college, David Balvien and his son, Alex. Something happened and they need a place to stay for a while.* Dumping the noodles back into the pot, she brought them back, setting them on the stove and turning to her aunt.

"Oh? Un flirt pour elle? Ou pour toi? Ou est-ce l'amour?" *Oh? Romance for her? Or you? Can I call it love?* She asked a twinkle in her aging eyes, a smile curling on her lips.

Marie laughed, shaking her head, "Non, tata, rien de la sorte." *No, Aunt, nothing of the sort.*

Mélanie pouted a bit, "Quel dommage, tu devrais en tomber amoureux, Marie, cela te donnerait des ailes." *What a shame, you should fall in love, Marie, it will make your heart fly.* She said patting her cheek lightly.

"Oui, oui, je vais essayer, tata." *Yes, yes, Aunt, I'll try.* She said with a roll of her eyes.

"Alors, t'es venue toute seule ou bien est-ce que je vais pouvoir rencontrer ces fameux David et Alex ?" *Now did you come alone or can I meet this David and Alex?* She asked, raising her eyebrows.

Marie set the lid on top of the pasta pot, "Alex est venu avec moi, il parle avec Evelyn à l'extérieur ; David et maman visitent une location à présent." *Alex is with me, he is talking with Evelyn just outside; David and Mamma are looking at a home right now.*

Mélanie's eyes danced as she took off her apron, "Viens, j'ai envie de rencontrer ce garçon." *Come, I want to meet this boy.*

Rolling her eyes skyward, Marie followed behind her aunt as she made her way to the front door, Princess close on their heels.

Mélanie wasted no time pushing the front door open and walking outside into the warm breezy air. She made her way across the yard, pushing a few scattered chickens out of the way as she went. Princess barked at them happily, his tail wagging back and forth as he chased them. "Evelyn!" she called, trying to spot her daughter, but instead only finding her husband and little boy, "Félix! Est-ce que vous avez vu Evelyn? Elle est avec un garçon qui est arrivé avec Marie." *Have you seen Evelyn? She's with a boy that came with Marie;* she called, going over to her husband and son.

Félix looked up from his son he was talking to and smiled at his wife, "Ah non, mais je pense que François l'a peut-être vue. François?" *No I haven't, though I think François may have, François?*

The little boy with dark curls looked up from his wooden airplane, "Papa?"

"Est-ce que tu as vu ta sœur ? Elle est avec un garçon." *Have you seen your sister? She's with a boy.*

François made a cute face as he started thinking. Finally he remembered seeing where they went, and remembering the boy he had shown his airplane to. "J'aime bien le garçon; il a dit que mon avion était très chouette. Evelyn l'a amené au bord de l'eau." *I liked the boy; he said my airplane was very nice. Sister pulled him to the water.* He said proud of himself for helping.

"Merci, mon grand," *Thank you bubba.* Marie said as her aunt pulled her off in the direction of the small pond that resided by their milking cows.

"Là ! Ah, qu'il est beau." *There! Oh what a lovely boy he is.* Mélanie said clapping her hands together, spotting them sitting on a patch of grass.

Marie stopped walking as she watched them. Alex was sitting with his feet in the water, playing with a piece of grass while Evelyn sat close, her face was smiling as she played with a strand of his hair, twirling it around her middle finger.

She didn't know why, she didn't know how, but at that moment, she felt a pang of jealousy course through her. Sure Evelyn flirted with all boys, it was in her nature, but this just made Marie uneasy.

Mélanie stopped her pursuit of the teens and looked back at her niece, noticing the look in her eyes as she watched them by the pond. Smiling gently she walked over to her and put a soft, yet worn, hand on her shoulder, "C'est pas l'amour?" *Not love?* She asked, Marie shook her head silently, "Alors pourquoi cette tête ?" *Then why do you look like a lover who has just been betrayed?* She paused for a moment before continuing, though she too turned and watched the pair. "Les gens disent que c'est le cœur qui le sait quand on est amoureux. Et, chez les français, ceci doit être vrai pour la plupart des gens. Mais ce n'est pas le cœur qui sait, ma chère Marie, c'est l'âme... et ton âme, que te dit-elle? " *Most say it is the heart that can tell when you find that one special person, and being French, that is most likely true to most everyone. But my dear Marie, it is not the heart that knows, but the soul, and yours is calling out.* She finished giving the girl's shoulders a light squeeze before walking over to the duo.

Marie sighed, letting her thoughts reel as she tried to process what her aunt had said to her, and what she had, has, been feeling for the past few minutes

Chapter Seven

Alex smiled at Evelyn as she told him of her school days and of the trouble, she usually ends up causing. She reminded him of his brother. Daniel would like her, he thought as he listened to her talk.

"Evelyn!"

Alex and Evelyn looked up as a lady with red hair, grey peppering her temples, and brown eyes come up to them. He also noticed Marie was behind her as she came to a stop in front of them.

Alex took his feet from the cool water and stood up brushing jeans off. "Hello." He said sticking out his hand, the lady shook it. "I'm Alex Balvien, a friend of Marie's."

"Wonderful to meet you, I'm Mélanie, Evelyn's mother and Marie's aunt; you may also call me aunt."

Alex grinned, "Yes, alright aunt."

Mélanie waited for Marie to join them before speaking, "Marie has told me lots about you, though not to much that you can't tell me later after diner."

Marie looked at her aunt form the corner of her eye, what was her aunt up to?

"You will stay for dinner won't you? I haven't seen my niece in six months; you won't take her away from me will you?"

"You haven't seen *me* since the beginning of the year!" Evelyn cried.

Mélanie rolled her eyes, "I've seen you since the day you were born."

Alex laughed, "Of course we'll stay."

"Ah! Merveilleux!" *Wonderful!* She said giving him a large warm smile before she turned on her heels and walked towards the house, Evelyn behind her. "Come! Dinner is ready and you need to wash," she called behind her just as she disappeared around the corner of the house.

Alex looked at Marie, "What did she say?"

She said 'Wonderful', and what she meant by we need to wash, is simply that we need to wash our hands of the dirt that has been collected, and to also cleanse our mouths with water so we may fully taste the richness of the food." Marie explained as they started for the house.

"Wow, the French people have odd traditions. No offense." He said with a chuckle as they reached the front door, Félix and François coming up behind them.

Félix gave a hearty laugh as he opened the door for them to pass, "I do not think it is a French tradition, my boy, only one my wife has made."

The three of them laughed, François only staring after them curiously as they all walked into the house, Princess greeting them as they entered.

★★★★

"Evelyn, si tu t'assieds près d'Alex, je te casse personnellement les jambes." *Evelyn, if you sit by Alex I will personally break your legs,* Mélanie said under her breath to her daughter as she stopped her from sitting next to the boy.

Evelyn looked at her mother with a glare, "Je t'aime aussi, maman." *I love you too mother,* she said sarcastically, taking a seat next to her little brother.

"Marie," Mélanie called to the girl as she entered the dining room, "come, and sit by Alex. It's the only seat left, dear."

Marie raised an eyebrow, looking at her aunt. She is definitely up to something, she thought, taking the last seat next to Alex who was also by Mélanie.

"What is your name?" Félix asked Alex.

"Alex Balvien, sir, my stepfather and I are staying with Marie and Mrs. Dumas. They are currently looking at a house not too far from here." He said while taking a bite out of the marinated chicken and grilled zucchini with sweet onions. "This is wonderful – or how did you say it? Merve… a something." He finished with a chuckle. "Sorry my French isn't that good, actually it's terrible."

Mélanie gave him a pat on the back, "it's *Merveilleux* and thank you, I'm glad you're enjoying it." She took a bite of the pasta, "You French is… so-so… no, you're right, it's terrible."

Marie gave him a reassuring smile, "Don't worry, Alex, if you move here it will get better."

After learning of the dark-haired boy's name, François finally got up from his chair and went over to him. François tugged on his shirt, calling his attention.

Alex smiled down at the boy, "Yes?'

"Tu veux jouer avec mon avion avec moi?" François asked.

Alex looked at Marie, "What did he say?"

Marie told Alex what François had asked, "He asked, will you play with his airplane with him."

Alex looked at the boy, "yes." He said nodding his head.

François giggled in happiness and ran back to his seat.

"Alex," Mélanie whispered to him taking his attention away from her son, "what do you think of Marie?"

Alex's eyebrows knitted together as he looked at his elder, "what do you mean?"

"I mean what do you think of her, her personality, her looks and charm. What do you like most about her? What do you think about Marie?" She asked again making sure not to be over heard.

Alex thought, "I don't really know," He said looking briefly to the girl in question, "I guess she's just a happy person overall."

"Happy most times yes, but she has had troubles."

"Her father's death?"

"Yes, I see she has told you then. Do you like Marie in anyway more than say a… friend, do you, could you, see her as something more perhaps?" She couldn't help but want to ask questions, Marie was her most loved and favorite niece and she deserved to be loved by some who was not family, and this boy might just be the key for that.

Alex shrugged taking another bite of his chicken, chewing slowly as to think about what she asked. Swallowing he answered, "Truthfully… I still don't really know. I've only known her for two days."

"It doesn't take a life time Alex, only a moment."

"What do you mean?"

"Well… then why don't you think about it, I'm sure you'll know very soon."

Alex glanced at Marie, watching as she laughed at something François had said. He noticed the way her nose wrinkled as she laughed, or how her eyes light up when she talked about something she cared for. Alex didn't know what had just happen; whether it was in the conversation he had with aunt or if it was just that he was finally noticing it; he knew *something* had just happened.

Chapter Eight

The house was filled with laughter and warm happiness as Marie and her family sat around the living space. Alex was on the floor, playing with François just as he had said he would, though every now and then a look of confusion would cross his face as François would clap and laugh a word or praise in French. Mélanie and Evelyn where on the love seat, across from the spot where Marie and Félix were sitting on the couch, whispering in hushed tones while glancing at Alex then at Marie with curious glances.

Marie smiled as she overlooked her family as they conversed together, her heart swelled with love at the moment… she truly did enjoy her life… no matter what has happened, or what is to happen, she truly was content with how her life was.

"Marie…." Said the cool rasped voice of her uncle, Marie gave a small special smile to her uncle, brushing the palm of her hand across his sun worn cheek. "Sweet, dear Marie…." He said, closing the lids of his eyes briefly.

"Yes uncle…." She said folding her right leg under her as she turned towards him.

Félix just sighed and smiled. "You are ever growing more and more beautiful as time passes… my little seed, forever flowering in these old hills."

Marie lent forward and wrapped her thin arms around his broad shoulders, squeezing them tightly. "I missed you too uncle."

"My little seed, would you care to take a walk with me?" He asked pulling back. Marie nodded silently and grabbed the white and blue flowered shawl that lay folded on the small en-table, and stood up sliding her small hand into her uncle's.

No one, save Alex who watched her from the corner of his eye, noticed as they left, lost in their own conversations and activities.

★★★★

Félix and Marie stepped out into the still, warm, summer air. Both breathed deeply as they felt a slight breeze touch their skin as it blew. The pair walked in silence for awhile, content with the peace that surrounded them... it was a quiet calm that settled in their souls, something usually only they felt at times.

They walked the property, just listening to the night. Félix linked his arm through Marie's and guided her to the pond as they passed it for a second time. "Time has passed my dear and you have not come to see me once during this time that has gone by?" He stated in a curious voice as he stared at the moon reflecting water.

Marie sighed. "I'm sorry uncle, truly, I've been meaning to come see you, all of you, but I've been busy." Félix nodded in understanding.

"I am not accusing, sweet." He added with a chuckle, "Just curious."

"Curiosity killed the cat, uncle."

"Ah, but the cat found out what it was looking for, though, before he died."

The girl just shook her head and laughed lightly. "Yes I suppose he did."

After that, a silence crept in and they sat, sitting contently by the water side on the grass not saying a word but just enjoying each other's presence. The crescent moon in the sky lit up the dark night like a star, and Marie couldn't help but close her eyes and lay back on the ground, arms stretched above her head as her body relaxed.

Félix looked down at his niece and smiled doing as she did and laid back, hands folded on his slightly rounding stomach.

"Uncle…." Félix turned his head to Marie, giving her his attention. "…How do you help someone get over a nightmare?"

Confused by her question he turned his head back to the stars, thinking of an answer. "When Evelyn was very little she had a nightmare about a rabbit-"

Marie giggled, "Yes I remember her telling me the next day. What an evil little bunny it was." The memory crossed her mind and she couldn't help but giggle again as an image of a mean looking bunny with glowing purple eyes wafted through her memory. She quieted after a moment. "What did you do to help her go back to sleep?"

"I let her explain the dream and then stayed by her side until she fell asleep, being there for a person in a dark hour is sometimes the best thing you can do."

★★★★

Alex and Marie said their good byes' as they walked out of her Aunt and Uncle's house. Mélanie and Félix both hugged the kids as they left; Evelyn gave Marie a quick squeeze before she sauntered over to Alex, who was momentarily smiling at François as he rambled on. Marie watched the exchange with a silent emotion, the knowledge of her aunt watching her closely went unnoticed.

"Evelyn, that's enough, come inside now." Félix said in a gruff voice. Evelyn glanced at her father with a small huff, and turned back to Alex with a flirtatious glint in her eyes as she gave both corners of his mouth a quick peck before walking away.

"Bonne nuit my lucky cousin," she said as she passed Marie with a wink.

Mélanie rolled her eyes and ushered her son and daughter into the house but not before saying good night to her niece and to Alex.

The two teens stood there in front of the house for a moment before Alex made a comment that they should go. "I'll drive this time?" Marie nodded her head in agreement, turned to the truck, and slid into the passenger's side while Alex sat in the driver's side, slipping the keys Marie handed him into the ignition.

★★★★

The ride home was, unlike the previous hours before, a quiet one, the hum of the engine lulling to them gently. Alex kept his eyes on the road, occasionally looking over at Marie who sat beside him, head leaning against the window with her eyes closed.

"Marie?" He whispered as to not disturb the silence. She hummed lowly; he could see her body relaxing as sleep took over her mind. He just shook his head, "Never mind."

★★★★

Alex parked the truck at the end of the road leading up to the house, and got out. Walking around the side of the car he gently opened Marie's door and unbuckled her seatbelt. She awoke with a sigh, opening her eyes slowly as she stared at the boy in front of her.

"I fell asleep, didn't I?"

He nodded and helped her out of the vehicle as she shook the sleep from her. "It is getting late though." He said looking up at the dark sky. "Come on, our parents should be back by now."

Marie took a deep breath letting it out as she made her way up the gravel road slowly, Alex falling into step beside her, their arms bumping every now and then as they took their time walking to the house. They were quiet for a while before Alex spoke up. "You're cousin scares me." Marie let out a loud laugh and smiled at the boy, "Yes, she has that impression with everyone. I tried to stop her... but Evelyn has a bad habit of not listening." She explained as Alex made an understanding sound. "She's nice though. She reminds me very much of my brother." He said voicing his earlier thoughts. Marie tilted her head, looking up at Alex. "Will your brother come here once... once your mother...."She couldn't finish her sentence so settled for looking at Alex with curiosity.

Alex walked ahead before stopping and turning to look at the fields

The Good The Bad and Everything Inbetween

that lay on either side of them, hands in his pockets as he watched the wave like dance play off the long grass in the moon light. He thought for a moment, when his mother would eventually pass. What would happen when that happened? Would Daniel come to live here or...? He couldn't think about it just then.

A small soft hand slid into his own, giving it a gentle squeeze. "I am sorry. I shouldn't have asked you that." Alex just shook his head looking down at her, "It was a good question." He paused before speaking again, "Right now, I don't want to think about something as sad as my mother's death. It has been a wonderful evening that I enjoyed so much. Your family is… is something I wish my family could be."

"Oh? And what would that be?" She asked.

"Crazy." Marie laughed. "But it is a good thing," He continued as he pulled her once again in the direction of the house. "Your family is so warm and whole. Your aunt is always prying but never too much. Your uncle is gentle and warm, and your cousins are wonderful to be around… though Evelyn does still scare me." Marie shook her head good heartedly. "I have a feeling that if you're whole family was to congregate together for a day or so that it would end up being a very interesting couple of hours."

Marie gripped Alex's forearm as she stumbled over a rock, Alex steadying her. After regaining her balance, they continued. "Well then, you are in luck my dear friend." Marie said turning to face Alex as she walked backwards… probably not the best thing to do in the dark on a rocky road. "For generations my family has hosted a party at the end of summer, right here at our home. With colorful paper lanterns, food and music, the music courteous of my uncles and my great aunt Anna who loves to sing the most horrid songs she can find. Oh it's wonderful!" She exclaimed with happiness as she threw her hands above her head. "Laughter and my wonderful yet crazy cosines' whom have a tenancy to adding alcoholic beverages to the drinks they serve to the adults, little do the adults know, they just think their drunk off the summer air." She said with such a devious twinkle in her eyes and a smirk to match that it made the other laugh aloud.

Alex could imagine such a night as that and it made him slightly giddy at the chance that he may able to attend it. "I will be living here, do you think my father, brother and I will-"

"Of course you will!" She said cutting him off. "My mother already thinks of you and your father as family, why would you not be able to attend? Though… you will have to learn some French not all my relatives are as fluent in English as my mamma and I."

"Well then," He said, not being able to contain the smile that bloomed on his handsome features. "I guess you will just have to teach me."

Marie smiled back, "Oui, I suppose I will." The two turned up the walkway as they came to the end of the road, the front door now in their site and only a few yards away a clear yellow light shining through the kitchen window.

As Alex tested the front door, the knob turned easily in his hands and swung open to a dark house. Curious, the duo stepped through the threshold, Marie shutting the door behind her. Voices were whispering to each other from kitchen area and Alex and Marie went to observe what was happening.

"Thank God you are here." Anaïs said in a desperate tone, as Marie and Alex walked into the only lit room in the house.

David was leaned against the edge of the counter silently; a blank mask covered his face though few dry water marks streaked down his cheek. Alex looked to his stepfather then to Anaïs with questioning eyes.

"An hour ago, your brother called,"

Alex grinned, "Well, is it good news then?"

Marie gave an audible gasp from the background and Alex could feel her walk up beside him, and wrap her arms around his in a comforting manner, as Anaïs said her next words. "Alex… he didn't have good news about your mother."

Chapter Nine

Previously, that evening....

"Paging Dr. Kaulitz, please report to level three. Dr. Kaulitz, please report to level three."

 A young man in his late teens sat on one of the several cushioned chairs that waited in the hospital hall, with chocolate brown hair, tanned skin and deep green eyes that looked up at the intercom that spoke, his full pink lips pulled into a straight line, his eyes void as he turned his attention to a group of doctors' and nurses' as they ran past with a patient in the middle being wheeled away in a gurney, disappearing moments later behind swinging doors.

 The cushioned seat he sat on felt stiff as he stared at the room door in front of him, his heart beating like a drum that couldn't slow down, it just kept going faster and faster till it felt like it would stop at any moment. A man in a white coat came out, peering over his rectangular spectacles as he came to stand in front of the sitting boy.

 The doctor peered down at the clip-board he had in his hands and then back to the boy. "Daniel?" He asked, his voice a cautious questioning at first. Daniel looked up at his mother's doctor, Dr. Fiedler, with no emotion. He was tired and mentally cold, he hadn't eaten since last morning when he had gotten the call. There were dark bags under his eyes and paleness to his tan complexion. "Yes?"

"Deine Mutter ist nun stabil, obwohl wir nicht für wie lange weiß." *Your mother is now stable, although we don't know for how long.*

"Ich kann meine mutter jetzt sehen?" *I can see my mother now?* Daniel asked, standing up in the process.

Dr. Fiedler nodded, "Dein mutter ist sediert, du musst ruhig sein." *Your mother is sedated, you must be quiet.* Daniel nodded, "Natürlich." *Of course.* Dr. Fiedler gave the boy one more look before turning away.

Daniel rubbed the back of his neck as he walked to his mother's room, pushing the door open and stepping in, closing it behind him as he entered. The heart monitor beeped slowly as Simone's chest rose and fell with steady, though laboured, breaths. Daniel walked quietly over to the chair that rest by the hospital bed and sat down, taking hold of his mother's tepid hand. The gauze wrapped around each of her wrists scrapped against the soft skin under his own wrist, and he sighed, turning over her left hand gently, tracing the thin line of red with the pad of his thumb. "Mum… bitte… nein weitere…." *Mum… please… no more….*

As a few hours past, coming and going slowly, Daniel soon fell into a restless sleep, his upper body bent over the hospital bed, his head resting on his arms.

He slept; dreaming vivid pictures of bright gold's and yellows. He was in a field of long grass, his mother stood yards away from him but he could see an easy smile on her face, and the corners of her eyes wrinkle as they danced… then she vanished. And as he stood there in the center, his body rested, alone for miles he didn't mind. It was as if he stood there for an eternity until a *Beep---* sounded like a bullet through his mind and he jolted up.

Daniel pushed back his chair as he stood hurriedly. His heart hammering in his chest as his mother's heart monitor became a flat line. His throat constricted when he saw her pale weak body. "*DOCTOR!*" He screamed as he shook his mother's empty form.

A nurse ran in seconds later having been startled by the cry. One glance at the women patient in the bed and her heart fell for the boy who stood next to her. She was clearly dead. Though taking not another thought about it she cried into the hall, "Dr. Fiedler!" Spotting the doctor turning into the hall.

Dr. Fiedler looked towards the nurse, noticing the hurriedness in her voice, he jogged over, his white lab coat flying behind him as he turned into Simone's room. "Schnappen Sie sich die Paddel!" *Grab the Paddles!* He instructed while coming around to Daniel's side. "Daniel bitte Schritt zurück." *Daniel please step back.* Daniel did as he was told, turning to stand in the far corner of the room with his arms wrapped around himself as he watched his mother's doctor remove her gown, he turned away; though still listened as the doctor called "Clear!".

Again and again, he called it but still she didn't response. The boy looked at the scene in a slow trance, the doctor calling it, the nurse writing down the time of death. It was as if his mind could not process the motions he was seeing.

Dr. Fiedler sighed, rubbing the bridge of his nose and facing the teenager who stood behind him. "Daniel... Ich bin so leid, der Stress war einfach zu viel für Ihr Körper. Es sieht aus wie Ihr Körper ging in to Intensive schock. Es gibt nichts, was wir tun können. Es tut mir leid." *Daniel... I am so sorry; the stress was just too much for her body. It looks like her body went in to intensive shock. There is nothing we can do. I am sorry.* He paused before continuing, though in English this time. "I will need you to fill out some forms later, though for now, I will give you a moment."

Daniel nodded mutely, feeling a hand grip his shoulder shortly before two sets of footsteps sounded through the room and disappeared. He took a deep breath, scrubbing his face with his hands before taking hesitant steps towards the body.

He stared down at her pale face, the blood already draining from her complexion, and heaved a dry sob. Sinking to his knees, he grabbed hold of her tepid hand and held it close. "Mamma," he cried, and just like that, the tears started to flow. His head dropping to the bed, He cried.

Chapter Ten

The kitchen was silent as David explained what had happened. Marie could feel herself start to shake softly as the images of that evening played out in her mind; feeling this Alex put an arm around her, drawing her near to him. Marie looked up at him with a drawn face and noticed how tear after tear rolled down his face with silence, though his emotions showed no sign of noticing them.

"He said to call you when you had the time." David finished.

Alex nodded his head slowly as if in a trance. "Can I borrow your phone?" He asked looking to Anaïs.

Anaïs produced a portable home phone from on the counter and handed it to Alex. "He said he was calling from his mobile, I assume you know the number?" Alex nodded a second time. "You can make your call in the living room if you wish." Alex didn't answer, but turned on his heels and strode form the eerily quiet kitchen space.

Marie spoke up, her voice seeming to echo loudly, "Will he be alright?" She asked David.

David sighed, "I don't know Marie... I don't know."

★★★★

Alex sat on the arm of the couch as the phone rang his tears having cleared away though his throat felt dry and his heart hammered in its confinements. A click at the other end sounded and the breath in Alex's throat caught. Pushing it down, he took a deep breath exhaling it before speaking in a choked voice. "...Dan...Daniel?" He said in broken words.

"*Yeah..., I'm here,*" came the quiet voice of his brother at the other end of the connection.

Alex blew out a puff of air, dropping his head into his free hand while still keeping the phone attached to his ear. "*Wie... was....?* How... what...? He asked reffuring back to his native laungage for a second.

Daniel gave an audible groan though muffled by what Alex supposed to be his hand. "David must have told you already. She tried to kill herself."

"Yes, he told me. Marie and I had just got arrive back at the house when we found Marie's mother and David in the kitchen. They explained what had taken place... I'm so sorry Daniel that you had to see that."

"Well you know what it's like so I can't really say I'm alone in this, though it's hard... you know?"

"Unfortunately, brother, I do know; it's not easy."

"No, it's not."

"How are you holding up?"

"My nerves are shot at the moment. Head is spinning as if I'm drunk and I am exhausted."

Alex made a sympathetic noise, "from what I know, those feeling will pass in a few days, though everything became numb for me, so I truthfully don't know how you'll take it."

"I'll have to see what happens then."

They were quiet, letting the silence hang between them.

Daniel was the first to speak. "Out of curiosity: how is it there?"

"It's nice," Alex answered. "This place is, different, I don't know. The people are friendly enough and warm. Maybe slightly different from the people we are use to associating with, but a good different. You know?"

"I do know." The two gave a short laugh.

"You'll like it here Dan."

"We'll see soon enough. After the funeral ...."

Alex sighed having had a momentarily laps, though the thought of it nagged at the back of his head like a needle poking at his skin. "When will the funeral take place?"

"A week. I had to handle some paper work, but there's still some left that David needs to fill out that I can't. I talked to him about it and you and he will be flying out here tomorrow in the afternoon."

The dark haired male just nodded his head though unaware that his brother couldn't see it.

"Alex?"

"Oh right, yeah I understand. I guess I'll see you in a few hours then huh?"

"Yeah, I'll see you then."

"'K, if you need to talk to me and I'm not there yet, call me okay?

"Ok, I will."

"I love you. Goodnight Daniel."

"Night Alex. I love you baby brother."

Alex hung up, slowly bringing the phone down from his ear and letting his hand fall heavily in his lap. He swung back and fell across the red couch with a mute thud. He stayed there, content with just the feeling of letting his body just melt into the soft cushion.

His thoughts began to whirl together with a sudden storm. He clenched his lids shut and rolling off the couch he stood. As he did he noticed his drawing from earlier today and gave a small smile. The picture was shadowed though light all the same, the shading; fading in and out in the pencil sketched drawing. A simple picture held beauty.

He grabbed the picture, folding it into forth's and tucking it into his front pocket, walking out of the living area and up the stairs to the second floor.

★★★★

Alex knocked on David's door, looking to the hardwood as he

waited for his stepdad to answer, snuffing the toe of his shoe a few times. David answered after a minute seeing it was Alex, let him in.

David shut the door as Alex walked into the familiar room. "How is Daniel doing?"

The younger sat down on the bed, looking at David as he sat next to him, their combined weight causing the mattress to sink. "He's shaken right now. He's feeling what I had felt. I don't know what will come after that though." David nodded, "And you? I expected you to be... well." He said gesturing to his and then to the dark sky that viewed from the window. Alex rolled his eyes, "I'm not stupid– ok maybe I am a little, but I'm not stupid enough to go running off into the fields that seem to go on forever."

David shrugged, "You never know, you did it the first night."

"I wasn't planning on running away into the night David, I just needed air."

His stepdad shrugged again, "You're taking this oddly well. Why?" He asked curiously.

Alex got up from the bed, leaning against the dresser, arms crossed against his stomach. "I'm tired of it all, I'm just glad it's over, that she's not hurting anymore," he said. "I don't think I– any of us– could have taken much more. That sounds selfish, I know, but you can't go through something like that and not feel like your drowning slowly and no one is there to drag you out of the undertow."

David listened carefully as Alex talked; not interrupting once to make a comment of his own, he just let him talk. He let him let it go.

Chapter Eleven

The morning came of swift wings, like a breeze, it flew into the Dumas cottage and woke the sleeping occupants, one by one. David and Alex woke that morning just as the sun rose, the warmth of the sun filling the rooms, filtering in through the windows.

The pair made their way quietly down the stairs past Marie's bedroom, the girl having yet to wake up, and into the entry hall. Anaïs was there, waiting for them, her robe securely knotted at her waist as she stood there, her hair falling over one shoulder; a white paper bag was in her hands.

Anaïs looked at the two men, "we'll miss you," she said simply.

David gave a nod, "we'll be back, with the missing part of our family. You and Marie will be able to meet Daniel when we get back."

"We would like that," the woman said, "here, I made you and Alex breakfast," she gave the paper bag to Alex who took it gratefully, already feeling his stomach begin to wake up.

"Can you," Alex started, pulling out the picture he had tucked into his pant pocket, "give this to Marie when she wakes up?" Anaïs nodded, and Alex gave her a smile of thanks.

"Well, we'd better be going," David said, shifting his bag in hand.

"Do you know when you'll be back?" Anaïs questioned, as she opened the door for them.

David let Alex speak for him as he took Alex's bags in hand and

The Good The Bad and Everything Inbetween

started walking down the path with them, walking to the taxi that waited for them; he had called last night and made a pickup appointment. "Two weeks is what he said," Alex answered, stepping outside, "we don't know for sure, but it should be just two weeks."

Anaïs nodded, "Marie, will miss you," she said, with a small smile.

Alex gave her a smile in return, "I will miss her too, goodbye Anaïs."

"Goodbye, Alex."

★★★★

Marie woke up just an hour after sunrise, the rooster just starting to crow; her eyes opened and she felt her body start to wake up, she lay there not moving, not until her mind began to think again and the thought of Alex leaving suddenly reached her and she sat upright, dashing from her blankets as she reached her door and pulled it open, running to the kitchen, her feet slapping against the flooring.

"Mum!" Marie called, trying to find her mother, "Mum?" She asked again, this time quieter.

Anaïs appeared, dish towel in hand as she dried her hands off, "you called?" She asked with an amused expression.

"Did they leave?" the younger questioned, coming around the kitchen table to stand before her mother.

Her mother nodded, Marie's spirit fell, ashamed at herself for having not woken up earlier. "Though," Marie's head shot up at the words, Anaïs hiding her smile as she reached into her robe pocket, "Alex, did tell me to give you this," she said handing her daughter the folded paper.

Marie looked at her mother as she took the paper; Anaïs covered her smile as she turned away and let her daughter be. Marie watched her mother retreating before she unfolded the paper and beheld the drawing she had wanted to see the day she had left Alex alone in the living room. It was just as beautiful as she thought it might have been, and more. The picture held a certain beauty to it, the shades of grays the pencil had made molded together as if shifting together in a sea of light; the light streamed in through the living room window and hit the desk in just the right manner, while the wood of the desk was knotted in a complicated manner. At the bottom of the paper was Alex's scrawled hand writing:

Beautifully Complicated

Marie ducked her head, with a smile she folded the picture back up and stepped out of the kitchen area to return to her bedroom. Marie licked her lips as she entered her room, shutting the door firmly behind her as she walked over to her nightstand and placed the picture in her drawer. She began to undress, and change into clothes for the day's events.

★★★★

Anaïs looked at her daughter as she entered the living room, closing the magazine she had been paging through, "what are you going to do today?" She asked, as she turned up her face as Marie leant over and kissed her cheek.

"Aunt's house, Evelyn and I are going to go into town, the flea market is today."

"Hmm, do you want me to call Evelyn to let her know you're coming over?" Anaïs asked, Marie hummed a yes, "well, enjoy yourselves, bring back some apple's, will you?"

"Yes, alright, I love you" she said before exiting the room, leaving her mother to her reading. The morning air was already dry with a warm breeze as she stepped outside. Her loose clothing was light on her skin as she walked down the road towards the truck.

It was right where they had left it the previous night, with light steps she made her way towards the truck and opened the door, taking the keys from the seat as she slid in. Starting up the ignition, she put the truck into reverse, pulled out of the long driveway and onto the street; following the same path she and Alex had taken to her aunt's house.

The drive, though, was not like the last; it was silent and still save for the noise from the engine. No music blared from the speakers of the old truck and no loud, over produced singing followed it; Marie stayed quiet on the drive, her window rolled down, and the wind cool on her face. She reached her aunt's house in little time, finding her cousin on the porch, waiting for her.

Evelyn stood when she saw Marie pull up, and walked off the porch, coming around to the passenger side when the truck came to a stop. "Why didn't you just call yourself?" She asked as she shut the truck door, Marie pulled away from the house and back onto the road.

Marie shrugged, "I didn't think to."

Evelyn snorted, "You didn't think to," she muttered, "you know, I had hardly any time to get ready."

"Oh?" Marie looked over to her cousin, taking note of her peach colored dress and loose hair that hung down her back, "you look fine to me."

The other raised an eyebrow, "compared to you, I believe I look more than fine," she sniffed. Marie's lips curled into a small smile that she hid from Evelyn as she drove.

★★★★

Alex stared at the back of the airplane seat he was situated behind, his mind telling him he was ready to go back to France; the young man took a look out the plane's window, watching as Germany past under them.

"Hey," David said, "we're going to be back in no time."

"Yeah," Alex agreed, "I just can't wait for this trip to be over."

David looked at his stepson; the elder couldn't see what was going through the young man's mind, although he knew his thoughts must have been muddled and murky. A conflict of wanting to go back, and a desire to move forward, a complicated situation. David touched Alex's arm, turned his head and made himself comfortable in his seat as he closed his eyes and began to sleep.

Alex gave a glance to David's sleeping form, and just as he had predicted, Alex's thoughts and emotions raged inside of him like a war.

Chapter Twelve

Marie slowed the truck to a stop on the side of the road, pulling over onto the grass alongside a row of cars. The market happened for three days, large and grand it was, it held wondrous items and gadgets that anyone would like. New and Old, bought and handmade; it was a place where everyone came, from towns and neighboring cities; it would be crowded until the last item was bought.

The duo got out of the truck, Marie throwing the keys onto the seat just before she closed her door and made her way over to her cousin. "Mum wants me to bring back apples," she said as Evelyn scooted in between two cramped together white tents, Marie followed behind her, turning her body sideways to fit through the space.

"Mère wants the same," Evelyn said as she stopped at one of the booths as an aging lady with wrinkled sun aged skin and white hair held up a handmade beaded necklace to her. "What do you think?" She asked, clasping the necklace around her thin neck.

Marie looked at the multiple strands of light honey wood beads and then to her dress, it complimented her skin tone and dress, "it looks wonderful," she said, giving her a smile.

Evelyn grinned and reached into the neckline of her dress and pulled out 3 notes from her bodice, handing it to the lady, "Merci," Evelyn said thanking the lady. Marie laughed as she watched her cousin adjust the top of her dress, "what?' Evelyn asked raising an eyebrow. Marie just shook her head and laughed quietly. "Fine, don't tell me." Marie just laughed again; Evelyn rolled her eyes and chose to ignore her, taking her time to look at a booth that held an assortment of fruits.

★★★★

Anaïs was busy in the garden, pulling up carrots, when she heard the gate open and a pair of feet step onto the stone path. Anaïs set the carrots aside in her basket and stood brushing the dirt from her hands and wiping the sweat from her forehead. She found her sister Mélanie walking over to her, Anaïs grinned and met her half way, wrapping her arms around her, "I've missed you," she said pulling back.

Mélanie smiled, "I have missed you too, when Marie came by the night before I realized my time for staying away was long overdue."

"Yes, well, I should, could, have come over," she said kneeling by the carrots once more, Mélanie joining her, helping to pick out the orange vegetable from the soft soil.

"How have you been?" Anaïs asked as she brushed dirt from the food.

"Good, life is life, my life at the moment is good, but tomorrow it may change."

"You never know."

"No, you do not."

The two sisters stood; Mélanie took the basket from her sister and turned towards the house. "You know I am perfectly capable of handling the basket," Anaïs said, catching up to her sister's retreating form.

"Yes," Mélanie said, "but I felt like holding it."

Anaïs shook her head and smiled, shutting the cottage door behind her as Mélanie set the basket onto the counter of the kitchen. "Here, let's put them on this," Anaïs said, taking a dish towel and spreading it out onto the countertop. Mélanie dumped the mass of carrots into the sink and Anaïs turned the water on. The cool contents washed over the vegetable, the dirt slowly starting to wash off. The two sisters each picked up a carrot or two and began to scrub them; the time past and they looked at one another with a smile, just enjoying their time spent together.

✦✦✦✦

The flea market had become crowded over the time spent there; Marie and Evelyn scooted and pushed their way through the crowd. They had gloriously ripe green apples and oranges in a bag, and courteous of Evelyn, Marie now had two new accessories both of which her cousin had insisted buying for her; Marie couldn't refuse and let her pay for the simple yet lovely items. One was a knotted ring with a turquoise stone in the middle, while the necklace was a brass gold oval locket.

"Do you think we should go now?" Marie asked Evelyn as they walked away from a candy filled booth, they had been there for little over two hours, maybe more.

Evelyn nodded, "Yeah, I'm getting hungry."

"There," Marie said, pointing to a booth selling sandwiches, "let's get one." The pair walked over and picked out two already made sandwiches, Evelyn paying the man behind the table.

They took their items in hand made their way through the crowded market, pushing past the bodies to reach the two tents in which they had slid past in the beginning. Turning sideways, each girl moved past the cramped space of the white tents and into the open air.

"Is it just me, or does it feel as if I am breathing for the first time?" Evelyn asked as they walked slowly up the road to the truck.

Marie chuckled, "It was getting a tad over whelming," she said going to the bed of the truck and opening it. Evelyn hopped onto the bed, Marie following suit, helping her cousin with their bags, taking the sandwiches out in the process. "Here," she said, handing over her turkey sandwich and opening her own.

Evelyn took a bite from hers and hummed contentedly, "You

know, I think this is the best sandwich I've ever had," she said with a mouthful of bread.

Marie laughed, taking a bite out of hers, "I couldn't agree more." They smiled at one another, chuckling to themselves as they continued to eat, people passing them with curious stares as the two cousins laughed and talked with each other.

Chapter Thirteen

The plane had landed half an hour ago, Alex and David had picked up their luggage and hailed a cab from the airport. Alex was staring out the car window watching as the numerous buildings of the large city of Berlin past by them in a whirl wind of color and people. He had unknowingly missed his birthplace, somewhere a hole inside of him had filled, yet it was only a small portion of the gouge, which was filled, the rest had to remain opened for now.

Alex followed the path the driver was taking with his eyes, watching every turn and stop they came across; and soon, all too soon, they came to a stop just forty-five minutes later in front of a suburban house in a tiny area that was tucked away from the noise of the city. Alex got out of the cab slowly as David paid the man for his work; the cab driver and David got the bags from the trunk and brought them up to the house; the cab driver got back into his car and pulled away from the curb, leaving Alex to walk up the walk way in a quiet manner. He took the time to look around him, taking in the green grass that was long and uncared for, the flowers had weeds throughout them and the trees were untrimmed; the house looked grey rather than white, the young man's heart clenched as he looked upon the state of his childhood home.

"Alex?" David asked as he opened the front door.

"Yeah?" He answered walking up behind him.

David handed Alex his bag, "why don't you take those to your room."

He only nodded as he took his bags from David, his stepdad took his own and walked into the threshold, disappearing around the corner; Alex peered into the entry hall before cautiously stepping in and walking deeper into the corridor, he paused to look into the living room briefly, though continuing on up the stairs to his old room.

It was an odd feeling to be back in his room, like a comforting dream and a nightmare that had come back to haunt him. Alex set his bag down and took a seat on his old bed; the room smelled stale, dust coated everything, no one had cleaned in there since the event that happened that day. He looked around his old room and studied the bare walls and the desk and side table; then his eyes glanced to the floor, a barely there stain was visible, though just barely enough for his eyes to see it but once he saw it he couldn't look away, it was the brightest thing in the room.

A hallow knock sounded on his door and David entered, Alex looked at him, "yeah?" It sounded like he had been saying that allot since they got here.

"I'm going to the hospital," David said, "you want to come?"

"Wouldn't the body be at a funeral home?"

"It's arriving today, they just had to preserve it until they were opened, and we have to pick your brother up."

Alex winced at calling his mother 'it', though nodded all the same, "yeah, I need to see Daniel."

David nodded in understanding, "Ok, then, come on."

Alex stood, took one more glance around the room, itching to crawl away from it, and exited the space, closing the door behind him.

★★★★

The son and stepfather entered the hospital, the doors opening automatically. David walked over to the receptionists desk while Alex continued to the elevators, he pressed the up arrow watching as the numbers counted down until the doors opened and he stepped in;

David saw Alex step into the elevator and rushed over, entering the compartment moments before it shut and began to move.

"What floor?" Alex asked. David leaned over and pressed the three.

They waited in silence, something unknown hanging between them. The double doors opened and they stepped out, Alex following David as he turned left, walking down the corridor, their footsteps making hardly a sound on the tiles.

Alex stopped when he saw his brother sitting on one of the chairs in the hall, he was bent forward, his hands on his knees. Stepping forward, he swallowed and came to stand in front of his sibling. Daniel looked up at Alex, Alex saw the dark circles under his eyes and his pale skin, and his heart broke for his brother, knowing the emotion he was going through.

Daniel's shield broke and his courage came crumbling down, and just like that his eyes filled with tears and one slipped down his cheek; Alex dropped to his knees and pulled him close, Daniel hid his face in the crook of his brother's neck and cried.

****

Marie and Evelyn walked through the door of Marie's home, to hear the sound of laughter coming from the living room. The two girls looked at one another and followed the sound, finding their mothers' on the couch surrounded by paint cans and furniture.

Marie recognized the old chairs and tables, "weren't those in the attic?" She asked pointing to the furniture.

"Mhm," Anaïs said humming.

Marie nodded, "ok, and why are they out?"

Mélanie cut in before Anaïs could speak, "well, David bought the house your mum and he were looking at yesterday, well technically they had already looked at it the day you and Alex came over to our house, well... I guess that means last night; anyways, they had already made a deal with the owners over the phone and were going over there to settle it."

"David, I'm sure, does not want the furniture from his old home—"

"To start over you need a completely new slate to start from," Mélanie interrupted.

Anaïs nodded in agreement, "anyways, we figured we might as well do him the favor of making his home a home."

"So I bought paint," Mélanie said, "and your mum and I have more than enough furniture in our attics to fill a house for three men."

Evelyn and Marie ginned to one another, "sounds like fun," Evelyn said setting the bags aside, "can we help?"

Mélanie smiled, "well of course, you and Marie can do the painting of all the rooms; think you can handle that?" Marie and her cousin nodded excitedly, "good, you can start now. Go get changed, we'll load up the truck."

The two young women grinned and rushed away from the room, forgetting their bags as they hurried up the stairs to Marie's room.

Evelyn shut the door as Marie walked to her dresser and riffled through the drawers until she pulled out two pairs of old, light, loose jeans and a pair of white tank tops. She handed a set to her cousin and put her own on the bed as they undressed and redressed in their new clothes. It was just barely eleven in the morning and the sun was high in the sky lighting Marie's room; the two girls took a few minutes to sit on the bed.

"You know what I love about this? This painting and decorating business our mum's wanted to do," Marie nodded, and Evelyn continued, "I know Alex means allot to you."

"That's the only reason?" Marie questioned, tilting her head, her blonde hair falling over her shoulder.

Evelyn nodded once, "He makes you happy."

Marie smiled, "thank you." Evelyn shrugged, "you can be selfless when you want to be."

"Hey," Evelyn chuckled pushing her shoulder good naturedly.

"Come on," Marie said standing, "we better go they must be nearly done." She pulled Evelyn from the bed and the two walked from the room.

★★★★

The funeral home looked like an ordinary home, the outside was white with blue trim and shutters around the windows, and the only difference was a white painted wood sign in front with the words "Marshall Funeral Home" written on it. Alex, Daniel, and David stepped through the threshold glancing around the building, it looked normal though as they stepped further into the house, to their left was a room that displayed coffins while the room to their right was a large gathering room with chairs decorating the inside.

"I don't like it in here," Alex muttered, mostly to himself.

Daniel nodded while David stuffed his hands into his pockets, "I know the feeling," his stepfather said.

Alex gave a brief glance to his stepdad and stopped. A man with little hair on top of his head and large glasses that magnified his eyes came up to them.

"May I help you?" Asked the man, with a thick accent.

David nodded and pulled the man aside as they started to speak in rapid German, Daniel and Alex looked at one another and went into the coffin room. They looked at one coffin after the other, studying the wood work and the color.

"This feels weird," Daniel said, speaking up in the quiet room.

Alex couldn't agree more, "odd?"

"Very."

The two brothers strode around the room and came to a stop in front of one another, "How long are we staying in Germany?" Daniel asked as the two stared down at a dark cherry wood coffin, brass siding on every corner of the crate.

"David hasn't really told me, I think two weeks at most."

Daniel turned to Alex, "*Two weeks?*"

"Boys?" David said as he walked in, "Mr. Addler and I are going to look at the body," he said coughing slightly. "Do you want to come with us?" The two brothers hurriedly shook their heads no. David nodded in understanding, "right, after we take a look, Mr. Addler and I are going to discuss the funeral; if everything is in order it should take place in two days." David finished and left his stepsons' presence.

Daniel turned to Alex with pursed lips, "*two weeks?* He's planning the funeral already, and in a few days our mother is going to be buried in the ground, and we're going to be moping around Germany for two weeks!" Daniel hissed.

Alex waved his hands helplessly, "I don't know what to say, Daniel."

"Just...," Daniel shook his head, "I don't know, it just doesn't seem logical for us to be staying here for two more weeks, nothing is keeping us here. The house, what happens to the house doesn't matter; I've been living at the hospital mostly for a while now anyways."

His twin just stared at the coffin before them, "I don't know Daniel, we'll see what David say's tonight."

"Yeah," Daniel agreed, "alright."

★★★★

Afternoon sunlight streamed in through the windows of the room Marie and Evelyn were situated in, their bodies lain out on the white carpeted floor of the second room they had painted that day, the chemical smell of freshly painted walls wafted out through the open windows in the room. The two girls didn't say a word to each other as they lay there, their bodies lax. They had white and shades of pale yellow streaked on their arms and splattered on their clothes; empty paint cans were strewn around the room along with around the house, their mother's having taken the liberty of painting the kitchen area so they could move some of the stuff they had found, out of Anaïs and Marie's living room.

They were starting to drift off to the mellow breeze that decided to come into the room when a crash was over heard from downstairs, and the two girls sat up on their elbows looking at one another than to the open door. "We should probably...?" Marie gestured to the hall.

Another crash a string of curses flew to their ears and loud chores of laughter followed shortly. Evelyn nodded and helped Marie up as she stood, "probably best if we do."

The girls took the flight of stairs down to the first level and walked into the kitchen, only to find their mother's both on the floor sitting in a pool of pale yellow paint, Anaïs's back was covered along with the side of her face while Mélanie's backside was all but covered and as bright as the sun.

Evelyn snorted out a laugh along with Marie as the two young woman observed their mother's. "Brilliant," Evelyn chuckled out as she and Marie clung to each other to stay right side up.

Mélanie just rolled her eyes and looked to her sister, "we'll put a rug over the stain." That only caused the girls to laugh harder.

Chapter Fourteen

The day's past and soon the funeral had arrived; the sky was an appropriate shade of grey as it threatened to rain, the clouds blanketing the sky in a low overhang. Alex and Daniel shared a hotel room with two queen beds and very little space to walk around. The day they had come back to the house from the funeral home, Daniel had asked their stepfather what he planned to do with the house, why they were staying for so long. David had replied by handing them a bank notice stating that David had signed the house and everything in it, over to the bank. "We don't need anything form this place," was all he said. The boys left it at that.

Alex stood in front of the window from their hotel room on the 6th floor, the view looked onto another old building and Alex sighed, straightening his cobalt blue tie, re-adjusting it against is black dress shirt. His eyes survived the outside world, his thoughts wondering as Daniel entered their shared room, two tangerines in his hands. "Here," he said handing one of them to Alex.

Alex took the fruit from his brother, though didn't bother to peel it, "thanks," he said, tossing the item back and forth in his hands.

Daniel took a slice from his and popped it in his mouth, glancing at his brother, "What's wrong?" He asked in a low tone.

Alex jaw worked as he silenced the movement of his hands, "we're going to bury our mother in a couple of hours...." Daniel didn't respond.

✯✯✯✯

Marie woke Evelyn up the next, her cousins sleeping face was turned towards her, her was mouth parted slightly as she snored lightly. Marie smiled and carefully got out her bed, exiting the room and closing the door silently behind her. Her cousin and aunt had stayed the night. The two young woman having had a long night of helping their mother's peel paint out of their hair and off their skin.

Marie stepped carefully down the stairs and into the living room, finding her mother on the couch with a cup of coffee in her hands. The girl smiled and walked over to her, joining her mother on the couch. "Good morning," she said.

Anaïs smiled at her daughter as she watched her get comfortable on the couch. "David called, just an hour ago," she said taking a sip of her caffeinated coffee.

"Oh?" Marie questioned, tilting her head. "What did he say?"

"Funeral is today, and that they are going to wait two days, just to make sure everything is situated, before they come back."

"Then...," Marie said slowly. "That means we only have two days to get everything ready for them."

Anaïs nodded, "we'll be fine, you and Evelyn can handle the painting," she said this as she pulled out a piece of yellow paint from her hair. "You're aunt and I can handle the decorating."

"How are you going to put a bed and dresser in every room, along with kitchen supplies, and clocks, and everything else that is needed in a home?"

"Well Mélanie and I found lenders."

"How did you find people with spare house items?"

"Yesterday, while you and Evelyn were at the market, we had the idea and then we just needed supplies. I'll call everyone in a hour or two, to tell them to bring it over today rather than next week."

Marie took a deep breath, "I guess we will make do."

Anaïs ran her fingers through her hair and made a face, pulling another string of dried yellow paint from her hair, "Indeed we will." Marie chuckled and leaned forward to help her mother pick through her hair.

★★★★

The air was humid as the rain threatened to pour. Alex, Daniel, and David stood at the grave, the dark cherry wood coffin lying beside the open pit, a bouquet of pink and yellow flowers rested on top of the wood. The brother's wore identical black slacks and black button down shirts, Alex wore the blue tie while Daniel wore the green one; David had worn all black.

The priest stood next to the grave, his bible opened up to the prayer he was saying, though the words fell on deaf words. The three men stood next to the grave, the three of them deaf to everything but the sound of silence.

Alex stared at the coffin, his blood rushing to his head.

"Mommy! Mommy!" A dark haired little boy called as he raced towards his mother.

A petit lady with honey brown curls turned around and scooped up her son, "Ja?" Yes?

"Schauen Sie was ich gefunden!" Look what I found! He cried, holding out his cupped hands to revile a small frog in the center.

The lady smiled and she kissed his forehead, than his nose, and finally his cheek. "Was ein ziemlich kleinen frosch." What a pretty little frog.

"Alex... Alex, here," Daniel said, shaking Alex form his trance, and handing him a flower pulled from on top of the coffin. Alex took the flower and watched as the priest gestured for four men who stood nearby he had failed to notice on arrival; the men walked over and took up either end of the straps that lay under the coffin, and heaved the heavy weight up, carefully guiding the wood to the dirt pit. Alex could see how heavy it way by the way the men's necks' and arm's bulged, he looked down at the flower, turning it between his fingers.

"Daniel," he said, his brother turned to him. "She's never coming back." Daniel didn't say a word to his brother but wrapped his arms around him and laid his head on his shoulder as the brother's watched their mother get lowered into the ground. David looked at his stepsons and it became even more difficult to hold back his tears that he had obtained when they had arrived at the graveyard.

The men slid the straps away and stepped back to grab the shovels, "come on, Alex," David said, as he and Daniel stepped forward to throw their flowers into the grave. Alex stepped forward as his brother and stepfather stepped back, and looked down at the grave.

"Bye," he whispered, and tossed the flower into the grave. He felt Daniel come up beside him and put a hand on his shoulder.

"Come on." Alex let Daniel guide him away from the grave; he, Daniel, and David all walked away.

Chapter Fifteen

Two day's past faster than the four woman had hoped for, though with help from their neighboures, they had managed to pull it off. The house was complete. Evelyn and Marie had painted all 5 rooms in the house, the two bedrooms, bathroom, kitchen, and the office; Anaïs and Mélanie, as they had said, contacted everyone who had promised them furniture or any other spare household item and made arrangements for them to all come over and help. The house had been filled with people—young and old and in between. They all came to help, one big group of friends and people who were related in some sense.

Anaïs and Mélanie had congregated outside with a glass of wine in their hands to celebrate their hard work. They had just put the finishing touches on the house with their daughters, who had stayed inside to walk through the house and make sure everything was in place.

"They're going to be here tonight, right?" Evelyn asked as she and Marie walked down the stairs and towards the front door. Marie shrugged. Evelyn stared at her curiously, as she opened the door for her cousin and allowed her to step outside before following suit. "Marie?" Marie looked at her and then to the road. "What are you thinking about?"

She was quiet for a minute, just watching the road as they walked down it. She licked her lips, "what if he's different?"

"Everyone is different, Marie, you can't exactly change that."

Marie shook her head, "no, what if he's different from how he left?"

Evelyn cocked an eyebrow at her cousin in question, "what do you mean?"

"What if," Marie said, "what if he's the same as before? When he first came here, he was rude and broken… and then—" Marie stopped for a moment, blinking her eyes as water unknowingly filled them, and she smiled shortly, "and then he became sweet, and kind, and I just don't want him to go back to hating life." Evelyn stared at her as she listened. "He wasn't even at his lowest when I saw him, but the sadness, and the emptiness, and hatred at the world that he tried to conceal, it tore me. I remembered what it had felt like when my father died," she took a breath as Evelyn slipped a hand into hers. "I just don't want him to be mad at the world anymore."

Evelyn gave her a small smile and squeezed her hand reassuringly, "don't worry so much. Things change, and then they re-change, and then they change again. It's like the food chain or the circle of life, you can't stop anything from happening, you can't stop a person from feeling the emotion he or she feels; it just has to happen, and when it's done, we will truly see the final results."

Marie's lips switched into a smirk. "The food chain? The circle of life?" she asked, as she held back a chuckle.

Evelyn laughed, "They were rather crappy metaphors, weren't they?"

The other agreed and laughed, "Yes they were."

★★★★

The hours past, and the late afternoon sun that hung high in the sky was hot upon Marie's back. The young woman wiped the thin sheen of sweat from her forehead and continued to walk forward; the tall grass brushing gently at her bare legs as she walked through the fields by her house, stopping occasionally to pick one of the many flowers that surrounded her. In her hands were a bundle of long steamed flowers of purple and red; Marie brought the bouquet to her face and inhaled deeply, the intoxicating smell of their sweet sent made her smile.

"*Marie!*" Marie turned, finding her aunt standing at the edge of the field. "*David called! They are on the plane; you need to come and wash up, and get ready!*" She called.

"Coming!" She cried back. Stepping carefully through the tangled ground, through the gentle grass; making her escape from the hot overbearing sun.

She made her way to the front door and pushed it opened, stepping into the cool house. The sweat at the back of her neck and on her face cooled instantly as she walked further into the house; the sound of pots and pans sounded through the walls of her home, and echoed everywhere else. She walked into the kitchen area and watched as her mother and aunt bustled around the spacious area, from one pot to another, they stirred and sautéed the food as it cooked. Marie watched in amusement as her aunt started to sing, her mother jumping in moments later. Moments like these, were the ones she cherished the most.

She set the flowers down onto the counter silently and pulled away from the area and let them be; taking her time to walk to the stairs, slowly yet gradually making her way up them; not pushing herself, just leisurely going about it. Slowly, she pushed open the door to the bathroom and shut it behind her, resting her back against it shortly; taking a white towel from the cupboard and setting it over the shower rod as she undressed herself, turning the water on. Marie picked her clothes up and placed them in the wicker basket that stood in the corner near the window; the sound of the curtain rung through the tiled room as she stepped into the porcelain bathtub. Cool, fresh, water touched her skin as she brought her face beneath the spray, washing the sweat away from her flesh. She scrubbed her body clean and washed her hair in lavender sent; the water was turned off and she stepped out of the bathtub, bringing her towel to her face, patting it dry before wrapping it around her body.

She opened the door and walked to her bedroom, finding her cousin there, sitting on her bed. "Evelyn?" Her cousin looked up from the picture frame she was holding, she set it placed it back on nightstand and stood up.

"I'm going to take a shower before the two down stairs get a chance to, by the time their done, they're going to need it," she said shaking her head.

Marie smiled, and stepped aside so her cousin could pass. The door shut behind her and she walked to her bed, letting her towel drop onto the quilt. She noted two outfits lay across the bed, Evelyn having taken the liberty of choosing her clothes for the night, and she own as well. Marie gave a short smile and slipped her undergarments on, taking the cotton white dress and stepping into it, reaching behind her to pull the zipper up. It was soft and light, with a loose skirt. She looked in the mirror and smiled as she blue and green eyes smiled back at her, her tan skin glowing with warmth. Her reflection bit her lip and turned away, going to the bed and sitting down as she opened her drawer and took out the folded picture. Quietly she unfolded the paper and stared at the picture in her hands, a drop of water suddenly staining it. She placed the picture on the nightstand and took her towel, wrapping her hair up in it, leaning back onto her pillows. Marie smiled as she smiled at the thought of the coming hours.

★★★★

"Marie...? Marie?"

Marie stirred, haivng fallen alseep for a short period of time. Evelyn came into her view as she sat up, taking the towel from her head. Her cousin was dressed and made up, looking every bit beautiful.

"What are you doing sleeping?" She demanded. "David, Alex, and what's his name are going to be here in thirty minutes and your not even ready!"

Marie just rolled her eyes and got up from the bed, "I'm going, stop rushing."

Evelyn huffed, as she watched her cousin go to the mirror and check her reflection, "I am not rushing, we just need to get the dinner table ready."

"Where are mum and Aunt Mélanie?" She questioned, looking at Evelyn in the mirror; her cousin stared back and shrugged.

"Mine is probably in the bath, and yours is probably finishing up the dinner," she said, straightening her light blue dress she had on.

Marie looked over her shoulder as she turned about to face the young woman, "well then what are we doing up here still? Come," she said taking her cousin's hand in her own and pulling her forward. Evelyn just rolled her eyes skyward and sighed.

★★★★

The girls' entered the kitchen to find Marie's mother freshly showered and dressed, though still hard at work completing the meal she and her sister had put together.

"Aunt Anaïs?" Evelyn said as the two girls stood there watching her.

Anaïs turned at her name and smiled when she saw her niece and daughter. "Oh good, you're ready, I need you and Marie to set the table, and possibly just straighten up everywhere."

The two girls nodded and turned away from the busy woman, leaving her to her work. Evelyn took the dishes from the cupboard and handed them to Marie as her took napkins and silverware out. Marie placed the plates while Evelyn did everything else. The girls' worked quickly and quietly, as the time ticked by. The clock left them with just minutes to spare as they finished straightening the house. They grinned at each other and took a seat on the couch.

"So who is other person coming with David and Alex?" Evelyn asked as she put her feet on the coffee table.

Marie followed her example, crossing her ankles, "his name is Daniel, and he's Alex's fraternal twin."

Evelyn smirked, "let's hope he's just as delicious to look at."

"Why don't *you* stop talking about guys' as if they are a part of the food group," Marie said shaking her head good naturedly.

Evelyn just gave her a Cheshire grin, "hmm."

Marie chuckled and swatted her arm, "stop."

"Oh, so you're not disagreeing?"

"With what?" Marie asked raising an eyebrow suspiciously.

"That Alex is delicious."

Marie blushed, "he's not delicious, and he's very handsome." Evelyn just stared at her, giving her a look. Marie stayed silent, though under her cousin's gaze, it was hard to resist and after a long pause, she caved and nodded.

"Ah!" She squealed, "I knew you and I were related!" Marie couldn't help but laughed as she watched her cousin.

"Girls', they're here," Mélanie said as she walked into the living room, her hair still wet from the shower.

Evelyn gave Marie's hand a small reassuring squeeze, and helped her from the couch as the three woman walked into the hall. Anaïs was already at the door, inviting them in.

Marie watched with a still heart as David walked in, and then a man she hadn't met before, though whom she assumed was Daniel, followed next. Alex didn't appear and her eyes searched the doorway for him; and just like that his form appeared from out of the shadows and she was greeted by his tanned face and dark brown eyes. An automatic smile was placed on her face and she watched as he stood silently behind his brother and stepdad. Marie's smile soon faded when she noticed the way he was acting. She pulled Evelyn aside and whispered lowly, "something is different."

Evelyn looked at her and then to Alex, "what's different?"

Marie just shook her head, "I don't know."

"Well come in, come in," Anaïs said, standing aside so the three men could congregate into the living area. "Dinner is ready, if any of you are hungry?"

"I am," Daniel said raising his hand shortly.

Evelyn's interest peaked, and she looked at the young man, her eyes surveying him. A small smile appeared on her features as she looked at his chocolate brown hair and deep green eyes that were complemented by sun kissed skin, just like his brother's. Evelyn grabbed her cousin's hand and whispered, "I like him."

Marie looked at Daniel, and smiled, "I thought you might," she whispered back, smiling secretly.

Anaïs ushered everyone into the dining room, "take a seat anywhere," she said, taking her own seat at the end of the table nearest to the wall. Evelyn sat next to Marie while Daniel sat across from her and Alex across from Marie, David sat at the other end and Mélanie took her extra seat next to her daughter.

The dinner progressed smoothly, Daniel chattered with Anaïs and Marie, though kept most of this attention on Evelyn, who in turn couldn't help but smile at him every time he glanced at her. Marie watched the connection with a smile of her own, the girl, however, couldn't place her finger on the emotion she was feeling every time she looked at Alex; the young man had stayed quiet since he had arrived. She prayed he would talk to her, though he avoided her eyes and didn't say a word.

Marie's spirits fell during dinner and she picked at her food for the rest of the night, Daniel caught the switch of her mood and glanced at her puzzled.

After dinner, Daniel pulled Alex aside as everyone went into the living room. "Your acting weird," he said bluntly to his brother.

Alex frowned, "am I?"

"Yes. You are. Or that's how it looks," he said in a low voice as to not be overheard by the others.

"Well I'm sorry, but I can't change how I'm acting."

Daniel gave him a bewildered look, "of course you can!"

"I can but...."

"But what?"

Alex gave him an angry glance, "I don't know!" He shouted. Alex turned on his heels and walked out of the room, opening the front door and slamming it shut.

Daniel winced at the loud sound that echoed through the now silent house, everyone in the other room having heard the last bit of the conversation.

★★★★

Mild summer air rushed over Alex as he ran out into the twilight night, his blood cooling from his short outburst. His jaw clenched and unclenched as he walked over to the nearest tree and kicked it hard with the toe of his shoe. "Shit!" He cursed loudly.

"Alex?" Marie's hesitant voice came from behind him.

The young man ran his fingers through his hair and closed his eyes, turning to the girl. "What?"

Marie bit her lip rethinking over her decision of following him, though shook her head and held fast to her decision. "I wanted to talk to you," she said coming closer. "Are you ok? I saw what happened just now."

Alex shrugged, "I'm fine."

Marie nodded, "that's good. Is everything all right? Between us, I mean."

"Not everything is about you, Marie," Alex snapped, turning his back on her once again.

Marie flinched, "I'm sorry, I was just curious…."

"You need to stop, Marie, just leave me alone. I need to think a few things out right now. Just stay away from me for a while." A door shut from behind Marie and Alex looked behind her, shaking his head he turned from the scene and walked away.

A hand fell on Marie's shoulder; the girl looked behind her, up into Daniel's green eyes, her own multicolored eyes filling with tears. "He didn't change," she whispered.

Daniel shook his head, "I'll talk to him." He walked past Marie and ran after his distressed brother.

Chapter Sixteen

"Alex!" Daniel called. "Alex! Wait, dammit Alex, wait!"

Alex turned around sharply, "what!"

"Why did you say that to Marie? She has done nothing to you!" Daniel said, stopping in front of his brother.

"She has no right to pry!"

"You have no right to yell at her!"

Alex groaned in frustration, "I don't know what to do right now. I can't keep my emotions in check right now, they are everywhere."

Daniel put a hand on his brother's shoulder, "your upset." Alex looked away. "I understand, though you *don't* take it out on these people who have taken us into their home, fed us and made us feel welcome. Now you may know them more than I do, but I know these people care for us. Marie cares for you."

Alex looked at him, his eyes clear of his previous anger. "I messed up… I just need time," he said with a sigh.

"Talk to her tomorrow. Don't ruin something that makes you happy." Alex nodded in understanding.

"Boys, come on we're going," David said as he walked past the boys' to their red rental car that was parked in the driveway; an air of frustration hanging onto the man as he past.

Alex and Daniel glanced at each other before hurriedly getting into the car, Daniel in the front while Alex took the back.

The car was quiet for a few minutes, a tense silence hanging over them; but before long David spoke, "Alex." Alex looked away from the window and glanced at his stepdad in the rearview mirror. His voice was steady and calm as he spoke his next words, "I'm tired of your attitude, your choice of grieving is fine, to seclude yourself from everyone, but you have to get past this. She's gone now; it's for the best that—"

"How can you say that?!" Alex asked astonished.

"Well would you have liked it better if she were in pain, and miserable for the rest of her life!? Stuck in a mental ward until the day she finally dies of old age!" David yelled, stopping the car suddenly and turning it off; everyone jolted forward from the sudden stop.

Alex looked away and shook his head.

"What!" David demanded.

"No! Ok," Alex shouted, his voice seeming to echo in the small cramped space. "*No*. I would never want that for her, I'm just trying to deal with the fact that she's never going to get better, she's never coming back!" Alex's voice choked for a moment. Daniel could feel his eyes fill with unshed tears. "Before, I knew she was alive, and I could handle that; but *now*, now I know that she isn't alive, she's buried in some cemetery in the ground rotting!" The young man said through clenched teeth, a small sob escaping. David was silent. "She's never coming back, and I'm trying to understand that; for some reason I keep feeling as if she will suddenly appear, though I know she won't, and that's what hurts the most."

Alex couldn't speak any longer, his voice void of words, having said all that he could say. David started the car up; as he drove the rest of the way to their new home, Daniel watched his brother in the car door mirror, knowing he felt the same as he did.

David pulled up in front of a two story house, and turned the engine off, putting the car in park. The three men got out from the car and grabbed their luggage from the trunk, making their way up to the front door. David opened it for them and Daniel and Alex stepped forward into the threshold.

"Wow," Daniel said as he found the light switch and flipped it on.

The house was completely furnished and freshly painted. Alex just looked around surprised.

David came up on Daniel's left, "they did this?" He questioned aloud.

"Who else," Alex said.

The three of them walked quietly into the house, taking in everything. "Um," David started, "Alex, Daniel, your sharing a room, its upstairs, mine is down here. I guess we'll see each other in the morning." The two young men nodded and took their bags, making their way to the stairs. David watched for a brief moment as they progressed up the stairs, before taking his own bags and heading to his room.

The boys walked down the hall, past one open door that led into what looked like an office, and to another opened door that held a bedroom with two twin beds in it. Daniel pushed the door open further and walked in with Alex; the two set their bags on the floor at the foot of their beds.

"Unpack tomorrow?"

"Yeah," Daniel agreed. "It's been a long day."

With tired, heavy limbs, the two stripped to their boxers and pulled back their quilts on slid in between the cool sheets. They settled themselves and didn't say a word to each other as they quieted. Both knew neither was asleep, their thoughts reeling, their emotions in a rage from the past week's events.

Alex turned his head towards his brother, though the dark room making it impossible to see him. "Hey, Daniel?" He heard his brother turn towards him.

"Hmm?"

"Goodnight."

They turned away from each other's invisible forms and continued through the night in a silent state.

★★★★

Alex woke that morning before everyone else, a change in his attitude was clear as he showered and dressed before borrowing the keys to the rental and driving to the Dumas house. It was a beautiful day with a light breeze that felt cool against his skin. He took his time walking to the door when he arrived, though when he stopped in front of it he hesitated before knocking upon the wood.

No one answered, so he knocked again, and again, no one answered. Alex stepped back and looked up at the house, shaking his head. "Great," he muttered, stepping away and pacing himself as he walked back to the car.

A door opened from behind him, "Alex?" Said the soft voice of Evelyn.

Alex turned around, an apologetic look on his face, "oh, I didn't know no one was awake."

She shook her head, "no, Marie and I have been up for about an hour, talking about last night."

"Oh," Alex murmured, bowing his head in shame.

"No, no, would you like me to get Marie?"

"Would you?" Alex said with a slight smile.

Evelyn gave him a friendly nod, "sure, though wait out here, everyone else is asleep." The young girl disappeared back inside the house, letting Alex wait by the door.

Minutes past before a fresh face Marie stepped out of the house; she greeted Alex with a kind yet hesitant smile, tugging lightly at her white blouse that was complemented by a pair of light, old faded jeans. "Hello," she said, speaking first.

Alex started to speak, but stopped himself, the silence was awkward. Finally he spoke. "Do you want to go for a walk?"

Marie nodded, "yes"

Alex held out his hand to her and felt as she slowly slid her palm into his. Marie led the way to a worn path through the fields, tall grass surrounded them, and soon it hid them form view as they wandered further into the land.

"I'm sorry about last night," Alex said, being the first to break the silence.

"My mother and aunt were very worried; they stayed up most of the night talking about what happened. I...," she trailed off. Alex looked at her as she steered them off the path. "I thought maybe it was me, but then I realized it couldn't have been. When you left, you left me with hope, for us...possibly. Though when you came back, it was as if that hope had been killed; it hurt what you said to me, but I can't disagree with you."

"No, Marie," Alex said dropping their hands and stopping the girl, turning her to face him. "I was wrong; I shouldn't have snapped at you, I was out of line."

Marie just took his hand in hers again and continued on, "You're grieving, it's understandable."

Alex scoffed, "no, I have grieved, but it's over, she's not coming back, I have to understand that." He said as they stopped again in a small secluded area.

Marie walked ahead of him and knelt down in front of a large stone. Tracing it with her fingertips, "I remember when I had just put my father in the ground, how hard it was, and how angry I was, at everyone; it was as if I could not control how I dealt with my emotions, I was silent and bitter at everything," she said, looking at the stone. Alex came over and knelt down next to her. Realizing it wasn't just a rock, but a gravestone, with her father's name on it: *Élie Dumas*. The girl looked at him, "I was just like you, it's hard, and I know you're not over it, not completely." Alex was silent. "I, will listen, I will..., I just want you to know that I will be there for you." She said with an exasperated sigh.

Alex was silent as Marie peered at him, finally the boy nodded and looked at her again with a smile on his face, "I know." He lent forward, placed a hand around the back of her neck, and brought her face forward so he could kiss her cheek, "I know," he murmured. He looked into her blue and green eyes and with a small smile, he and Marie looked down at the grave. Alex was smiling inside and out, he had been given a second chance to live again, a second chance to love again...a second chance at loving wildflowers.

Never Let Me Go

One

Life and death are nothing but two items of the same circle, having one, but soon to have the other, 'tis natural in the state of life. Though one is shorter than the other; leaving us with no room to examine our actions that have preceded us through time. No one truly understands what he or she has lived through, or that they never have enough time to figure it out.

England, mid 20's…

The fields of the countryside were tall and lean with the wild grass and blossoming flowers that grew through them. A mild wind crept through the air and caressed Jolene Hart's flesh as she walked through the seemingly endless fields; a feeling of walking stark naked as the light summer dress of hers seem to vanish in the wind, her skin feeling refreshed as if nothing was left untouched by the seductive wind.

Her finger tips brushed across the tops of the grass as she walked forward, taking small steps, small breaths, as she walked. The sun shone in a cloudless sky and illuminated her deathly white skin a glow of the brightest yellow; warming her thoroughly.

"Oh…," she murmured quietly as she felt the sun's heat. Eyes closed, she rose her head to the sky, neck arched up into a graceful curve.

The moment, no matter how wonderful, was too soon broken by the sound of her friend Mara's voice.

"Jolene! Do you know how worried I have been? Trying to find you, and here you are in the fields while sick!" She all but cried out as she hurried over to her friend.

Jolene gave a slight smile and closed her eyes once more to the sun, "hush, Mara," she muttered. "The air will do me good."

Jolene could all but hear Mara's eyes roll and feel the burning of her eyes in the back of her head. With a sigh, she surrendered, "fine. Though promise me I will be able to come outside for a few minutes occasionally. I do hate not being able to go outside."

Mara gave her friend a smile and putting her arm around her body, "yes well we'll see. I'm sure the fresh air will do us both good occasionally, a break from that stuffy ol' cottage. "

"Yes, Mara, fresh air now and then will do us both some good," Jolene agreed, letting her friend guide her back to the house.

"Now come on, back to bed with you."

The mild English air soon left and the caressing seductive wind was all but gone from Jolene as she entered her aunt's cottage just a ways from where she had been previously.

Her aunt Taliss, gloriously plump in her aging years with pink cheeks and blonde curls, bustled into the living space as Mara and Jolene entered. Giving the girls a look and more, she just shook her head and swept an arm around Jolene's middle. "You know better than to go off without telling us where you're going," she said shuffling the sick girl to her bed and applying pressure to her shoulders to make her sit down on the spring mattress.

"Oh aunt, you know I mean nothing by it, but you know you wouldn't let me go outside if I had asked," Jolene explained with a sigh as she laid her body back and stopped when her head touched the soft feather pillow.

Aunt Taliss just tilted her head to the side and gave her niece a look of bemusement, "you, my dear, do not know what I would have done," she said giving her side a light tickle.

Jolene giggled some and smiled, "yes, alright, I'm sorry aunt. Next time I will tell you."

"Yes you will," Aunt Taliss said with a pointed look and a small smile before walking to the door. "Now go to sleep, I want you better by the week's end!"

Jolene nodded with a grin, "I will try my best, aunt." With no other words or action, Aunt Taliss shut the door to Jolene's bedroom and soon the girl of 19 years, was left alone with nothing but a desk, four walls, a dresser for clothing and a singular window to look at.

"Well...who ever said being sick was absolutely boring, is an absolute idiot," she muttered in a sarcastic tone giving a breathless cough as she spoke, then soon more came and the breathless coughs became painful ones that felt like daggers. The coughing continued and Mara rushed in with a glass of warm water and honey.

Sitting closely to the coughing girl, Mara set the glass down and helped Jolene sit up as she hacked out coughs. "Here you go dear," she said in a soothing voice, tipping the clear glass up to Jolene's full pink lips.

Jolene choked for a moment on the water and honey, but soon the contents went down without complaint and the coughing stopped, her throat's inflamed aching too followed through and began to calm.

When the coughing subsided, Jolene wiped at the tears that had gathered in her eyes and gave her friend a grateful smile, "Thank you, Mara," she said gratefully, leaning against the wall her bed was pushed to.

Mara sighed and gave Jolene's shoulder a light squeeze, "I wish you would get better soon," she whispered, dropping her hand to her lap.

Jolene couldn't help but just shrug, "I can't stop what I have no control over."

"Yes, well, this must end at some point. Nothing lasts forever; if it did then nothing would have a beginning."

The girl in her bed gave a soft smile, "I agree," she murmured. "Nothing lasts forever, that is why God made death."

Mara scowled, "Don't speak of death, Jolene. You'll jinx yourself," she said, muttering the last bit.

"Well I guess I just won't speak anymore of the matter for now," she said, settling into the bed.

"I don't want you to speak at all, not with that cough you have," Mara stated standing up as she did so. The bed lifted as her weight freed the mattress from the body mass. Her brown curled hair hug loose in a mass of chocolate color to her waist as she leant down and gave a sweet kiss to Jolene's forehead.

Jolene's eyes closed shortly as her friend's lips touched her skin, her eyes fluttering open when the pressure disappeared. "Thank you, Mara again for the honey water," she said in a drowsy state, her voice slurring in the slightest. She hardly heard Mara whisper a, "Your welcome, dear," before she left the room, shutting the door silently behind her.

Jolene stayed, melted, into her mattress as the warm honey water took it's affect on her body and soon her eyes closed and refused to open again to her will; her mind becoming a blank screen and soon, all too soon, she was the prisoner of a dreamless sleep.

Mara settled into the carved wooden chair that rested in the kitchen area, the cushion aunt Taliss had stitched comforted her bottom from the hard plank of the wood seat. With a defeated sigh Mara's shoulders sagged and her eyes closed.

"Oh do not worry child," aunt Taliss said as she went to obtain the seat across from Mara's; setting two cups of tea down and a small plate of biscuits down, "my niece will get better it's just a matter of time."

Mara opened her eyes and took a biscuit from the plate, "she seems to be getting worse, aunt Taliss."

"All things get worse before they can get better."

"Yes but...," the girl gave a short nod, "your right."

"As always," aunt Taliss said with a smug little grin.

Mara chuckled, "yes aunt Taliss, as always." When they quieted Mara took the time to peer around the kitchen area; taking in the brightly lit room with the shine of the sun streaming in through the windows, the white and red and yellow colors that decorated the space with patterns of flowers and people. Copper and iron pans and pots were hung on the wall while a stove was pushed into the corner for the heat in the winter. The floor was stone and easily kept clean during all season, an array of flowers stood proud in the middle of the block counter that sat primly in the center of the kitchen. Mara turned her caramel eyes on aunt Taliss once more, "Thank you for housing me, aunt Taliss," she said, hoping aunt Taliss could hear the love and gratefulness in her voice. She had become orphaned at the age of 16 when her parents passed away from fever. Jolene's aunt had willingly taken her in after their death's, saving her from the children's home and the work house. Though still after three years, she could not help but still thank the woman for her kindness.

"You are a friend of Jolene's," aunt Taliss said, waving away the thanks. "I have known you since you and Jolene was just young enough to run. Do not thank me for taking you into my home; you are as much my blood as Jolene is; I should be thanking *you* for making my, our, Jolene so happy. I couldn't have asked for a better set of nieces then you and the girl in the room just down the way," aunt Taliss finished with a curt nod and lifted her cup to her lips and took a rather large sip of her tea.

Mara sat with her back straight now, a look of pure happiness shinning in her eyes as she stared at the older woman before her, a smile tugging at her lips. For minutes, she just sat there staring.

"Have you become frozen, girl?" Aunt Taliss asked peering over her cup.

With those words, Mara stood from her chair and threw her arms around the woman before her in a tight embrace. "Thank you, aunt," she whispered into her neck. She breathed in deep, the smell of vanilla filling her senses before she pulled away and once again took her seat; glancing out the bay window that was presented before them, watching the site of the fields and the singular dirt road.

The girl didn't notice as aunt Taliss took a sip from her tea, hiding the smile that curled at her mouth as she too, watched the fields and road.

The hours past, the morning turned to noon and soon that too turned to dusk. Jolene awoke to the darkening sky, eyes blinking back the haze and rubbing at her eyes to take the sleep from them. She sat up in her bed, pulling back the thick blanket she had been covered with in the previous hours by either Mara or aunt Taliss; maneuvered her legs to the side of the bed, her feet touching warm hard wood as she sat straighter.

Jolene stretched her arms above her head and then twisted her back, taking out the kinks that had gathered; moving a piece of her blonde hair, she had inherited form her aunt, away from her face and letting her wide hazel eyes scan the room before she stood and walked to the window.

The countryside of Marlborough was beautiful as twilight set in; sky darkening to a cloudless night that let the stars gather in mobs to create a twinkling affect. Jolene's eyes danced over the dark sky from her window pane, watching the heavens come to life before her very soul.

Jolene knew nights like these were precious; the skies in England were always filled with large fluffy white clouds and, on more occasions, a grey overhang that fell like a lid over the nation.

She coughed lightly, covering her mouth waiting for it to subside. When it did, she sighed and looked to the heavens that were presented before her, "What is happening?" She asked in a quiet whisper that seemingly echoed in her scarcely filled room. She didn't expect a reply, God was far too busy to answer her questions and she didn't completely mind that thought.

Her mind started to fog over again with a sudden exhaustion that over took her body and, with heavy feet and drooping eyelids, she drug herself to her bed and pulled the quilt back, crawling in between the neatly made sheets. Just as her head laid itself upon the pillow her eyes shut and she was soon fast asleep.

The busy bustling in the house was what woke Jolene the next morning, the fog in her mind soon cleared as she wiped away the sleep that lay in her eyes. Sitting up she pulled the covers back slowly, coughing lightly, and made her way to door; though first taking her time to look out her window, the morning sun coming up, rising higher and high in the sky. She smiled and gave a gentle content sigh and continued forward. When she opened her room door the sound of talking made its way to her ears, and she walked forward towards the kitchen.

The house halls were empty, room doors were open and curtains throws back as sunlight started to stream in through windowpanes with golden light. Jolene followed the voices to the kitchen and stepped into the spacious area. Jolene glanced around the place and noted her aunt Taliss cooking up the bangers while Mara sat at the table that lay by the window. Her eyes were set upon the window and a cup of tea lay in her hands.

"Good morning, aunt Taliss," Jolene said, going over to kiss her aunt's cheek, turning to look at Mara who seemed to not notice her presence, "Mara?"

Mara didn't move but continued to peer out the window. Curious, Jolene went forth and glanced over Mara's shoulder to see what had caught her friend's attention, "Mara?' She said again only this time near her ear.

Mara jolted and turned her head sharply, "oh Jolene, you scared me!"

Jolene raised a brow, "I did call your name."

The girl blushed and turned around to peer out the window once more, "I'm sorry, I'm just watching," she muttered.

"Watching what?" Jolene asked; all she could see were the road and the fields beyond it.

Mara stood and took Jolene's chin in her hand and turned her head to the walkway that lead to the house, there standing at the small wooden gate was Doctor Fergus McGraw and his two sons Travis and Collin, seeming to be disusing something.

"Is that Travis? I thought he was at university in the Americas?" Jolene asked stepping closer to the window just as Mara did.

Aunt Taliss clucked her tongue, coming to stand with the girls, "Aye, he was, but he's back now for the summer season. Collins will be staying too, though be joining his brother at university in the fall."

The two girls turned to gap at the woman. "How did you know that?" Mara asked bewildered.

Aunt Taliss shrugged her plump body, "Lady's tongues wag at the thought of gossip. It seems to me that two very eligible young men are a very good source of gossip to the wives and daughters," she finished with a twinkle in her green eyes. Jolene and Mara laughed turning back to the window.

"They have grown up, haven't they?" Mara asked looking over her shoulder to aunt Taliss. Aunt Taliss nodded in agreement and went back to her cooking.

"Yes they have grown up," a preoccupied Jolene said watching as the trio made their way up the path, "Oh, their coming up!" She said, and both she and Mara scrambled away from the window to sit at the table, Mara pouring Jolene a cup of tea in the process.

"Aunt Taliss, why are they here?" Jolene asked taking a sip of her tea, humming contently when the contents warmed her body.

Aunt Taliss looked up from her cooking stove, "I called for the Doctor, though I presume the boys must have wanted to come along."

Mara looked up from the table she had started to trace patterns on, "why?"

"Hmm?" Aunt Taliss question.

"Why did you call for the Doctor?"

"I called him because I want him to look over Jolene. I want my niece to become well, don't you?"

Mara nodded and went back to tracing the patterns on the table's white cloth when a knock came from the door.

The two girls looked up from what they were doing and watched aunt Taliss with wide curious eyes; curious as to what, they weren't too sure. They held their breath as she opened the door and ushered the gentlemen in.

Standing to greet their guests, Mara gave a bright smile to Collin who in turn gave one of his own. Jolene's eyes were on Travis as he made his way to stand near her. "Hello, Jolene," he said politely, giving her a small warm smile.

"Manners, Travis!" Dr. McGraw scolded.

"Oh no, it's quiet alright Dr. McGraw, please, no formalities."

"Yes but the boy needs to learn a few," he said with a smile.

"Father, we've known them since we were kids," Travis said shaking his head and looking at his father before turning back to the girl before him. "How are you, Jolene?"

"I've been better," she said coughing lightly.

Dr. McGraw's eyebrows drew together and he came over to the pair, his Doctor's bag jingling slightly; placing a hand on the girl's shoulder, "come lass, lets' have a look at you," he said and steered the girl away from the other.

Travis turned to the three that were left in the room, "how has she been? When did this start?" She asked looking between aunt Taliss and Mara, Collin stared in turn, his curiosity becoming him, though, held his tongue.

The aunt shook her head, "It's been weeks, we've been giving her warm honey water, and it helps to a point but only for so long. We've been keeping her in the house and in bed most of the time, trying to get her to rest; she just doesn't seem to be getting better."

Collin and Travis looked at one another, Mara looking between them, a single question running through their minds, "What will happen to her?"

Jolene sat on the cushioned seat near the window giving the Doctor as much light to work with as possible; waiting patiently as he looked through his black leather bag, pulling out a small rounded mirror on a long handle and other such items.

Dr. McGraw came and kneeled in front of her, "open wide, sweet," he said. When she did, he stuck the long handled mirror into her mouth. Jolene watched his face as he did so, noting the way his brows pulled together and the frown the tugged at his lips. When he was done, he sat back on his heels and hummed.

"What is it?" She asked.

"I'm not sure...," he muttered thoughtfully and stood once again, going to his bag. "Can you tell me what has been happening? How does your body feel?"

Jolene thought for a moment, "I've been tired far more than usual, coughing to very painful extents and sometimes I feel chilled. I don't really feel the need to eat anymore either and sometimes I become feverish."

The Dr. looked troubled when he turned back to face her, "I see. Will you excuse me for a moment?"

Jolene nodded and the Dr. left the room, leaving her to wait.

Dr. McGraw made his way to the kitchen, watching his two sons' and the other two ladies' of the house crowd around him.

"Well? What is wrong with my niece?" The aunt near bought demanded.

"It's hard to say," he said rubbing the back of his neck. "I can see nothing wrong except the color of her skin seems to be lacking. Though other than that, I can't seem to find anything seriously wrong with the girl; my instincts tell me different. What she described, it seems to be something much larger."

Travis shook his head, "Then what?"

Dr. McGraw sighed, "I don't know."

Jolene sat in her chair trying to take in a breath as small coughing fits emerged one after the other, having come moments after the doctor left.

The fits became larger and soon pain started to erupt through her lungs, she leant forward and covered her mouth with one hand the other went to the chair's side to keep from falling forward. The coughs continued for what seemed like hours to the girl, the pain was intense as they soon slowed to a stop and with heaving lungs, she sat back against the chair. The taste of metal was in her mouth and she winced at the flavor. Pulling her hand from her mouth, she cried out as her skin had turned the color of the red flowers her aunt grew on occasion.

"*Doctor!*"

The group of five heard the scream and rushed out of the kitchen and into the living space.

"Oh!" Mara cried out as she saw the blood covered on her friend's hand. Collin put an arm around her and shuffled her out of the room.

Aunt Taliss stood there with a hand to her breast a look of horror etched onto her skin, "Jolene," she whispered, taking a step towards the girl.

"No!" The Dr. cried. "No, not until I give her the proper treatment."

Aunt Taliss reluctantly backed away and left, giving her niece one last glance. Dr. McGraw gave his son a sad a look, "You have to leave too, Travis."

"No."

"Now, Travis," a thread of steal falling into place as the doctor said those two words. The son gave in to the order.

When they were left alone the doctor took a bottle of pure alcohol and soaked a white handkerchief with it. He took her blood coated hand and began to scrub at it. "Has this happened before?" He asked as he cleared the blood away.

The pale frightened girl shook her head, "no," her voice shook as she spoke, "Never."

"I didn't think so."

Jolene sat there frightened and suddenly very chilled. She didn't know what to do, she was lost. The doctor took notice of the girl and her state; with a father's feelings coming forward, he brought the girl close and gave her a hug, "It's alright, lass. You will get over this."

Jolene felt a tear roll down her cheek, "thank you Dr.—"

"Please, call me Fergus," he said pulling back.

The girl settled back into the chair, calm once again, though still chilled. "Thank you, Fergus."

Fergus gave her a smile, "Your welcome, lass. Now lets' get you healthy again."

Aunt Taliss sat slouched in the kitchen chair, her shoulders hunched and head bowed though no tears came forth. Mara cried, fearing the worst for her dear friend and sister. Collin stood next to the weeping girl, a hand around bought her shoulders as he leaned against the table. Travis stood pacing the floor, his gaze solely focused on the patch of ground he stepped onto next.

"Travis, you will wear a trench through Miss Hart's floor," Collin said in the quiet air, the sound of his words seemed to create a shattering affect to their ear drums and they all but winced though not saying a word.

Travis stopped his pacing and took to leaning against the wall and staring at the entrance which his father would soon be coming through.

The seconds ticked into minutes, and soon those minutes turned into a single hour, when the doctor finally appeared no one said or did anything, they stayed where they were and waited for the man to speak.

Fergus cleared his throat, "She has tuberculosis."

Still they stayed quiet, none of them seemed able to speak and in that silence the doctor went on.

"Its quiet advanced, and it isn't uncommon for the bleeding to just now show itself. Symptoms are exactly what she described: feverish, lack of appetite, unusually tired; and one she may not have noticed, but, loss of weight. The poor girl is unnaturally thin," he sighed, "the best you can do is give her the medicine I have prescribed her; I had a small vial on hand though I will stop by with a larger one tomorrow. I escorted her to her bed just a moment ago and she should be asleep by now. When she wakes I want her to go outside, she should go out in the fresh air whenever she can. The country's dryer air will be good for her."

Aunt Taliss stood form her place on the chair and closed her eyes briefly before striding forward to the doctor and placing a hand on his shoulder, squeezing it gently. "Thank you," she said with sincerity.

Fergus gave the woman a kind warmhearted smile, "I have known Jolene since her and Mara were tots, running through those fields. I would do anything for that girl."

Aunt Taliss nodded, "I know," she said and back away, taking her place once again.

Mara sat in her seat not raising her head as she asked, "Is she going to die?"

Fergus gave the girl a pitied look and went to kneel in front of her just as he did to Jolene a few minutes past, "If we keep her in a dry climate and give her, her medicine then no, love, she will not die. But God holds the cards to what may really happen, I am only a doctor and only try to make her better. If God wants her to live then she shall, if she is to die, then so be it. That is the way of life."

Mara gave a dry sob and turned away; Collin wrapped his arms around her and held her close to him as she shook with repressed tears.

The doctor shook his head, "I have done all that I can do, now it up to the rest of you."

"Collin and I will help," Travis interjected, breaking his silence.

"Aye, boy I think that will be a good idea," he said giving his son a caring look. With one last glance at the surrounding faces he turned to the door and opened it, "I shall leave now, Travis, Collin, you'll come with me today but tomorrow you should come along when I give Miss Hart her medicine." His sons nodded in agreement and followed their father to the door, though Collin giving the top of Mara's head a sweet kiss before he followed suit. "I will come around ten, expect me then," Fergus said, and with that he swept from the room and down the walk way. Travis shut the door, giving the women a glance back just as the door shut.

Jolene's back was turned to the door as she curled up on her side, facing the wall. Her eyes were dry of tears as she stared at the white wall; hands folded in front her chest with the covers pulled up and over her shoulders. She listened to the voices talking amongst themselves from down the hall, their words drifting to her ears in pieces, though none that she could make any sense of. The medicine was starting to take effect and her eyes began to droop as her heart began to slow to a steady hibernating pace; her breathing became deep and unheard as she gave into the drug that now filled her veins.

The young girl paced the floor of the brightly study while aunt Taliss sat in one of the two cushioned chairs that sat primly next to a long window that reached from the floor to ceiling with long drapes hanging from it. Aunt Taliss was currently reading the paper she had left untouched touched on the kitchen counter, scanning the headlines and then the articles.

Mara pushed away a chocolate curl and looked at aunt Taliss, "Why do you read that?" She asked, gesturing to the paper.

"If you don't read the newspaper, you are uninformed," she stated, not bothering to glance up at the girl.

"Yes but if you do read the newspaper, you are misinformed. So why bother reading it?" Mara countered back as she started to pace once more.

Aunt Taliss finally took her eyes away from the morning's newspaper and watched the girl for a few moments, "I am reading it not because I want to but, because I have to do something to keep my mind preoccupied; and child, come and sit down, you're making me dizzy."

Mara huffed and walked over to the chair across from the other and sat, turning her head as she did so to look out the window, "Will she survive?" she asked in a soft voice, not taking her eyes off the blue sky that seemed endless at that second.

A sigh came from the aunt and she folded the paper and put it aside, "I don't know, child. For now we just have to do as the doctor says."

"When she wakes up later in the day, I'll take her to the mountain."

"That sounds like a marvelous idea, Mara," aunt Taliss said leaning back into the chair's long back and sighing deeply, "I think I will rest my eyes right now," she murmured closing her eyes, "So tired from today's events."

Mara watched as the older woman fell asleep, the day's early events having taken an exhausting turn for aunt Taliss. The girl stayed in the chair across from the sleeping aunt, picking up a book from the table that the newspaper laid on; with no words and no sounds, she opened the book and began to read.

The morning soon passed and the afternoon crept upon country cottage. The house was silent, no creeks and no moans were heard, no voices talking, not a whisper was spoken; just the complete silence. Jolene finally woke that afternoon though not as pleasantly as she would have liked. Without warning she rolled off the side of the bed and the ground came up from below to meet her; she squealed in surprise as she landed. Her quilt lay on her, tangled around her body and with little struggle she managed to free herself form the cloth's confinements.

When free of the quilt she sat atop of them with her legs crossed and her hair disheveled, the tie at the neck of her nightgown had come undone and was now falling off her shoulders. Her mouth was cotton dry as she opened and closed her mouth trying to moisten it. "Bugger," she muttered, standing and kicking the quilt. She passed herself slowly as she made her way to the door and opened it, leaning against the frame for a direct second; shoving off of it she stumbled through the cottage's halls, keeping a hand on one wall for support as she tried to keep her balance whilst entering the kitchen and going over to the water spigot.

"Jolene?"

Jolene turned at the sound of her name, coming to the face of Mara. "Hullo my dear friend," she muttered, turning back to the spigot. The medicine had yet to completely wear off and was making her slightly discombobulated.

"Here let me do that," Mara said rushing forward to help her with the water, when it was flowing Mara took a cup and filled it; handing the filled glass to the girl next to her.

"Thank you," she said, taking the glass and consuming the water in just seconds.

Mara watched waiting for her to finish. When she was done, the girl took the cup and placed it in the dirty dishes bucket aunt Taliss had placed on the counter some years ago. "Are you feeling alright?"

"Mhm," Jolene hummed, "I will be a complete version of myself once this blasted medicine wears off completely."

Mara chuckled at her tone, "I want to take you somewhere."

Jolene gestured to the door with hands, "Then take me somewhere if you must, anything will do so long as I can get out of this cottage."

"Are you fine to go like that?" She asked pointing to her white cotton nightgown, "We aren't going far."

"Just grab my coat," she said fixing the shoulder of her gown and tying the string that held it in place.

Mara turned and left, returning moments later with a dark green tweed coat with cuffs at the end of the sleeves, large black buttons down the front and the flap of the neck fanning across the shoulders; and a pair of flat tan shoes. Jolene slipped into the coat with help of her friend and placed her feet into the almost ballet slipper like shoes.

The two slipped out the door and down the walkway, taking to the country's dirt road. The two of them must be a sight to be seen if someone spotted them coming down the lane. Both girls wore their hair down, while one was in a nightgown and though the other in a simple summer dress and was not in least bit an odd sight; the very thought of a girl strolling around in broad daylight with nothing but an almost sheer nightgown was un thinkable.

"You know people will think we are crazy," Jolene mentioned, looking an arm through Mara's.

Mara shrugged giving her a sidelong glance, "when were you ever to care what people think?"

Jolene gave a small smile in her friend's direction, "noted."

The two girls walked and walked taking their time in the fresh air; Mara smiled as she looked to the sky, Jolene, however rejuvenated she was from her sleep felt her body soon become exhausted. "Are we there yet?" She asked, restless to find a place to sit for a moment.

"Nearly, we'll cross here," Mara said pointing to the partially worn path that started at the edge of the road and then ascended a small hill.

Jolene recognized the place they were at, picking up the ends of her nightgown, she turned to Mara and grinned, a sudden burst of energy pulled from her and she sprinted forward, leaving Mara to call after her. Jolene didn't listen and ran forward, leg muscles pushing her onward as she climbed what she and Mara called the mountain. Her breath was coming out in gasps by the time she reached the top, and she bent to her knees, catching her breath and letting her heart beat slow.

"Jolene!" Mara gasped out as she finally caught up with the girl, "don't do that again! I am not one for running," she laughed.

Jolene shook her head, "you didn't have to follow me."

"Noted," Mara said with a roll of her eyes.

The two girls stood straight and walked to the very top of the mountain. The sun was at its highest peak and it was one of those rare cloudless days with warm air and a small wind that like to tease their skin once in awhile with its presence.

The mountain overlooked the whole of the country side, nothing but fields and mountains could be seen for miles; shadows played over the plains like a wave, floating and shifting every which way, never staying still; making the area come to life like magic.

"It's beautiful, isn't it?" Jolene stated in a questioning manner, taking a place on the mountain with her legs crossed in front of her.

Mara sat behind her, legs on either side of her friend's; Jolene leaned into her and relaxed as Mara folded her arms around her waist, her head resting atop of Jolene's. "It is, it always will be."

Jolene stayed quiet for minutes, not saying anything, hardly breathing in case she might shatter their little world they had created in that moment. But soon the reality of her, their, situation came bearing down on her and she turned her head so she could see Mara.

Mara glanced down at her friend, "Yes?" she asked.

With a nonexistent smile curving her lips she raised a rand to Mara's cheeks and laid it against the soft skin, caressing it ever so gently, "can you promise me something?"

"Anything."

"You always say you never make promises you can't keep, but can you promise me," Jolene took a deep breath, "promise me you will never let me go, ever. You'll hold me just like this and never let me go?"

Mara tightened her arms around her waist and sighed while pressing a kiss to her forehead, "Jolene, I will never let you go."

"Do you promise?"

The girl nodded, "I promise."

That was all Jolene needed to hear. Turning her head back to face the shifting fields, she leaned back and melted completely into her friend's warm, welcoming embrace.

The next day came at dawn, and the cottage was alive and full as aunt Taliss made a feast for breakfast; laying out the contents and such in the dining room. Mara bathed and dressed, helping Jolene to do the same, washing her back for her and taking the time to pick out a lovely dress the color of the nicest shade of blue, with white cuffs at the end of the sleeves that fell to her elbows.

The girls stood in front of Jolene's mirror, Mara standing behind her with her shin resting on Jolene's shoulder. "You look lovely, Jolene," Mara said, giving her a smile.

Jolene smiled back at the reflection, "thank you." Mara pulled away and offered her arm to Jolene, the girl took it, linking her arm through Mara's,

"Come on," Mara said and pulled Jolene away from the mirror; the door squeaked quietly on its hinges as Mara opened the door, letting Jolene pass first before following.

Travis fidgeted with the collar of his shirt and clearing his throat as he and Collin stood in front of the Harts' cottage.

"Travis?" Collin said looking at his brother, "Calm down."

"I know, I know," Travis said opening the gate's latch and walking up the path, "I am calm," he said over his shoulder before he knocked on the door.

Collin rolled his eyes heaven ward and came up behind his brother just as the door opened and aunt Taliss bright face welcomed them in.

"You boys are early!" Aunt Taliss said hurrying the boys over to the table in the kitchen and setting two cups of freshly made tea in front of them.

"Our father had to make a house call in the city, so he gave us this," Collin said pulled out a brown glass bottle of medicine, "to give to Jolene."

Aunt Taliss took the bottle from Collin's hands and set it aside, "thank you, I'll give it to her when she and Mara get back; Mara took Jolene outside, it seems the girl is going to be making a regular habit of it," aunt Taliss said with a smile.

Travis looked behind him, peering out the window as if to try and see the girls, "They're in the fields?" he questioned, his head swerving back around.

Aunt Taliss gave a whisper of a smirk and nodded, "Yes, Travis, there in the fields. You can go see them if you want...."

"Yeah, I think I'll do that. Thank you, Miss Hart, Collin you want to join me?"

Collin shrugged and stood, "Someone has to keep you out of trouble; thank you for the tea Miss Hart," he said gesturing to the cup of untouched tea. "Oh and is it alright if we invite the girls' to brunch?" he asked, "Mandalin Conwell came by yesterday and invited us to brunch at her house."

Aunt Taliss grinned, "Yes you may, Collin."

With a finale nod, the two walked out the way they had come and aunt Taliss watched as they broke off the house path and followed the field's grass to around the other side of the cottage. Aunt Taliss watched them disappear and laughed quietly to herself, "Young people," she muttered and closed the door.

Mara had lead Jolene away from the house, leading her to the center—or what they liked to think was the center—of the tall grass. The two girls lay on the ground, Mara resting on her side, her elbow propping her up; Jolene sat cross legged while a group of white flowers lay in her lap as she linked them together.

"Do you suppose days like these will always last?" Jolene asked, keeping her eyes on the white flowers.

Mara stopped pulling up bits of grass, playing with a long stem between her fingers, "Nothing lasts forever... I think living for the moment you're in will last forever."

"Memories fade."

"No, they just get pushed away for a little while, but they come back."

"What about the ones you don't want to come back?" Jolene questioned, her brows pulling together as her hands stilled for a moment and she looked at Mara."

Mara sighed, rolling onto her back, "I guess you just have to hope that they don't reappear."

Jolene continued linking the flowers one by one. When she was done, she held up the necklace of flowers and smiled leaning over Mara, placing the necklace over her friend's head.

Mara sat her head up and placed it more securely around her neck, "I love it," she muttered laying her head back down with her eyes closed.

"Collin? Travis?"

Mara's eyes opened and she looked at Jolene who was staring beyond their little circle with her head tilted in curiosity. Sitting up the girl brushed her hair over her shoulder and crossed her legs.

The two young men drew closer and stopped at their little indent in the grass, "Ladies," Collin said giving them a hello smile.

Jolene and Mara gave him and Travis a smile in return, "Collin, Travis," Jolene said.

Mara gestured to the ground before them, "sit?" Travis and Collin entered their circle and lowered themselves to the ground, "So is your father talking with aunt Taliss?"

"No," Travis started, "he had to make a house call so he left us to the job of leaving you, Jolene, your medicine; also your aunt said it was alright that Collin and I to invite you to brunch at Miss Conwell's estate."

Mara and Jolene looked at one another, "Mandalin...Conwell?" Mara asked hesitant.

Collin nodded, "you know her?"

Jolene sighed, "Yes, Mara and I went to secondary school her...."

"She wasn't what you would call our friend," Mara finished.

"Don't let it bother you; she's a very sweet girl now." Jolene and Mara shared a glance. "It is on Sunday, will you come?"

The girls thought for a moment though after a few seconds they gave in and agreed.

Jolene continued to cough up blood while slowly losing weight from lack of food as the week progressed; her hair, both she and Mara realized, was starting to thin and just barely were her cheeks starting to grow hollow.

The week passed in a blur to Mara but, for Jolene it felt as if forever had stayed in her room and kept her company. When Sunday came about Mara Helped Jolene dress in a pretty dress of deep red that reached just mid calf, with a pair of black, small heeled, pumps. Her hair was knotted in the back, kept away from her face, and light makeup applied to her cheeks and eyelids.

Mara gave Jolene a hug from behind, "There, all pretty."

"Not as pretty as you," She countered, tilting her head and smiling at her friend's reflection.

"We are both the same."

"Yes," Jolene agreed, "same." She turned and brushed off a piece of lint from Mara's dark green dress, her eyes lighting up from the color. "We better go," she said quietly, "the boys are probably waiting for us." Mara hummed and took hold of Jolene's arm and led them to the kitchen area.

"Ladies," Collin said as the two women entered.

Travis gave a slight smile as he saw Jolene and strode over to her; taking the place of Mara and gently leading her to the door. "You look beautiful, Jolene," he whispered so no one could hear.

Jolene ducked her head as they went outside, her cheeks blushing lightly from the complement, "thank you," she murmured, letting him help her into the automobile.

Travis shut the door just as Collin helped Mara in, and got into the driver's seat; Collin used the crank in the front of the car to start it up, when the engine roared to life, the boy jogged to his side of the car and got in as Travis pulled away from the country cottage.

The Conwell's estate was much larger than that of Jolene's aunt's cottage. It was made up of large grey stone with green ivy crawling up the side, large honey coloured doors stood proudly in the center of it all, surrounded by stone and windows that were placed neatly into the stone.

Mara sighed, "Come on, Jolene."

Jolene nodded and got out of the cab—with the help of Travis, who generously held out his arm for her to take.

The Estate loomed over them with a daunting presence, though with the sun shining merrily the cold stone of the building made it seem chilled.

The large front doors opened and out stepped a woman dressed in a white dress that came to her knees, black shoes graced her feet, and a layer of black pearls hung draped around her neck, Mandalin Conwell.

"Ah, lovely, you're... here? Travis? You brought guests." Mandalin stated more than a question. Her smile she had once donned was now strained, though it hardly showed; neither of the men noticed, though Mara and Jolene exchanged side-glances before following their group into the large house.

The inside was just as cold as the outside, everything was in its place, nothing touched and no dust was to be seen. The colours were all white with little to no other colours save creams; flowers in vases were scattered here and there while curtains draped to the floor in elegant waves.

"Come, the dining room is just this way," Mandalin said, gesturing to the entry they were approaching.

Jolene's footsteps echoed in the living area, against the cold tile of the floor; whilst did the others. She coughed lightly, covering her mouth; Mandalin looked over her shoulder as she came to a stop, a slight smirk appearing invisibly on her lips. Travis and Collin passed their hostess as she stood to the side of the entry of the dining-room. Mara passed and Jolene was left to face Mandalin when she stopped her.

"What a pretty dress, Jolene," she said sweetly.

Jolene flattened her hands over her dress, smoothing away non-existent wrinkles, "thank you," she said timidly, expecting to pass, Mandalin wasn't finished.

"It's a shame though," she said with a smile, "that, that color doesn't suit you. Red just isn't your color," with that she turned on her feet and joined the others. Jolene looked down at her dress, and then touched her cheek self-consciously. Was she too pale? Did she really look horrible?

"Jolene?" Mara asked interrupting the latter's thoughts.

Jolene brushed away her concerns and gave her friend a small smile, "coming."

Travis, Collin, and Mandalin were already seated around the long table when Mara and Jolene joined them.

"Well, look at you two, all buddy- buddies," Mandalin said with a sticky smile, gesturing to the last empty seats, "please, sit."

The two girls shared a brief look before setting themselves down; each muttering a thank you. Just as their bottoms touched their seats Mandalin rang a bell that resided near her, and four maids came out, each holding a plate set with food; a butler following suit with a tray of glasses filled to the brim with clear, cool, liquid water.

"So, Mara," Mandalin started, "I heard just after secondary school, Fred Marsh, proposed? If so, why aren't you married?"

Mara cleared her throat, taking a sip from her glass as the butler placed it in front of her. "I broke that off," she muttered.

Mandalin's lips tipped up into a small smile, "hmm? I'm sorry, dear, what was that?"

Mara's swallowed thickly, and gave a tight lipped smile, "I broke it off."

"Oh my," she said acting every bit shocked, "that's scandalous, rejecting an offer from a suitor—"

Jolene cut Mandalin off before she could say anymore, "It's the 20's, Mandalin. Fifty years ago it may have been "scandalous" but today," she paused," today it is perfectly fine."

Travis and Collin sat staring at the three women, looking between the three. They knew they should step in, though from what they could see the girls could defend themselves from Mandalin's insulting, covert, tongue.

The rest of the meal passed just as the beginning did, quiet and with near silent remarks on Mandalin's part. When everyone was finished, Mandalin ushered everyone into the parlor, leaving the servants to clean up. The five of them took up sitting areas here and there, placing themselves scarcely apart, though of course Mara took up a seat neat Jolene, creating a defense against Mandalin, just in case she may have the urge to poke and prod at their mistakes and choices in life she didn't agree on.

"So tell me, Travis? How is university in America?" Mandalin questioned after pouring herself a small glass of brandy from the crystal decanter; taking a sip and sitting herself down beside him on the loveseat.

The two young women who sat opposite them, near the window, rolled their eyes upward and took to conversing with Collin who was standing awkwardly by himself.

"Look at her, hanging all over him," Collin muttered to the girls.

"You're jealous, Collin?" Jolene teased, Mara scowling at her slightly.

Collin shook his head, "no, I'm not. Though to think she thought the very idea of Mara rejecting an offer is scandalous when she herself is draped over my brother, throwing herself at him."

Mara and Jolene each took a turn to glance over at the embarrassing site, "Scandalous," Jolene muttered.

The four of them exited the way they came as they left the estate, Mandalin standing just outside the door, watching as the men helped the women into the buggy. Travis came to stand in front of Mandalin, wishing to thank her for her hospitality as Collin started the buggy. "Well I hope you enjoy the rest of this wonderful day," Travis said with a kind smile, meaning it sincerely.

Mandalin shrugged carelessly, "I suppose," she said stepping down the steps and closer to Travis with a sly smile, "though it won't be very pleasant without you here."

Travis was unaware of Jolene staring out the buggy and towards the pair, her mouth set firm; Mandalin noticed this from over Travis shoulder, and with a small smirk and without hesitation, she leant forward, placing a kiss on the corner of Travis's mouth. "Have a nice day," she said sweetly and turned on her heels, sweeping back into the cold mansion.

The large doors shut with a thud and everything was quiet save the hum of the buggies engine. The three occupants of the automobile stared at Travis; the male stood there for a moment, slightly stunned, before coming to and turning around, taking confused steps towards the others.

"Are you finished yet?" Collin asked, giving his brother a deadpan look and raising his brows before rolling away.

Jolene coughed lightly, her face still set firm, and gave a glance to Mara who looked at her sympathetically; having seen the encounter between Travis and Mandalin. With a silent smile, she scooted near to Jolene and wrapped her arms around her, laying her head on her shoulder as the buggy made its way down the dirt road, bouncing along without a care, or notice, in the world.

Collins pulled up in front of the cottage, helping Mara out and escorting her up the path to the door. Travis came around, trying to copy the actions of his younger brother but Jolene made it impossible as she pushed past his offered hand—feeling faint for a moment as she got her bearings and her feet firmly placed on the ground. With her face set, she marched past the man who stood beside her, stumbling slightly; a pair of hands reached out to steady her, she brushed them away sharply.

"Jolene?" Travis called after her as she furthered herself from him; he rushed up to her, blocking her path to the door.

"Go away, Travis," she said with an angry bite, she was jealous, a simple feeling with so many emotions she didn't wish to admit to herself.

"Jolene!" He said again, though this time in a demanding voice, stopping her as she once again tried to push her way past him. He held her firmly in place, his hands keeping a firm grip on her upper arms. "Blast, woman!" He cursed as he felt the toe of her boot encounter his shin. That didn't stop him, though, from stopping her progression around him. "Jolene, what is the matter with you?!" He exclaimed.

She scowled, mostly at herself for her stupid feelings, "oh leave me be, Travis, why don't you go back to your Mandalin," she all but snapped in a huffy voice, but before long she could feel her cheeks grow warm, she hadn't meant to say that.

"*My* Mandalin?" He asked bewildered.

She rolled her eyes, "Oh don't think we didn't see you and her in the parlor, Collin, Mara, and myself were there too, Travis!"

By then Collin and Mara had come to stand in the door way quietly, peeking to see what the yelling was for.

"Do you think we should stop them?" Mara asked.

Collin shook his head, "no, let them be; besides it's entertaining."

Mara tsk-ed and grabbed his arm, "Your worse than a female, let's leave them be," she said dragging the reluctant man away as the two started at each other once more.

"What did you expect me to do?! Push the girl away?" He exclaimed.

"I would have!"

"Yes, but a gentleman doesn't!"

"Please! You weren't acting ever the bit of a gentleman in the parlor, nor on the stairs!"

"I was too!"

"She said *Mara* was scandalous, *really*! Does the woman not own any respect for herself!"

"Jolene, I don't have the slightest clue what you're talking about!" Travis sighed bringing his voice down, "look, yelling isn't getting us anywhere, can you tell me what this was all about? Why you were acting like a mad woman just now?"

Jolene blushed red, ashamed of her behavior. "I can't...."

Travis had to lean forward, not catching her words, "hmm?"

"I can't say...." She muttered again.

"Can't say what, exactly, Jolene?" The young man said, leaning on his heels and pushing his hands into his pant pockets.

With a sigh, she gave up knowing he would never quit, "I was jealous," she said clearly.

Surprise came over Travis's face and a small chuckle ran past his lips, "jealous?" He chuckled again at the word, "of what, exactly?"

Jolene huffed, suddenly annoyed with herself for getting into this situation, "Mandalin, I was jealous of the blasted woman!" she said cursing freely, Travis not the least bit affected by it.

Travis tilted his head, giving her a confused side smile, "Why would you be jealous of Mandalin?"

"She," Jolene started with a sigh, "she has everything. Beauty, wealth, charisma," she looked away, "she has a healthy life and she has…you."

Suddenly it all made sense to Travis and with a small smile he bent his head and tucked his finger under Jolene's chin, forcing her to look his way, "Jolene, my dear sweet girl, her beauty is cold and hard, her beauty could never compare to yours."

"I'm not beautiful," she said trying to turn away again, he wouldn't let her.

"You are a thing of angels, Jolene." The girl gave him a dead look, he laughed, "alright then, not angels; but to me, you are more beautiful than Mandalin. Her wealth makes her uncaring and inconsiderate for what she has, and her charisma—for what you think she has—affects me like a dead fish." Jolene gave a laugh to the thought of Mandalin being thought of as a dead fish. Travis brought his hand up to the girl's cheek as she smiled, "Health, she may live longer or she may die younger than most, but she will never have lived as full as you. You see the beauty in the smallest things, Jolene; she doesn't; what is the point of living if you cannot enjoy the wonderfulness of life?"

"But she has you!" she protested.

He just shook his head, "she never had me, not like you do."

With those simple words, her heart felt faint and her mind began to spin. She didn't know if it was from her happiness, the sun at her back, or from her lack of good health; but just as he said those words, her soul started to raise itself from her body and her vision started to blur, and as soon as it started it ended. She fell into a dead faint.

Fergus surveyed the unconscious girl in front of him, her thin body having been brought in by Travis who had said he caught her just as she fainted. "Where did you take her?" He asked to Collin who stood behind him with Travis, Mara, and aunt Taliss.

"To Mandalin Conwell's estate for brunch," he said simply.

His father shook his head, "she should have stayed home."

"I'm sorry, father, I should have known better," Travis interjected.

"Yes," Fergus said, turning to the others, "yes, you should have. But what has been done has been done. This girl needs time to rest and let her body regain some of its strength."

The group was silent as the younger party nodded their heads shamefully and turned to leave; aunt Taliss stayed behind to go to her niece's side, taking the girl's hand in her own. Fergus came up behind the older woman and touched her shoulder in a gentle manner, "come, Marie, she will get better, but now she needs rest." Aunt Taliss nodded and, reluctantly, pulled away from the unconscious girl.

For the rest of the day the house was silent, the girl never stirring, no matter how many times Fergus checked up on her. Finally, night broke through the days light and covered the sky in a blackness that left the stars to light up the sky. Aunt Taliss made it a point to keep the men at the cottage, housing them in Mara's room; who offered it up, opting to stay in the aunt's room.

As the others went to bed, Travis went his own way, creeping lightly into Jolene's room, the wood of the floor creaking in protest for a moment's breath. He waited a moment more, listening for any sign of movement in the house; there was none. With no final thought, he crept forward the rest of the way and sat at the edge of her bed, gripping her hand tight in his.

"Please wake up, Jolene," he whispered. Blinking back tears, he swallowed thickly and bent his head in a silent prayer; his chocolate brown hair falling over his forehead softly. The girl didn't stir once; a silent tear trickled down Travis's cheek as he lifted his head; Jolene opened her mouth and gave a productive cough, Travis's face flinched as he felt a warm drop of liquid fall close to his mouth, and hot breath of her blew on his face. With eyes closed, he wiped away the liquid, and lifted his eyelids to look at the red drop of blood. "Jolene," he said with a sigh of defeat. Her hand fell from his limply and he stood; he bent his form over hers, "this is yours," he whispered and closed the distance, kissing her lips softly and carefully as to not wake her, they were dry and warm and he smiled as he lent away.

Mara sat in front of aunt Taliss's vanity mirror, brushing her dark curls; thinking quietly to herself. Aunt Taliss lay comfortably in her bed, the lantern light bright enough for her to read, and for it to light up the room in a yellow glow. Mara sighed and put down the brush, "aunt?" She asked, looking at the woman in the mirror.

"Hmm?" Aunt Taliss hummed, glancing at the girl.

The girl paused, "why do we close our eyes?"

"Come here, girl," she said patting the space next to her. Mara stood and walked over to the bed, crawling onto the bed and sitting faced towards aunt Taliss. "Now what is the question?" Aunt Taliss asked.

Mara took a breath, "why do we close our eyes?"

Aunt Taliss leant forward, cupping the girl's cheek; the girl unconsciously closed her eyes, "because every feeling, every moment, every special time, is when we close our eyes."

"Like what?"

"Well," Aunt Taliss started, "a kiss for example, a hug, a dream. You close your eyes when you sleep so you may dream, a kiss is a special feeling that only happens when your eyes are closed, it can't be special if you're watching, now is it?" Mara shrugged helplessly. "My dear, we close our eyes so we may see and feel something much larger then ourselves."

Mara was silent as she slipped between the sheets, her head resting on the pillow, her eyes tracing patterns on the ceiling. "Aunt?" Aunt

Taliss leant up and blew out the lantern's flame before turning on her side to look at the girl. "Even death?"

The room was dark but the younger girl could swear she saw the older woman's mouth pull up into a gentle smile, with a yawn she said, "yes, Mara, even in death." And she pulled the girl in her arms as they fell asleep.

The days passed and Wednesday approached them. Aunt Taliss was seated at the girl's bed while Fergus stood at her side, watching as she tipped a glass of warm honey water through Jolene's parted lips; the girl coughed and her eyes opened immediately. "Jolene!" Aunt Taliss explained in surprise at her niece's sudden awakening.

Jolene sputtered and Fergus moved aunt Taliss away from her as she coughed, "you could easily catch the sickness; you may want to stay back." Aunt Taliss nodded and let the doctor take her place. The coughing subsided and Fergus took the medicine he had prescribed to her and took the cap off, tipping the brown glass bottle up to her lips, holding her head, and giving her a brief sip of the medicine.

Jolene stared at the two with wide eyes, "hello," she said simply in a sleep enhanced voice.

"Hello, Jolene," Fergus said acknowledging the girl. He waited as she scooted around on the bed, becoming comfortable; before continuing, "Jolene?" The girl looked at him. "The day you went to Miss Conwell's estate, what did you eat?"

Jolene looked away, thinking back on the day, "I didn't eat anything; or I did but hardly anything at all. They served bangers and I remember the smell made me nauseous."

Fergus pursed his lips in thought, "so you haven't had any solid foods?"

Jolene shook her head, "none."

The doctor stood and aunt Taliss came over and took the medicine bottle from his hands, setting it on top of the dresser. "Mara, go and prepare some food for Jolene, I'll follow in just a second." Aunt Taliss agreed and left, sweeping out of the room with a light breeze. Fergus looked down at the girl, "you fainted because you were too active for a person with your condition. You need rest, not brunch at Miss Conwell's; you could have easily infected anyone."

Jolene gave a curl of her lips, laying her head back down on the pillow, "I could easily infect anyone here too, I don't see a difference," with her final statement the doctor lost her to an unconscious world he couldn't touch.

The days past and Jolene listened to the doctor's orders, and stayed in her bed. Mara and aunt Taliss came to her bedside regularly; Collin came by the cottage every day to keep Mara company. The pair grew closer and closer as the day's progressed while Travis could only stay by Jolene's side while his father was in the room. Fergus had made it a point to be in the room when anyone wanted to see the girl, in case something was to happen.

The air in the cottage was always filled with the scent of dread, as if at any moment in time something terrible could happen. The doctor proceeded to watch after the sick girl, and as the time past he noticed the girl eating less and less of her food, now unable to handle anything but her aunts honey water. Her body was pale and fragile, her bones prodding through her skin and blue veins visible along her arms. Jolene's cough had become more and more productive over the next two weeks, and Fergus started to worry.

Sunday came and aunt Taliss thought it would be a good idea for all of them to go to church, though Fergus made it clear that Jolene was staying home; they all agreed for her well being it would be best.

Aunt Taliss and the doctor proceeded to have a cup of tea before leaving; Mara, Collin, and Travis took this time to tell Jolene goodbye.

Jolene's door creaked open as her three friends stepped inside, Mara shutting the door behind her as she entered last.

Jolene's eyes opened as she heard them approach, and turned her head to look at them as they circled around near her. Collin gave her a small smile, Jolene returned it and watched as the young man backed up, walking to the door and waiting near it; Mara gestured for Travis to go next and he gratefully sat at the edge of her bed.

"Jolene," he started, the girl nodded encouragingly. He sighed and looked at the other two, "I have no words...."

She understood, swallowing thickly she said, "I know."

The man brushed the pad of thumb across her cheek and stood, walking over to Collin; the two brothers walked form the room, letting the two girls have their peace with each other.

When the door shut behind them, Jolene's face crumbled and her worries showed through; when she had awaken this morning, her heart jolted and something felt different today, she was afraid.

Mara brushed Jolene's blonde locks away from her damp forehead, tilting her head in a slight manner, "what's wrong?"

"I'm afraid," Jolene whispered.

Mara shook her head, "don't be, everything will be alright."

"I'm afraid I'll die alone," Jolene said quietly. Mara's heart clenched and she leant forward, giving her a hug as she buried her head in her neck.

"You will never, *ever*, die alone," she said through her clench teeth as she held in a sudden sob that tried to push its way free from her throat.

Jolene's arms lifted weakly and held Mara in place as her fingers tangled themselves into her chocolate hair, and she let tears slip past her cheeks as she sank herself into her friends embrace. A small hiccup emerged as she cried harder, "I don't want to die...."

Mara pulled back, her eyes red from her unshed tears, "you won't—"

"Promise me!" Jolene cried desperately.

Mara nodded continuously, "I-I promise, I swear, Jolene, I won't let you die alone," she choked out in a wet sob, a tear slipping past her barrier.

"*Mara?*", came the voice of aunt Taliss.

Mara cleared her voice, "coming aunt Taliss!" she called back, "I'm coming!" She looked at Jolene, the girl had passed out from her body becoming weaker; dried tears were streaked down her cheek and her black lashes were still wet. Mara closed her eyes and took in a deep breath, standing from the sleeping girl but not before placing a kiss to her cheek. She straightened her dress and smoothed over her hair, wiping away the tears.

"*Mara?*" Mara gave one last affectionate, loving, look to the girl and heeded her aunt's voice.

Jolene's eyes were open to a world of bright colors, the sky was the bluest it had ever been, the air as warm as the sun, the tall lean grass that surrounded her was green and vibrant. She was in the field near the cottage though it was nowhere in sight; only hills and grass were where she was. She was overcome with wonder as she stood there; a breeze blew by her, pushing her on towards what looked like the mountain. She walked and walked for what seemed forever; her finger tips running through the grass, feeling its cool touch. Her heart began to beat faster until it was like a hummingbird, restless and full of life. She walked and walked until she ran, until she couldn't feel her feet touch the ground, she ran until she ran so hard she stopped. Her breathing wasn't laboured, her lungs weren't heaving... her body wasn't dying. She was simply alive.

Her eyes opened wide as she felt her lungs compress, and her breathing was cut off like a knife slicing through her. Her mouth opened in a silent scream at the pain that came, she tried to breath but blood gurgled past her lips and flowed down her chin. She tried to take in a breath but her lungs painfully contracted together. Her body withered on the bed as she fought for air with no avail, tears streaming out of the corner of her eyes as she slowly suffocated to death.

In the final seconds of her life, her body stopped moving, her limbs becoming lax, and she gave up the fight. The last of her life gurgled past her lips, a tear slipped down the corner of her eye. She died.

A hand slid into both of hers as she stood on the mountain, she looked left and right and she saw the faces of both her parents; they were smiling and she couldn't help but smile a little bit back.

Aunt Taliss, Doctor McGraw, Travis, and Collin, all sat in the pews of the brick church, the priest blessing the sacrament of Christ; they all sat in a heavy silence. Mara sat between aunt Taliss and Collin, her body cramped between theirs, though it went unnoticed as her heart died a little in her as the worst feeling came over her, an indescribable pain and tears poured out of her as she clamped a hand to her mouth to keep the sobs silent. Her body heaved and she bent forward; the others looked at one another worried, aunt Taliss put an arm around the girl, trying to comfort her as best as she could.

Everyone went up to receive the sacrament of the body and blood of Christ, the pews were empty save but the four bodies that sat there as still as the air.

The cottage held an eerie quiet as the four entered. They entered slowly save Mara who pushed past them all and rushed to Jolene's room; Fergus followed her while the boys and aunt Taliss stayed behind, dreading what they would find.

Fergus found Mara in front of Jolene's door, staring at the wood. "Go on, girl, open it," he whispered not daring to speak any louder.

Mara took in a shaky breath and turned the handle of the door, it clicked open and she released it, pushing the wood gently. It swung open to reveal Jolene's ghostly form; Mara could see the blood on her chin and the way the sheets were twisted around her legs. Mara's body swayed as she stepped forward in a trance.

"Girl, don't touch her!" Fergus said hurriedly as Mara bent to touch the girl's brow.

Her fingers retraced, curling in her palm, "I promised her," she whispered. Fergus came up behind her.

"It's alright...," the doctor said placing a hand on the girl's shoulder, a look of bleakness coming over him.

"I promised her," she whispered again.

"It's alright...."

Mara turned to him, "I *promised* her!" She screamed, "It's *not* alright! I promised her! I would *never let her go!*" Fresh tears ran past her eyes and her nose began to run as she sobbed, "I broke it," she heaved out, "alone... I wasn't there, I promised her... I promised her," she repeated over and over again, falling to her knees, rocking back and forth, wrapping her arms around her middle as she gave a silent scream.

Travis, Collin, and aunt Taliss rushed to the room when they heard the shouting. They halted inside when they saw the body and then Mara's violently shaking form, Fergus walked over to them as they stared in horror. Fergus wrapped comforting arms around Marie as the older woman gave an anguished cry.

Collin knelt beside Mara as she fell on her hands, taking her in his arms. The girl resisted and pulled away, crawling to the edge of the bed, grabbing hold of Jolene's lifeless hand, pressing it to her cheek.

The room was quiet except for the small sounds of aunt Taliss's sobs. Mara pressed a kiss to the hand she was holding, turning the palm up so she may press a kiss to it too. "I'm so sorry," she whimpered out, "I am so sorry…."

They would never know why she was sorry.

Jolene was buried near the cottage, in a patch of tall grass with white and purple wildflowers. The day was sunny and warm, the wind was gentle and soft, and everything was set in a perfect day. The funeral was small, just the four of them as they stood in a half moon around the grave. The events of the days before playing in a loop in their minds, Collin had finally managed to steer Mara away from the body, the girl walking out of the room in heavy steps. Travis had left far before anyone could say anything to him, his body in a state of numbness. Doctor Fergus had steered aunt Taliss away from the room as she cried, setting her down in the kitchen as he made a call to the county hospital.

No words were spoken, no words were needed; they all just stood there in silence until Fergus and aunt Taliss turned and left for the cottage. Travis placed a purple and white flower by the gravestone and took Mara's hand in his own while Collin took the other. Mara let go, turned around, and began to walk further into the fields. Travis stayed behind as Collin followed suit, pulling out a handkerchief and put it to his mouth as he gave a heavy cough. When he pulled it away a splash of red coated the center and he looked over his shoulder, watching after the couple that walked together, hands held tight together; Travis turned back to look at the grave and folded up the handkerchief, pushing it into his pocket.

"You coming, Travis?" Collin called over his shoulder.

Travis nodded his head and turned, jogging to catch up to the couple.

They would never know why he chose to die.

Bury Me in the Frozen Ground; Bury Me in a Blanket of Rose Petals

One

"How do you want to die?"

Love Lauren looked up from her book and at her two best friends Bill McKenzie and Sean Howarth, a question etched on to her lovely white features. "What do you mean?" She asked tilting her head to the side as she looked at Bill, who had asked the question.

Bill gave a nonchalant shrug of his shoulders. "Well… how would you want to die?"

"Hmm," Love took her bottom lip between her teeth in thought. "I'm not sure really… I guess I would want it to happen the way it would happen. If that makes sense?"

"Then how about this: How do you want to be buried?" Sean asked cutting into the conversation.

Love cast her eyes down, her eyelashes fanning against her white cheek in black spikes. "How would I want to be buried…?" She murmured quietly. The boys had to lean forward to catch her next words, "In the ground… when it's cold and there's snow everywhere… I don't want to be buried in a coffin; I want to be buried in the soil. I want to wear a dress of white silk and I want a blanket to cover me."

"A blanket?" Her friends asked in unison.

"Of roses. Red rose petals that blanket me lightly." She said taking a light breath.

Sean and Bill exchanged glances before letting a small smile form on their lips. It was like Love to think of something such as a blanket of rose petals.

Love looked curiously at her friends, "Why do you want to know this?"

The two shared guilty looks. Bill sighed trying to think of away to go about this. His father worked in their town's local hospital as one of the head doctors. So when something came up with someone he knew than he was always the first to know. Love had her six month check up last month at the hospital; his dad was her doctor for the day. Bill hadn't found out until a week ago when he finally asked his dad what was wrong.

"Dad?" Bill asked as he walked into the kitchen which caused his dad to look up from his cup of coffee on the counter.

"Yeah?" He asked in an empty voice.

"What's wrong? I mean you've been acting weird for the past month… what's up?" The teen asked while taking the carton of milk out of the fridge and a glass form the cupboard.

Gordon McKenzie sighed scrubbing his face with his hands. "Bill I have something to tell you." He said simply, putting his full attention to his son.

Bill raised a pierced eyebrow in question, set the carton of milk down, and allowed his father go on without interruption as he poured himself a glass of milk.

"About a month ago Love had her six month check-up she has twice a year. " Bill nodded encouragingly when his dad paused. Gordon squeezed his eyes shut before going on. "This one… wasn't exactly like the other ones…." He said giving his son a look.

"What, do you mean 'not like the other ones'?" Bill asked a quiver in his voice as he thought the worst.

The sound of the winter morning wind howling outside could be heard throughout their two bedroom one-story house. Everything was quiet for awhile as Gordon stared at his coffee cup, unmoving for a few minutes before he finally spoke. "You see Bill in X-rays, things don't always turn up on the negatives… sometimes we can't even see them with other tests that have stronger results. We sometimes don't see them until it's too late…."

Bill swallowed the lump that had started to form in his throat. He clutched tightly to his glass of milk which caused his knuckles to turn white from his grip.

"Love has a heart problem— one too large to fix. She has a cancer called Cardiomyopathy. I give her about a month at most, maybe less." Gordon said with sad eyes as he looked at his eighteen year old son with despair. He felt guilty having had this knowledge with him for so long and not telling anyone. The elder of the two took a deep breath trying to calm his never ending nerves that seem to course through his body with sorrow. He had watched Love Lauren grow up, hell; he had been there for her birth having helped in the delivery room, even though it wasn't his department. And now this. It was like thousands of bricks had been crushed over his heart when he had gotten the results.

"Dad?"

Gordon looked at his son who was currently cleaning up the glass on the floor, mopping away the spilled milk. "Yeah?" He asked quietly.

"Can I tell her?" He asked, his voice was small and weak as if he stood up glass in hand, his eyes holding back unshed tears. "I want to be with her, I want to tell her with Sean."

Gordon nodded with understanding. The three of them were closer than twins. It was like when one of them got hurt the other two felt it, if something happened to one the others would know instantly. It was like their souls where connected, linked together to form one.

"You're bleeding Bill." Gordon said looking at his son's hand that held the glass, small drops of cherry blood red fell from his white skin and onto the marble tiled floor.

Bill looked down at his hand with clear eyes, "So it would seem." He said opening his palm to revel a small cut that lined from one end of his hand to the other. "So it would seem…."

Sean fiddled with the hem of his black t-shirt knowing what Bill was about to say. He had told him an hour after he had found out, and had about the same reaction Bill had; however, instead of holding back he let it go. He cried right in the middle of the street cross walk, with the car's blaring their horns at him to move. He didn't. He just stood there crying.

"Bill? Sean? What is it?" Love asked setting her book on the coffee table that sat in the middle of her living room, coming to kneel down in front of the couch, and placing a gentle hand on their jean clad legs.

Bill's eyes misted over, "Love, my dad got a report back in from your physical." He said clearing his throat. He was trying to put on a strong front and feeling as if he were failing miserably at it.

Love shifted and sat on the edge of the coffee table. Her wide dark blue were eyes peering at him curiously. "And what did it say Bill?"

He couldn't look at her at that point, her blue eyes seeming to look through him. "That... that you're going to die." He whispered, broken.

Sean felt a tear slip down his cheek unknowingly. He swallowed and looked at Love's face. It was clear; no sign of shock or sadness was there. "Love...?"

Love shook her head slowly as a gentle smile came on her lips. "No Sean, I'm not worried nor am I scared." She paused, "I'm not afraid of dying Sean... Bill..." She used two fingers to move his face towards hers, "...I'm going to be alright."

"We told you your going to die! And you're saying you're going to be alright?!" Bill yelled suddenly angry. She had always been the most content with what happens with life and death, but it still angered him that she could care so little about her dying.

"I am Bill." She said calmly not in any way affected by his sudden change of mood since she grew up with the random switches.

Tears rolled down in a steady stream as a small hiccup sounded through him. He sniffed feeling his heart shatter, "How? I don't want to lose you."

Sean interjected, "You have cancer of the heart, Cardiomyopathy, and Gordon says you have a month, maybe less, to live."

Love leaned forward giving her best friends a reassuring hug, her thin arms wrapping themselves around their larger bodies. "I know this is happening for a reason, one I don't know, but I know it's happening. And I'm going to let it happen I'm not going to try and stop it. When I'm gone you both will still have each other, and I'll still be there even if you can't see me... but I'll be there." She whispered into their ears. Right now her friends needed reassurance that everything would turn out for the better, rather than them reassuring her that she wouldn't die. She wasn't afraid of dying. She always thought it was one more step she had to take; she was willing to take it.

The three of them broke apart and sighed simultaneously causing them to laugh. Bill smiled, his previous sadness and anger wearing off. He asked, "So, what are we going to do now?"

Love tilted her head thoughtfully "Live right now until the time comes to sleep."

"That sounds like a great plan." Sean said with a smile and standing up with the others. "So where to?" He asked. "It's only twelve."

"How about the park?"

The chains on the swing set creaked softly as the three of them pushed their booted feet through the snow covered ground, pushing themselves slowly on the swings.

The sky was a clear blue and no clouds rested in the sky, but still the sun was hidden from their view. Love was in the middle while Sean resided by her right and Bill on her left. She sighed looking at the two in turn. "Do you want to know what I think about people who die in their sleep?"

Bill and Sean looked at her puzzled.

"What?" Sean asked.

Love looked to the sky with a grin as a white bird flew past. "I think people who die in their sleep are dreaming of flying. I want to fly."

The time past quickly over the next month and expanding into the next. Bill and Sean where normal around Love but inside they still held a deep worry that at any moment she might just disappear.

Love was currently tucked into the crook of Sean's armpit, her head resting against his shoulder as his arm draped over her white night gown clad body in ease. Bill had his head in Love's lap as she played with a strand of his jet black hair, his thin body curled into a ball on the couch cushions.

They were watching Miracle on 34th Street in their tradition for the Christmas holiday, a bowl of forgotten popcorn lay on the side table as they watched, not taking their eyes off the screen. Even as it began to snow heavily, the fat flakes dancing on Sean's living room wall against the color of the TV they still didn't look away from the screen.

A third of the way through the movie Love fell asleep, her body falling heavily against Sean's in a deep slumber. Sean looked down at her sleeping form and smiled to himself, stroking her hair in a loving nature. He leaned over and shook Bill quietly.

He looked up from his position on Love's lap and over at Sean who held a finger to his lips, he nodded and rose himself from the couch.

Sean stood up, making sure not to let her fall, and picked her up bridle style and carried her to his room. Bill followed behind soundly and helped pull back the dark red comforter of Sean's bed, allowing him to lay Love gently down on the soft bed so as not to wake her.

They covered her up as she took a deep breath and let it out while snuggling into the warm bed. They both looked down at her and each touched a part of her face. Bill caressed her soft white cheek and Sean stroked her hair once more before they turned and left as silently as they came. They shut the door behind them softly but left it open a crack in case something happened.

Love remained as still as the night outside that had soon calmed down after a few hours. Her breathing was low and unheard, her heart beat slowing... It gave a few great leaps before speeding up once again and then calming again. It strived for life but didn't push for it. So finally, it rested to a stop, giving in completely to death's welcoming hands.

As Love died in that moment, a small smile lifted her lips almost nonexistent and her last thoughts were of flying. In that moment she was soaring... soaring higher than she had ever before.

She was flying.

When Sean and Bill awoke the next morning something in them shifted uncomfortably, something they had grown accustomed to since they were little. They sat up straighter on the couch where they had fallen asleep last night when they finished the last of the movie. Looking at each other, they took a glance at Sean's bedroom door and shot to their feet, running over to the door and swinging it open.

They stopped half way across the room, staring at the white figure that lay still and silent in the bed. Her skin was whiter than usual, and her lips, still a pink color, now held a white tint to them. Her eyes were closed never to open again and her long lashes rested against her cheek bones.

Bill choked out a sob as he stood there holding a hand to his heart and his mouth. Sean just stared, not blinking. It was like a bad dream, one he couldn't wake up from. He didn't notice when Bill walked over to the figure and kneeled down beside her.

Bill reached out with an attentive hand and stroked back the dark hair that framed her face. She looked lovely still; in death her skin white as snow was framed by black hair and pink lips and once... dark blue eyes that seemed to shine with a kind of wisdom neither of them fully understood at times. He smiled at her empty form and whispered, "Hi there angel. I hope your flying."

He stood once more, walked out of the room, and past Sean who still stood there quiet as ever. As he past, he placed a reassuring hand on his friend's shoulder and walked out. He picked up his cell phone from the side table where the popcorn still rested and dialed the only number he could think of.

"Hello?"

Bill was silent for a moment. "Dad." In that, one word held a thousand meanings, but one was all he needed.

He could hear Gordon drop something as he got what his son had said, "What are you and Sean going to do?" He asked swallowing into the phone speaker.

"We're going to bury her. We're going to bury just as she wanted us to, as she wanted to be buried."

"With no family left there's nothing stopping you. I'll take care of the death certificate and everything else... Bill... do what you think needs to be done."

Bill slid the phone from his ear shutting it and throwing it onto the couch with a thud. He walked back into the room to find Sean keeling next to Love just as he had done, her cold hand resting against his cheek as he held it in his own.

Sadness creased through him as he walked over to Sean and rested a hand on his back. Sean looked up at him with tears streaming down his cheeks. "Bill...." He croaked out.

"Come on Sean. Go get dressed. I'll be back in a few minutes."

Nodding, Sean got to his feet as Bill left again, laying Love's hand back beside her as he did so. He walked over, grabbed his clothes from his dresser, and proceeded to walk out of the room.

Bill pulled up in front of the town's flower shop and walked in, ignoring the bell that chimed and the voice of the sales lady that spoke. He walked down the aisles before stopping in front of four dozen bright red roses.

"Can I help you with anything Sir?"

Bill pointed to the roses, "I want all of these." He said to the sales lady.

She raised an eyebrow but didn't question his action. She took a pair of keys from her pant pocket, unlocked the case that held the roses, and started to remove them.

Bill walked away towards the front and pulled out his wallet, taking his credit card out and placing it on the counter. The sales lady came over a few minutes later with two huge bundles of red roses, placing them next to him. She took the credit card and proceeded to fulfill the requirements for the payment.

After, Bill gathered the roses in his arms, tucked his credit card into his pocket along with this wallet and walked out, once again ignoring the lady as she said to come again.

Sean walked into his bedroom freshly clothed, carefully looking at Love as he entered. Going over he pulled back the red comforter and scooped her into his arms just as he did last night, her head lolling lightly before resting into the crook of his neck.

He closed his eyes briefly before walking out. He walked outside meeting Bill just as he came up the drive way. Bill got out and walked around to the back of his GMC and opened the back laying out the thick blanket he had folded back there, spreading it across the spacious back.

Sean came around with Love in his arms and gently laid her down, making sure not to knock her against anything. "Do we have everything?" He asked in a low voice as Bill shut the back.

"Yeah, come on."

Bill got into the driver seat while Sean slid into the passenger buckling his seatbelt as he did so. As soon as he was fastened, Bill pulled out of the driveway with care as not to go to fast, and onto the snow covered street.

Bill drove for forty minutes until he reached the edge of the woods where the three of them use to explore when they where little and their parents had taken them here to camp. He turned the ignition off but left the key in. Sean was already out of the car and pulling the trunk door down so he could reach inside and scoop Love back into his arms. He pulled the blanket with him and wrapped it around her thin frame.

As Sean walked through the edge of trees and disappeared into the section of woods, Bill shut the trunk door, opened the backseat side door, pulled out two shovels, and the roses. Soon he walked after Sean, slowly making his way through the snow that buried his feet a foot deep.

When Bill arrived, he saw Sean laying Love gently against a tree. He walked over, set the roses down next to her, and handed a shovel to Sean. "We should start digging."

And they did. They dug through the thin layer of ice that had formed at the top of the soil and through the snow and rocks. They dug until they didn't think anymore, they couldn't, and they kept going until the rectangle box like grave they dug was as deep as they were tall.

Both climbed out of the grave, soft dark dirt clinging to their skins, they threw their shovels a ways away. Sean went over to Love's body and picked her up. After going over to the grave, he knelt down and jumped back into the pit.

Before he unwrapped her cold body, he squeezed her tightly against him one last time knowing it would be last time he could hold her... touch her. He breathed in her sent, she still smelled of her lavender shampoo and he smiled breathing deeply once again before uncovering her body. She was still dressed in her white night gown, it wasn't silk but it didn't matter at that moment. The white of her gown seemed to match her skin, her ebony hair contrasting like a splash of black against her features.

Soothing out her hair, Sean laid Love down on the soft cold soil and smoothed out any wrinkles on her dress. He put her hand on her stomach, one hand folded over the other. Sean climbed back out, took one of the two bundles from Bill, and began to pluck the red petals from the stem. Letting them drop in a cascade over her body.

Bill was left with one last rose and with it he knelt down as far as he could and reached his hand down, letting the rose fall from his fingertips watching as it fell right over her folded hands.

They patted down the earth with their shovels making sure it was flat. Sean threw his shovel to the ground and went over to a section on trees bending his head as he did. Bill watched silently, and patiently, waiting for him to come back.

And he did come back moments later with a medium size, flat, smoothed, oval shaped rock. He brought it over and set it down at the head of the grave, digging it into the soil a bit so it would always stay there. He pulled black permanent marker from his jean pocket and offered it to Bill. "I took it after I changed. I thought we might need it." He said with a shrug of his shoulders, "You're better with words than I am."

Bill smiled, grabbed the offered Sharpie marker, and knelt down next to Sean. His back was hunched as he leaned over the 'gravestone' and began to write.

> **Buried six feet under in a frozen bed,**
> **she lies with a blanket of rose petals over her.**
> **Love Lauren**
> **1992-2010**

He capped the marker and stood up brushing the snow off of his jeans. Sean grinned for the first time that day as he looked at his friend. "Exactly how she would have wanted it."

"Exactly how she would have wanted it." Bill echoed back with the same grin.

The two picked up the rose stems and shovels and started to trudge through the snow. As they reached the edge of the woods, the trees thinning as they walked, they heard a burst of joist laughter that seemed to vibrate and echo through the wind that started to blow. A gust of warm air eloped them and they felt love tingle their senses.

And as the woods laughed Sean and Bill turned to look back in the direction of Love's grave their grins wider, they couldn't help but laugh along with the wind.

Snow

One

The wind was chilled as white ice started to fall from the sky in small, almost nonexistent flakes. Everything was covered in a white layer as Snow Ryan made her way through the blanketed ground, towards the abandoned factory that has stood silent for almost thirty years.

The sky was light grey with the outline of the sun peaking through the clouds; Evergreens surrounded the old factory with snow covering their green branches. The sound of satin and chiffon rustled through the air as Snow's wedding gown dragged across the icy earth. Her matching satin slippers soaked through with cold water, numbing her skin. Snow didn't feel the cold as she pushed on towards the factory, towards the large window that stood alone, open, and broken.

Her baby blue sweater doing nothing to warm her as she went over to the broken window and pushed aside the frame. Using her hands, Snow heaved herself up onto the worn splintered wood of the windowsill, leaning her back against the frame and sighing in contentment.

Snow loved this factory. It was silent and peaceful and, in that moment, was just the place she wanted to be. Her wedding gown cascading around her figure, her legs bent up on the sill so she could sit fully on the wood and with the point of her satin slippers, she toed off her heels and nudged them onto the ground with her freed toes.

Forty minutes ago, if she hadn't walked away she wouldn't be here.

She would be in the limo on the way to the airport for a flight to India for her honeymoon, newly wedded to George Listing….

Samantha Ryan fussed over her daughter's wedding gown making sure everything was in place before her walk down the aisle. Snow looked at her reflection in the full length mirror, her face wasn't that of a happy bride but of a conflicted one. Her mouth was set and her brows scrunched together in a manner that told people around her that she was in deep thought.

"Take that look off your face and pull your head from the clouds Snow; it's your wedding day. No thinking is allowed." Samantha said coming around to face her daughter, straightening the pale blue silk bow that rested primly in front of her form fitting three quarter length sleeves, baby blue, v-neck cardigan.

Snow looked at her mother for a moment, before turning her attention back to the mirror, her conflicted face starring back at her in confusion, "Do you think I'm doing the right thing… mom?"

Her mother was currently licking her fingertips and twisting a blonde curl so it bounced against her head. Snow sighed knowing her mother wasn't listening to her. Her attention was solely on her gown and hair. Brushing her mother's touchy fingers away from her, Snow huffed quietly and walked away, wishing for nothing more at that moment to have her mother go away and to see her best friend Tom.

"Sweetie you're not finished-"

"I'm finished mom, okay? Just enough is enough. I don't need to be poked, plucked, or pinned anymore, so just back off!" She said with a small snap to her voice. Snow's mom was starting to get to her and she really needed her to go away.

Samantha's lips pursed into a thin line, "Fine I'll be waiting in the front row. Get ready to walk down the aisle in five minutes." She said with a flippant tone and turned on her too high heels for a woman of her age, and strode out of the room with a firm shut of the door.

Once her mother was gone and the door was shut Snow let out a sigh of relief and walked over to a small counter that held a few glasses and a sink. Looking at it and then around the room she searched desperately for something strong to drink. It was a church so wasn't there suppose to be wine?

Snow bent down, looked under the counter cupboards, and found what she was looking for. "Ah-ha." She said with triumph holding the crystal wine holder in the air. Taking a white mug from the counter, she opened the stopper that was placed at the top, and poured herself a generous amount before she set the wine down and walked over to the couch that lay pushed against one white wall, a crucifix sat in the middle.

"Bottoms up." She muttered before taking a long swig of the alcohol. She grimaced at the taste of how watered down it was but still took another drink only smaller this time.

"Can I come in?"

Snow didn't look up as she heard George's voice come through the crack he had made in the door. "Yeah come on in."

George peeked his head around the door. "Don't you care if I see you in your wedding dress?" She shrugged taking another sip and finally just set it down not wanting anymore. "What's up with you? You've been acting bitchy for about a week now."

Snow looked at her fiancée with a raised brow. "How's that?"

"I don't know, I'm not you. But you just seem really standoffish lately babe."

Snow coughed out a laugh, stood up, and came to stand in front of the man she was soon to marry. "Standoffish? Wow, okay, no, I have not been standoffish babe, I've been confused because there was this thing that happened between Tom and I; you know our best friend? We'll then, I told you what he said but you didn't care. Jeez, George! It's thrown me through a loop. I don't know what to think about you anymore...." She paused taking a deep breath. "Do you even care?"

George just looked at her with a blank stare. "What are we talking about again?"

"Oh... my... God.... Okay, I'm talking about how Tom told me he was in love with me and said that I am too good for you and that I shouldn't marry you." Snow said folding her arms in front of her.

"Yeah... and?"

"That's what you said before!" She yelled throwing her hands up in the air. "Your best friend said that I shouldn't marry you, and you had no jealous or angry feelings over this?" She questioned in an astonished voice.

George shrugged, "No, not really." The piano started to play. "I have to go,

I'll meet you at the alter babe." He got up and walked out of the room leaving the door opened as he left.

Snow gritted her teeth together in annoyance, "He's going to be my husband and he doesn't care?" The piano got louder as the choir started singing Ave Maria. Snow could see the brides' maids her mother chose for the wedding, start down the aisle in a perfect line; the flower girl walking after the last one.

Clenching her eyes shut briefly she strode out of the room and towards the double doors, the woman waiting by them in a pink dress handed her a single white Lilli.

Snow closed her eyes for a second time and took a deep breath letting it out in a huff. "I'm getting married to a man who said he loves me; he's probably not the jealous type and that's alright…. Here I go."

She took the first step that made her heart pound, the rows where filled with relatives, family…, and friends she didn't even remember. The bride's maids pale blue dresses blurred her vision for a brief second before she glanced away.

This was it, she was getting married… right?

A flash of movement caught the corner of her eye and Snow stopped, the crowd turned at her sudden halt down the aisle. "Tom…" She breathed as she saw a figure leave out the side door of the church, a head of black hair peeking for a moment before disappearing.

Snow looked towards the alter and at Georg who was giving her a look as if to ask, "What the hell are you doing!" Honestly, right now, she didn't know.

"George let me ask you something."

The guest murmured to one another. What was she doing?

George shook his head. "What?"

She sighed and looked at her fiancée with eyes that were bright and intense as she asked her question. "What are you feeling right now?"

The guests turned to George, awaiting his reply.

"What?" A bewildered George asked, "Why are you asking me this… *now!*"

Snow just shook her head. "Answer the question."

"Fine," He said giving a frustrated groan. "I'm feeling anxious, were going to miss out flight if we don't hurry up and you're not helping by asking pointless questions."

The guests gave an audible gasp and Snow just stood there looking at the man she thought she would marry.

A small smile tugged at her lips and a laugh escaped. Snow placed her fingertips to her mouth and looked away then back again. Laughs bubbling to the surface, and before she could stop, she was laughing with the song ringing through the silent confused air of the white church. "Oh, George," she said stepping down the aisle and up to the man she thought she knew. Snow looked down at the ring that sparkled happily on her finger. Using two fingers, she slid off the diamond encrusted band and lifted George's hand, and faced his palm towards her. "Have a nice life." And with that, she left the silver ring in his open hand and walked down the aisle, a grin blooming on her features.

Snow exited the church with a rush of joy coursing through her. "Whoa." Her heartbeat skipped several times as she walked down the pavement steps. She had just reached the icy sidewalk when she heard a wild screech from inside and the sound of the church doors flying open. Snow turned to look at her mother's wild face as the woman slid on the icy steps in her too high heels, she clutched at the railing and walked over to her daughter with a stern face.

"Snow Cathrene Ryan, what in God's name do you think you're doing?!" She yelled, her voice echoing through the quiet street.

She thought for a moment before walking towards her mother and reaching inside her dress suit jacket, pulling out two airplane tickets to Mumbai, India and waved them in front of her mother's face. "Well mother, it looks like I'm leaving."

Samantha made a choking sound. "You... you can't leave! This is your wedding! You're marrying the man of your dreams—"

"Let me cut you off there. One, it's not my wedding, it's yours. And two, he's not the man of my dreams, he's the man of your dreams, the type of man you wished daddy was. If you love the guy so much, why don't you marry him?" Snow said in a perky voice. A minivan drove by and she flagged it down. "Hi," She said walking over to the open window. She peered in and saw only a lady who looked to be in her early thirties. "Do you think you could give me a lift somewhere?"

"Cathrene, don't you dare get into that car."

The lady smiled lightly and nodded, taking in her appearance of the wedding gown. "Sure, get in."

Snow smiled gratefully and got in. "Thank you so much."

"Snow!"

"I'm Jane by the way."

"Snow Ryan."

Jane pulled away from the sidewalk and back onto the street. "Where do you need to go?"

"Do you know where the abandoned mill factory is?"

"Thirty minutes away from here."

"Then that's where I want to go."

Jane nodded and turned right at the stop sign. "Mind me asking what you're doing in a wedding dress?"

Samantha stood on the sidewalk gaping at the sight of the minivan her daughter was in turn the corner. "That girl…." she muttered messaging her temples. How was she going to break this to the guests?

Luckily, for her just then everyone walked through the church doors and onto the sidewalk. George came to stand by her.

"Where's Snow?" He asked looking around the street as if she would magically jump out and say "Boo".

Samantha turned her head to the man and studied him for a millisecond. "Well George, where do you think?"

"I don't know, Sam."

The woman closed her eyes with an annoyed sigh. She truly hated when he called her Sam and not Samantha or Mrs. Ryan. "She's gone. George. Gone. Got it?"

"Wait… what do you mean, gone?"

Samantha shook her head and turned around walking back into the church. The boy really did have problems.

Jane and Snow talked the whole way. Snow explaining why she was in a wedding dress and why a church full of people had been outside all dressed in clothes not meant for the winter. Jane talked about her two kids, a boy and girl named Sarah and Michael, and told her about how her son and daughter had performed in their middle school's annual winter musical.

Snow smiled as Jane went on about her husband's work. It was nice to listen to someone talk about something that didn't involve wedding plans or her.

As the drive came to a close Jane quieted and turned to Snow as she pulled to a stop on the road. "Are you going to be okay here? Do you want me to wait? My husband is picking up our kids so I don't have to be anywhere in a hurry."

Snow just smiled and opened the car door. "Its fine, I have a feeling someone is going to turn up. Thank you Jane for the ride; for even pulling over really."

She laughed, "It's nothing honey, you looked like you needed to get away."

"Yeah," Snow said, glancing down, "I suppose I did... again, thank you."

"Not a problem, Merry Christmas Snow."

Snow smiled again, wishing her a Merry Christmas, and closed the door behind her, turning to the factory that lay silent in the air. The car pulled away and left Snow alone as it disappeared around the bend.

With a sigh, the runaway bride started forward through the white ground that lay frozen in a white blanket....

The wind was chilled as white ice started to fall from the sky in small, almost nonexistent flakes. Everything was covered in a white layer as Snow made her way through the blanked ground, towards the abandoned factory that has stood silent for almost thirty years.

The sky was light grey with the outline of the sun peaking through the clouds; Evergreens surrounded the old factory with snow covering their green branches. The sound of satin and chiffon rustled through the air as Snow's wedding gown dragged across the icy earth. Her matching satin slippers soaked through with cold water, numbing her skin. Snow didn't feel the cold as she pushed on towards the factory, towards the large window that stood alone, open, and broken.

Her baby blue sweater did nothing to warm her as she went over to the broken window and pushed aside the frame. Using her hands, Snow heaved herself up onto the worn splintered wood of the windowsill, leaning her back against the frame and sighing in contentment.

Snow loved this factory. It was silent and peaceful and in that moment was just the place she wanted to be. Her wedding gown cascading around her figure, her legs bent up on the sill so she could sit fully on the wood and with the point *of her satin slippers, she toed off her heels and nudged them onto the ground with her freed toes.*

Forty minutes ago, if she hadn't walked away she wouldn't be here. She would be in the limo on the way to the airport for a flight to India for her honeymoon, newly wedded to George Carter....

Had she made a mistake? No, she had not. If someone asked her years from now if she would change the way this day had played out, she would say "No, I wouldn't change a single thread that has happen today." Years from now, if she had married today, she would be divorced from George and eating deli chicken over the sink... but that was never going to happen, not now, not ever because of the single choice she made for herself and was not pushed because of her mother.

Snow tilted her head back, her silver blonde hair falling behind her shoulders as she let it out of its restricting up-do'. With a content sigh, she breathed in the deep smell of Christmas that hung around the area in folds which crashed over her like a wave that made her shiver with delight.

"I knew I would find you here."

Snow's eyes cast down, her lashes fanning across her cheek bones, and with a small smile, she tilted her head to the side to glance at Tom as he came nearer to her.

"And I knew you would find me here."

"Is that so?"

She hummed and watched as Tom came to stand in front of her, hands tucked into his dark jeans that hung snug on his hips while his white button up shirt lay untucked with the sleeves rolled up to his elbows, which showed cords of muscles that wound its way up his forearms, while a thick black coat hung over his arm. Snow couldn't think of a time when he looked more handsome.

Tom looked down at the girl in front of him in a white gown. He fingered the blue fabric of her cover and shook his head. "You're going to freeze to death if you don't cover up." He observed running his fingertips down her white arm to her fingertips with a single stroke.

"I have come to that conclusion," She said. "Though you're here now so I don't need to worry."

Taking the coat that lay over his arm and opening it up, he draped it over her shoulders as she leaned forward. "Hmm, much better."

Tom just shook his head. "You scared the crap out of me when you got into that woman's car." He said kicking the ground with the toe of his black dress shoes. "I didn't know where you were going at first but then I remembered how much you liked this place and I knew you would come here."

Snow looked up at the man hovering near her and with a gentle hand; she reached out and stroked his dashing features. "You know me so well, Tom."

"Well, not enough apparently because I don't know why you ran out of that church today. Care to explain why?"

"Well," She started, "I was thinking about what you said to me… you know that day when you said I shouldn't marry George. Well I told him about it after you left that day, and he didn't react as how I thought he would; truth be told, he didn't react at all. It got me thinking that if I was going to marry a man who didn't get jealous when his best friend said he was in love with me, that maybe I shouldn't marry this man and maybe I should walk away. I mean because I don't want to spend my life with someone who doesn't care."

She paused, "Then I saw you— yes, I saw you Tom, don't try to deny it." He shrugged sheepishly and gave her a crooked smile.

"I had to come, I'm sorry."

"Don't be, I wanted you there. When I saw you, everything just became clearer. So thank you… a lot." She added with a chuckle.

"You're welcome then. But ah, do you mind me asking what became clearer?"

"The fact that George was my mother's choice, not mine. That what you said about him not deserving me was true, and the fact that I'd rather have you in my life then not at all and that I would lose you forever if I married George… I would lose myself."

The wind blew and as it did so, the factory echoed with the past as the air rushed through its old and weathered walls and pipes.

Snow gave a fond look at the factory as it gave a haunted groan. "Do remember when the three of us use to explore this place? God I remember this time when you and I got lost in separate wings on either side of the factory and George got scared that we had gotten lost forever...."

"Oh yeah!" Snow laughed, "And he ran and got our parents by the lake, God, yeah we got into so much trouble for scaring him. But you and I found each other...."

"Yeah, I kept calling your name and you kept calling mine and we finally found each other a few minutes before our parents came rushing into here."

Snow laughed again, sighing as the memory wafted through her memory with fondness. "Seems like so long ago, like it's been a century... when it's only been a few years really."

"So many things have happened here... like our first kiss...."

Snow glanced at Tom with raised brows. "It was a game of high school truth or dare Tom, it doesn't count."

"It does to me; it was the first time I realized I was in love with you." Snow glanced away as he spoke and he turned her head towards his, his eyes meeting her blue ones. "If that kiss didn't count then how about one that will?"

Snow couldn't help but get drawn into his dark brown eyes, and with a surrendered sigh, she nodded. Tom gave an almost nonexistent smile and leaned down, his lips met hers in a small chaste dance. The kiss was soft and sweet as Tom held her chin softly. After a moment Snow drew back, resting her forehead against Tom's as her eyes opened and then closed again.

"How was that?" He breathed against her cheek with a whisper.

She took a moment before answering. "Perfect...."

Tom chuckled softly, playing with a strand of her hair. "You're going to inflate my ego if you're not careful there, miss."

Snow pushed away from him gently with a playful swat. "Thank you for ruining that moment."

He just stared at her as a smile played around the edges of his mouth. "So, what now?"

"Well… you see, George and I were supposed to go to India for our honeymoon and I sort of swiped these two first class tickets from my mother before I left."

"Is this your way of saying we should elope?" He said with a soft chuckle.

Snow swatted at him again, "No. I just think it would be nice to get away for Christmas… away from the ice and the cold… away from this town. India sounds like the perfect place to me. It's warm and far, far away from the people we know. It would just be the two of us…. Christmas in India."

Tom smirked and raised an eyebrow, "Sounds like fun, though what would we do when we get there?"

"Who knows?" She said with a careless shrug of her thin shoulders, "Wing it."

Without another thought, Tom bent and scooped Snow into his arms. She squealed and laughed out as he picked her up bridle style and turned away from the factory. "Well then, I guess we better go pack… when is the flight?"

Snow laid her head in the crook of his shoulders, the thick coat around her wrapped around her upper body as she twisted more comfortably in his hold. "Hour and a half."

"We'll stop by your place first since I assume you have your stuff packed by the door, am I correct?" She nodded. "And then we'll head to my place for ten minutes."

"Hey Tom," Snow muttered against his skin. Tom looked down at the girl he was carrying to his car and hummed. "Maybe we *should* elope while we're there."

Tom chuckled as he reached his black GMC and opened the passenger side, setting her carefully down on the tan leather seat. She looked up at him with a small smile on her pink lips as he said, "We'll… wing it while we're there."

Finding Balance

One

With everything that has gone on in my life, I would say it's safe to say that I'm definitely not perfect. Sure, to my parents I'm a straight A student, I come home on time and do as I'm told. Sure my teachers love me because I'm always on time for my classes, and that I always seem to be able to answer their questions, related to school or not.

I wear skirts below my knees and dresses that cover my body, I say Grace at every meal and I never talk out of line. My name is Annie. I'm the girl with bright red hair and pasty skin that likes to sing and put a smile on my daddy Warbucks face.... Or that's what they wished I could actually be inside and out.

On the outside I'm everything I just described, on the inside though is a totally different matter. On the inside, my name is Alex, I'm a 17 year old girl who likes to smoke behind the school building, and I love to wear my red dyed hair in layers with blonde streaks. My clothes, such as a skirt or dress, never reach to my knees, the longest I've ever had a skirt was an inch above them. I listen to fast music and I hate school with a passion that could kill. I'm just a girl with albino skin complexion, my eyes are blue and my hair is red. My clothes are most likely always going to be different and probably never going to match.

My name is Alex and most people tend to stay away from me thinking I'm this super smart freak. Truth is I have a split personality, or so I would hope. No, actually, I live in two worlds, one: where my parents and teachers and anyone else who doesn't know me, is happy with my outer appearance where everything is perfect and set in place. The second: me, myself and I. The one where no one knows me except for my best friend Angel, I gave him that name because really to me he is an angel, my personal protector. Or so that's what I thought. This side is where living and breathing are two different things, where trying to do both is nearly impossible.

I hate my alarm clock with almost the same hated passion I hated my school with. The stupid thing starts blaring every morning, weekend or not, at five in the morning with its freaking beeping sound. And of course every morning I would knock it off my nightstand with my hand while the rest of my body was still buried under my down comforter. But soon my still asleep mind would wake up like a splash of cold water when I hear my mother coming up the stairs after hearing my little commotion.

"Crap." I muttered under my breath while I hurryingly pushing aside my comforter and scurried to get up from my warm bed, throwing the quilt back into place to hid the evidence of my having just gotten up I straightened the pillow and smoothed out any wrinkles in the fabric. I had just finished and was walking over to the enjoining bathroom, when my door opened and in stepped my mother.

Having gotten up an hour earlier, my mother's hair was its perfect shade of blonde that hung in small curls reaching past her shoulders parted to the side. Her crisp white blouse was tucked in ever so neatly into her A-line beige skirt, while nude pumps graced her dainty feet.

In my mind I rolled my eyes and sighed, my mother was the perfect image of a gag worthy house wife slash business women, she had an office set up downstairs set aside from the rest of the house though why she dressed up for the "job" is beyond me.

"Annie." I seriously hate that name. "What was that noise I heard a minute ago?" She asked, her blonde brows rising to meet her equally blonde hair.

It was now time to play pretend, being the Oscar worthy actress

I am I put on my "I'm sorry" face and started to play the game, "I accidentally knocked my alarm clock off my nightstand." I said pointing to the old fashioned clock that was on the floor next to my bed.

My mother hummed a reply and bent to pick it up handing it to me after she straightened herself, "well then don't let it happen again, the noise could wake your father and he needs to sleep. And get ready. School is in two hours and you need to shower, get dressed, and eat; besides I don't want you looking like the Robin's girl. Any more makeup on that girls face and you might as well have stamped the word "Tramp" on her forehead." What does makeup have to do with my getting ready? Oh and have I told you that my parents are against all makeup? And the whole Robin's girl deal isn't even that big. She put a little bit of eyeliner on her eyes. Seriously, it was like, invisible. Mother turned on her $200 *Dolce&Gabbana* pumps and walked out of my room shutting my door behind her quietly.

I shook my head; my dad needs to sleep my barely existent ass! Yeah right, he goes to sleep at eight at night gets up at nine goes to work for three hours and comes home to watch the football game at two. How can that woman be my mother? She gets tossed around like a freaking rag doll and she likes it! Talk about Stepford Wives.

I walked over to my bathroom and shut the door behind me. Bending down I pulled my iPod speakers out from under my sink having to hide it from my parents knowing they would snoop through it. Pressing the Play button I let the hum of *A day to Remember's* guitar fill the room quietly as The Danger in Starting a Fire started to play.

Bobbing my head along to the beat I stripped my clothing, walking naked over to the shower, I turned the water on waiting for it to heat up before I stepped in, I let the water run down my body relaxing me wholly before I had to face the day as someone completely different then who I was.

I stepped out of the bathroom with a towel wrapped around me. My iPod was now safely tucked underneath my bathroom sink once more, and steam from my shower wafted out my bathroom and into my bedroom, evaporating.

Yawning, still a bit tired, I walked over to my closet and opened the sliding door, I peered in side with distaste. My whole closet was filled with beige and creams; it's not bad enough that my skin is like the color of a freaking piece of paper. Any other colors were yellow and pink and nothing darker than that, baby blues and peach where also thrown in with the other colors. It was as if I was a little made up Stepford Daughter, myself. I shivered at the thought.

Pulling out a white dress that came to my knees— if I *had* to pick a favorite it would be this one— and buttoned to my collarbone creating a small boat neck. I grabbed some underwear from my dresser and walked over to my bed taking the towel form my body and pulling my chosen items on. After I walked over to my closet again and slipped on a pair of white ballet flats with a silk white ribbon lacing through the seams of each shoe coming to a tiny bow at the end.

I was like snow, as my friend Angel had told me one afternoon. Snow that had red paint spilt on it because it was tired of being all white. I know it doesn't make much sense, but for me it did.

I didn't do anything with my hair; I just let it fall where it was in a wavy mess, which, yes, I would brush later before I got to school. My mother never let me go to school without looking, mind you, these are her words not mine, "Simply perfect darling." No, she always carried a hairbrush in the car in case of an emergency. Like what? The fashion police pulling us over?!

As I have said, makeup was a big no-no in my family so I didn't bother. Walking over to my door I pulled it open and walked down the hall and the stairs, my flats making, much to my dismay, more noise than they should have on our hardwood floors. So when I got to the bottom of the stairs I was met with the harsh glare of my mother, if looks could kill I would be long gone.

"I thought I told you to be *quiet!*" My mother hissed at me as I scooted past her and into the kitchen. I went and sat on one of the striped cushioned bar stools that sat neatly next to the island.

"I'm sorry; I guess we just have some loose boards. I didn't mean to, I swear ma." I am so good. All my mother did was roll her eyes and cross her arms, "Don't call me 'ma'. It's so lower class. I'm mother or

The Good The Bad and Everything Inbetween

ma'am." See what I have to put up with? "Yes mother." I said quietly. She nodded her head and went over to the fridge.

A noise from up stairs could be hear, ugh great just when I thought I was in the clear. My mother turned around her lips purse as she looked at me; lips pursed never meant a good thing. Just as my mother was about to speak, my dad came in scratching his slightly rounding belly in the process.

"Why is there so much racket going on at so early in the morning?" My father asked in a rather loud voice.

Mother turned to look at me with raised eyebrows a small smirk visible on her lips, "Annie? Would you like to say something to your father for waking him up?"

Dear old dad rounded on me giving me a look in the process; I gave him a small smile, "Good morning dad."

"Not so much when it sounds like the *Giants* are running through the house." He snapped. I wasn't that loud! Why that fricking- "Annie?" I turned to my mother this time, "yes?" I questioned, trying to take the monotone out of my voice. "Do you have anything to say to you father?" She asked again. I sighed and looked back at my dad. "I'm sorry I was so loud. I promise it won't happen again," Uh yeah how many times have I said this in my life? I turned back to my mom, "If you don't mind, can I walk to school this morning?" I don't think I could stand being around my mother anymore today. I could see her thinking about it, probably realizing that she wouldn't have to be around me either, "Yes, ok, but brush your hair. It looks like a wild animal just slept in it." How dramatic mother.

I walked out of the kitchen, silently this time, on tiptoes, and over to the downstairs bathroom grabbing the brush from one of the drawers. I brushed my hair out until it shone, well as much as possible, and put the brush back. I stared at my reflection before I left, taking in my appearance wondering what makes me do what I do on the outside and not just be me all the time. Shaking my head, I cleared my brain of the unpleasant thoughts and walked out, going to the front door. Pulling it open, the early morning breeze touched my face as I walked out, shutting the front door behind me.

The sun was starting to rise already though the colors of the sunrise still made a rainbow in the sky. This is what I liked, I liked the sunrise because really it was everything it could be, and every color there was to make someone happy. Not just a plain blue or a plain grey, it was every color it wanted to be, not afraid to be anything else. I wrapped my arms around my waist and continued down the sidewalk towards my prison, AKA school.

School: The epitome of hell. A place where everyone thinks they're going to be the next big superstar on Hollywood Boulevard when: **news flash**! Most singers now a day's can't sing to save their stupid pathetic lives they call perfect. No, my school is a big, ancient brick building that smells like the bleach the janitor uses every night to polish the floors. Which, speaking of the janitor, he just opened the school doors. Rushing over to the school steps, I ran up them and into the school, the metal doors echoing in the empty building.

OK. I admit that I liked the school when it was empty such as now, minus the janitor he doesn't count, if I wasn't such an outcast at this place I think I might actually enjoy myself, oh and have reasonably sane parents. Yeah I think I might like it, but since that's never going to happen it will have to stay an "I might like" forever.

I rushed over to my locker that was a ways down the hall, loving the fact that I didn't have to push, shove, and pull my way through a crowd of students to get to it. Turning my number lock on it I heard a click and watched at the bolt of my lock pop open. Grinning I took it off and opened the metal compartment, reaching in side I dug through my school books and this week's papers I've finished early, and pulled out a packet of cigarettes, my American flag lighter and a packet of mints. No time like this time for a smoke.

I shut the metal door and walked through the door across from my locker, it lead to a faster way around the school to the football field storage shack. And that was exactly where I was heading. Because technically there is not back to our school, there's a 360 wrap around of classrooms on all sides. So the only place to actually go without being seen is behind the football shack.

So instead of walking, I ran in record time, like I had been doing since I got here, and sat down on the surprisingly dry grass, my legs stretched in front of me crossed at the ankles. I took a stick from my packet and put it in my mouth, flipping my lighter open I lit the cigarette before flipping it shut again. I took a long drag, letting it out in a long stream; this is definitely what I need before everyone arrived; the nicotine calming my nerves.

I was almost down to the fag when he, the person who I didn't actually realize then, would change me and everything I know, arrived.

"And to think I thought I was the only one who did this," the voice said with a chuckle. I looked up sharply, afraid I was a deer caught in a speed way car accident. What I didn't expect was to see a boy with dirty blonde dreadlocks and large oversized clothes that looked like they belonged to a fat person (or a gangster), come sit next to me taking out his own pack of cigarettes.

"I'm Talan," he said extending his hand towards mine; confused I dumbly shook it staring at him. "Um… do I have something on my face?" Oops, I had been staring; I smiled at him and shook my head. Maybe he didn't know me. Wait, what am I thinking? Everyone in the school knows me; I'm the schools freaky little nerd. "What's your name?" Talan asked curiously.

"Ann- Alex" Maybe I should give him a chance…. "Cool. Hey Alex, I'm new here," Ah that's why, "and I was wondering if you could show me around, maybe tell me what teachers are nice and which I should try and sweet talk into liking me?" He said with a laugh giving me a cheeky grin, I liked this guy, he was cool. I nodded, "sure why not," really why not? He's new and doesn't know anything… or that I'm biggest loser in the school, yeah this could work out just fine… I'm totally being sarcastic right now.

Just then, I heard the slam of car doors and knew it was time to leave before anyone saw me, "We better go. They're pretty strict about not smoking," So not true, I mean even the teachers come back here to smoke. I once saw my English teacher lighting up just after third period. Talan sighed and stubbed out the butt of his stick against the shed and flicked it into the dirt, I did the same and followed him as he made his way towards the building.

Talan smiled- actually smiled, and not a grimace, Angel was the only one who usually smiled at me- at me as he said, "I like your hair, it's really cool." Yep, I defiantly liked this guy. "Thanks" I said back as we reached the door I had used before.

Pushing it open, we both walked in side by side, students already filling the halls with their crowds. Shaking my head at the sudden fullness, I made my way to my locker. I swear I really do hate time. It made two hours fly by like nothing. Opening it, I took my books out that I need for my first two periods the third one being free period. Talan waited beside me as I shut the locker with a slam, "So to the Student Building?" He shrugged, "I guess, I don't really know where to go." He said with a small nervous laugh. Right, ok I just had a blonde moment, "Sorry, yeah I knew that."

Just as we were about to make our way across to the other side of the school, none other than Courtney Evers, what a bitch name agreed, came up to us. Her black hair was perfectly straight, pulled back into a ponytail at the top of her head, while her face was covered in far too much makeup. What? Even I know when a girl has too much on- plus, its way too heavy and over done. Her crisp blue and white cheerleading uniform left little to the imagination as she stood there, hip cocked out arms folded across her silicone chest.

"Hey everyone, look, it's the little teacher's pet," Her bitch posse snickered; I just mentally rolled my eyes while still portraying a silent face. "Sooo," she drawled out in her annoying perky voice, "Annie, have you become an orphan yet? How is being miss little know-it-all all the time? Does daddy Warbucks just love it?" Again the bitch posse snickered, ok really why do I have to put up with such stupidity? Talan cleared his throat earning Courtney's attention along with rest of the wannabes. Great, so much for him.

"And, *who* are you?" Talan opened his mouth to reply but unsurprisingly Courtney cut him off, "Has Annie over here, been keeping you a secret?" She asked with raised pencil lined eyebrows, she walked over to him and pressed herself so close she might as well have been on top on him. Gag.

Talan took a deep breath, "Uh, actually I'm new, this is my first day," he said looking down at the girl with a smirk tonguing what I hadn't noticed before to be a lip rip.

"Well, what are you doing with *her* then?"

"Alex was going to help find my classes and what not, and also show me around the school campus." Oh fucking no. "Alex?!" That earned me a wonderful; again being sarcastic, shriek of laugher from the group. "She said her name was- oh my GAWD! Her name is not Alex its Annie just like the little red head orphan." Now I really did roll my eyes, is it a criminal offence to kill the head cheerleader?

Talan looked at me confused, I couldn't blame him. "Uh alright then, Annie said she would show me around."

Courtney rolled her heavily done green eyes and sighed, "Talan, trust me on this, alright, you don't want to hang around with her, you'll become an outcast and I really don't want to see that happen to such a gorgeous face such as yours," she said so sickly sweet it nearly made me hurl. She ran one long claw down his cheek smiling at him before she grabbed his hand and began pulling him away from me just as the perfect timing came, the bell rang. "Come on we don't want you to be late for class now do we?" The bitches actually had the nerve to giggle as they flounced away, Talan just looked back at me with a hopeless look in his eyes, and truth be told, it really was hopeless because I had nothing to say to the matter. If Talan had wanted to stay, he would have stayed.

Mrs. Norman stood in front of the class explaining why the square root of pi really has no end because in reality it goes on forever, so while she did that, I sat in my seat, second row down third seat to the far left, trying hard not to yawn and look like I was so bored. I was about to disintegrate in absolute nothingness. Fortunately for me, it was working far better than I thought it was because during class Mrs. Norman called on me, three times, asking me once what a certain problem was and to write the answer on the board, second, if I knew what clothing store my mother shopped at and three if I could please help Norbert Newman,(

who names their kids that now-a-days?)with a problem he was having on number fourteen. The little rat wasn't having problems it was just his chance to actually try and feel me up and win the bet that he and his little geek squad have had going on since freshmen year.

So all in all classes where good beside the little Norbert episode where I slapped him for trying to cop a feel, earning him a week's detention, serves the little pimple face four eyed freak right. Math was boring as usual and then came English; there I sat as, far back as possible in the class. Mr. Raine had a slight saliva issue and tended to spit everywhere when he spoke. And now I have free period which means right now I'm doing a nerdy happy dance in my mind, because this means no teachers around, well unless you count eighty year old Mrs. Wich- who by the way, snores when she sleeps.

I didn't have any homework so far so I just walked to my locker and put my books away , I shut it and was about to walk away when I heard my name being called out from across the hall, and it wasn't Annie- but Alex. I turned to see Talan pushing his way over to me finally coming to stand in front of me.

"I'm sorry about this morning," he said stuffing his hands into his pocket. I shrugged, there wasn't anything to be sorry about really, I'm sort of immune to it by now. "No, really I am. I probably should have said something." Just then, Courtney slithered up to Talan's side like the snake she was and wrapped her hands around his bicep.

"Why are you talking to Talan?" She asked narrowing her eyes to slits, oh, how scary.

Again, I shrugged, "I wasn't Courtney, I just bumped into him." She harrumphed flipped her ponytail from her shoulder, "Don't do it again, ok. Because I don't want you to rub off on him, which had a double meaning, if you didn't get that." Oh, believe me, I got it, you Bimbo. "Good, now that that's all settled and the trash has been taken care of, I want a snack. Come on Talan." She began pulling him away yet again from me, this time he didn't look back.

I swear she was like Satin's mistress or something, it was as if she could control who ever she wanted and they would always listen. Oh well it's not as I'll ever speak to Talan again after this anyways.

Two

I was wrong. So wrong, I admit it,ok. I thought that I wouldn't see Talan again after that "incident" in the halls, well, at least not talk to him, I mean, I can't really not see him since I see him at lunch and he's also in almost all of my classes. So technically, I thought I would never speak to Talan again after that. Get me now?

OK, so as I've said, I was so wrong. Of course it didn't happen right away, actually, it was two weeks later when he finally came up to me and said actual words…actually, it was today.

I'm at Angel's now; he lives in some doggy part of New York where as I live in New Jersey, home land of the Jersey cows. Moo. The small basement flat was as well lit as you could get a basement flat lit, meaning it was dim. There was garage sale couches and chairs, and a few tables he had gotten from a Good Will, and few prints he thought would look nice on the walls probably brighten the place up, I've told him many times that they don't and he should think of trying to find actual paintings and not prints. He always says he'll think about it and always ends up never doing it, he's just way to lazy for his own good.

Besides the crap furniture, which I can't really blame him for it because he's not what you would call rich or middle class, and the weird prints on his walls, it was an overall normal looking flat minus the slight stench of cigarettes and beer; everything was fine.

"You want a beer?" I looked over at Angel as he walked out of the bathroom and headed towards the kitchen. I shook my head, "no thanks, I don't drink, remember? Besides, what do you want to do? Kill yourself twice as fast, drinking and smoking are not the best combination Angel," I said for like the millionth time since I've known him. All I got was a roll of his eyes when he walked out sitting next to me, a cigarette between his lips and a beer in his left hand, "I'm perfectly fine babe, it's not going to kill me for a long time." I scoffed, "really? Wait five years and see where it gets you." I was seriously getting tired of this same old crap, and of course, the same old sentence being said to me every time we have this talk. Watch, I'll bet my life's savings he'll say something like this: In five years I'll be looking as gorgeous as ever, "In five years I'll be even better looking than ever before and chicks dig this whole thing anyways." See what did I tell you? I looked away from him as he took a drag out of his stick.

"What's up with you?" I turned to him confused. "You're all... moody and shit. Is it that, err... time of the month thing?" I blushed the shade of my hair, "NO! Ugh, I've just had some things on my mind. It's nothing; I'll be fine, just give me a few." He shrugged and set his beer on the cheap water stained coffee table pulling out his cell phone. I turned away again and got off the couch as he started to talk on the phone.

I don't get it, I really don't. Why do I even hang around Angel anymore? When I was younger, it was more of an act of rebellion against my parents. But now... now, it's just stupid. I pulled out Talan's number from the pocket of my jeans and stared at it, thinking back to only a few hours before.

Three hours before

I shut my locker and pushed my way through the thankfully thinning crowd of students, out of the back door across from my locker. Finally pushing the door open I walked out thankful for the fresh air, it was getting way to stuffy in the halls.

Making my way to the football shack I made sure no one was

The Good The Bad and Everything Inbetween

around before I sat down, pulling my beige skirt over my knees I took my packet of cigarettes from my waist band and pulled out a stick. Placing it in my mouth as I pulled out my lighter, raising it to my mouth I was about to light it but stop short as a thought struck me: why the hell do I even smoke? I started when I was twelve just out of pure spite because I was mad at my parents; we had gotten into a fight over my report card from school that day. I met Angel that day he was the one who got me into it, though not as hooked as he was. I was twelve he was sixteen and I thought he knew everything. I scoffed, shaking my head; he doesn't know everything that much was clear after about six months.

For some reason Angel just had his charisma around him that made him so... well irresistible, I guess is the word. He was like a magnet and I was the paperclip. I guess being twelve makes you a bit stupid and naïve at times, such as that time.

Shaking my head I threw my American flag lighter into the dirt hearing the soft "thump" it made. "Quitting?" I looked up and saw Talan coming to sit next to me, his legs out in front of him. I did the same crossing my ankles in the process. I shrugged, "Thinking about it, I don't really know why I started in the first place."

Talan breathed a laugh, "yeah, I know what you mean. I started because all these kids at my old school– when I was around fourteen, where doing it and I thought I wouldn't be popular if I didn't do it too, so I started smoking and now I don't know why I let myself believe what I did back then." I looked at him strangely, "why are you telling me all of this?" He shrugged, "I don't know, I've always thought you were pretty cool, you dress up everyday like you're about to go to church but you also have this bright cherry red hair with these blonde highlights. It sort of threw me for a second when I found out your name was Annie and not Alex... you look more like an Alex to me." I blushed a little and turned my head away grinning. "Also," he continued, "I could tell you keep secrets by the way you handled yourself with Courtney. No one else noticed but I could tell, it was like someone different was behind your eyes while you spoke in such a... monotone voice," He said with a chuckle.

I was comfortably shocked that he had been able to relate to me and figure me out so quickly, sure it took me by surprise but in truth, it was nice having someone to know me by just looking, without me having to explain myself, not having to go the long route around everything in between. "So what kind of secrets do you think I keep?" I asked, smirking a bit; I just couldn't help myself from flirting just a *tiny* bit, so shoot me.

He smirked back, "I bet you secretly think I'm a smoking hot, and hope that Courtney could just go jump off a cliff." He's... actually pretty, close. "The Courtney part yes, alright, I admit that I do wish that sometimes, but the smoking hot, err not so much you cute and all, but your just not my type." I said with a small teasing grin, I poked my tongue out at him. He poked his right on back. We laughed freely, knowing the school was almost empty so no one would be likely to hear.

After we quieted a moment later, I turned to him with a question that started nagging at me a few minutes ago, "Talan." He looked at me. "Why did you go with Courtney?" He was quiet for a second; I could see him thinking about the answer before he actually answered. "I don't know, and before you say 'like hell'," He's good, I shut my mouth, "I just want to say that, I've never listened to what they say about you, because I already know it's not true so give me that alright, and also I don't think you're a freak or a loser or anything else like that. I personally think your pretty cool, on both sides that you play."

Ok, now I was going to ask him, "both sides?" He nodded, "I see the way you hide apart of you away from people, well ,not me I hope, but like the fact that you smoke or why is your hair dyed that color, and you're a straight 'A' student and let's not forget you dress like a Stepford Daughter's robot," FINALLY! Someone gets my dilemma in my parents clothing choices, "and also the teachers love you yet you can barley stay awake in class."

"You notice all of that...? And you still didn't answer my question." Talan rolled his eyes; hey I wanted my questioned answered. "My old habits kicked in, my wanting to be popular just pushed the side of me wanting to be friends with you to the back of my mind. Reality is, is that I don't like Courtney, she's like the biggest slut slash bitch I've met, and I've met a lot of those," I raised my eyebrows, "popular remember, cheerleaders are pretty notorious for wanting the title. Any ways, I sort of told Courtney that I wasn't going to be hanging with them from this day on. I like you, a lot Alex, and I want to be friends. So yeah that's all."

OK, a lot was going through my mind at that moment, but the only thing that I could actually distinguish was the fact that he had called me Alex, and I swear I couldn't stop the grin from taking over my face. Sure, he's said it before but for some reason this felt different. "You called me Alex." He smiled weirdly, "yeah I did, but did you get anything I just said to you?" I just kept grinning like an idiot, "You called me Alex and you didn't even ask if you could, no one has said the name Alex without asking before; even Angel asked if he could." Still he looked at me weirdly, so bending over I wrapped my arms around him and gave him a hug. He wasn't the only one surprised, I surprised even myself, I have never done anything like this before, it was a first… and I really liked it.

"Oh?" Was all Talan said before he wrapped his arms around my waist and pulled me closer, "do you do this to everyone you talk to?" I chuckled a bit and shook my head slightly, "just me then?" I nodded, "well, I feel very special then." I pulled back and grinned. "You should," he grinned back, "well I do."

After that, we went onto talk about our different problems. His on how his mom left him and his dad when he was ten, and he hasn't seen her since. Mine on was on everything, my parents, their strict way of living, the way I dress, my smoking, his smoking and of course life in general.

A few hours had come and passed by the time Talan and I realized that we had to get going. I looked at the small watch on my wrist and glanced at the time **2:45** well crap we've been talking for almost three hours. It had been a half day at school so it let out at twelve instead of three today since tomorrow was the last day of school before summer break. "Hey I have to go." I looked at Talan and nodded following him as he stood up brushing his pants off. "Yeah same, so I'll um, see you tomorrow?" He nodded.

We started to walk around the side of the school building towards the parking a lot when Talan stopped. I turned to find him quietly cursing while he patted his pant pockets. "Lose something?" I asked walking over to him. He groaned, "No, I just left my car keys in my locker." I raised my eyebrows, taking his hand, I started dragging him to the other side of the school, so basically a 360 on the whole school. "Ah, Alex, what are you doing?" He asked when I finally stopped in front of a singular window low to the ground. "Most people would ask, 'Where are you taking me.'" I said with a laugh, he gave me a look which I knew meant 'and the difference is?' I shook my head and pointed to the small barely human width size window, "That's the window that leads into the boiler room, I've gone down there enough times for school supplies to know where this window leads out to, also that they never lock it." Talan smirked, "you use it to sneak out on occasions?" I rolled my eyes, "Come on." I knelt down and pushed the window up, "you first."

Talan knelt down next to me, "why me first?" I gestured to my skirt, "uh I'm wearing a skirt you moron, now come on I don't want anyone seeing us." Shaking his head humorously he slid onto his belly, using his arms he slid his upper body through the somewhat small opening, grabbing his legs I held them in till he found something to grab onto or in till he touched the ground. "Ok you next," He called a few seconds later after he disappeared from view. Nodding to no one, I did as he did and got onto my stomach, pushing myself forward I pushed myself half way in; I could feel my skirt ridding up every time I pushed through the window. Talan grabbed me under my arms and helped pull me from the space. At the last moment my shoe caught on the edge of the window, this is such a movie moment I all most gagged, "Ah!" I swear that yell came out by accident, wrapping his arms around me at the last moment Talan caught me as I fell the rest of the way in.

OK, why aren't my feet touching the ground? I opened my eyes which apparently I had closed in the process of a very gag worthy movie moment, looking up I realized Talan was still holding me, ok, maybe not so gag worthy, it was nice his body fitting with mine perfectly my arms of course to complete the movie moment, where wrapped around his neck. I looked up to meet his eyes finding them to be staring down at me, I smiled attentively and unlaced my arms from around his neck and regrettably stepped away from the comfort of his body. Talan smiled at me as if saying he felt the same thing I had, what exactly had I felt? I sighed quietly, my emotions where everywhere after that moment, great just what I need: to fall for a guy I barely know.

Clearing my throat, I walked around Talan and further into the boiler room, small bangs and pops could be heard from the boiler as I walked passed boxes that had been shoved into the corner from past years. Walking up the old wood steps I pushed open the metal door that lead into the east wing of the school.

I waited about for about four minutes before Talan joined me, "what where you doing down there?" I questioned following him down the hall where I presumed would be where his locker was. I could see him shrug, "I was thinking about something." Ok, uh, more info would be nice, "thinking about what?" He shrugged again, "Talan…" He didn't answer, "Fine, don't tell me, but I'll find out soon enough I always do." He chuckled, "whatever you say, Alex." I groaned, I hate not knowing things I guess that's why I'm so good in school, I actually like to learn shocking I know.

We reached his locker in just under five minutes; I leaned against the others while Talan opened his up and got his keys out, "so you ready to go now?" I asked as he shut his locker door with a slam, the sound echoing in the empty halls. He nodded, "yup come on."

We walked back to the boiler room; the walk was silent just as it had been on the way to his locker. We headed down the boiler room steps, past the actual boiler and its little pop's and bang's, I dragged an empty medium sized wood box under the small window. Talan smiled at me and stepped up onto the box and pulled himself out through the window, I went next climbing on top of the box I knelt down somewhat and crawled out Talan grabbed my hands this time and helped me to my feet. I kicked the window shut gently before we started to walk to the parking lot.

The walk was surprisingly short as we reached Talan's car in record time. "So uh, I guess I'll let you go now." When did I become so awkward! Talan looked at me curiously, "don't you have a car?" I shook my head, sadly my parents wouldn't let me have one, "my parents won't get me one." I saw him take his lip ring between his teeth pulling at it, he was thinking. "I could give you a ride if you want, where are you going?"

"New York." He coughed, "you were going to walk to the city!" I laughed, "No, I was going to take the bus."

"Oh well, I can't let you go on the bus, those things are seriously nasty, plus lots of perverts." I raised an eyebrow; really, I have been taking the bus for years, "And I would be worried about you, crazy, I know," no it's totally sweet, ew I'm going mushy, but hey I am a girl so you can't blame me, "but really I like you and I don't want something stupid and out of the blue happening. I would feel better if I could drop you off where ever you're going." He said a bit awkwardly, it really is quite cute. I smiled and hugged him quickly, "Thank you. Alright, you can give me a ride."

We both got into the car; Talan started the engine and pulled out of the school parking lot. I told him the address once he pulled onto the main highway.

We had talked the whole way there and of course once Talan turned on the radio we both started singing along to the music blasting from the speakers. You know for a guy who wears the type of clothing he does, he sure does like rock music, and well, every other type of music gene there is.

Everything turned quiet once he parked out in front of Angel's place. I turned and looked at Talan, watching him as he survived the area in front of him. I wouldn't say the spot where Angel's place was located was the nicest of places, actually, it was pretty low, that's why he bought his flat here the rent was very cheap. "Talan?" I asked touching his arm gently, he turned to stare at me, "Alex, you don't really want to go in there do you? I know I dress like this but I mean, even I know this isn't a safe place." I knew this was coming, "its fine Talan I come here all the time. Really I'll be fine." He sighed and shook his head; I could tell he knew he wouldn't be able to talk me out of it. Grabbing a pen from the visor and an unused napkin from the side of the door he quickly wrote, what I presumed was his number. "Here's my number," Yup, "If you want to meet up anywhere, not here, but anywhere else. Or if something has happened , give me a call and I'll come pick you up or if you just want to meet somewhere-" I held up my hand making him fall silent, "ok Talan, I get it, I'll call you ok?" He nodded and I could hear a sigh slip past his lips. Thinking a moment, I leant over to kiss his cheek in reassurance, it was the only thing I could think of, but Talan turned his head just as my lips were about to touch his cheek. His lips met mine in a small kiss that shot little bolts of electricity up my spin causing me to shiver a bit as if I had been shocked as I pulled back. "Uh, I, you, I have to go I'll call you though." He nodded a light blush on his cheeks, "I'll be in the city so yeah...call me."

I got out of the car waving a bit before I walked into the building and took the stairs down to Angel's basement flat. I now knew one thing for certain: I now definitely had a reason to feel mushy inside.

Present

"Alex, *yo* Alex!" I shook my head clear of the memory and turned to look at Angel, "what?" I asked slightly annoyed that he raised his voice for no reason while calling me. I looked over to the coffee table and noticed three new empty beer bottles, he's wasted, great. "I want to party, you want to party Alex?" He asked lying back on the couch, his words where slurred quite a bit making it hard for me to understand. "No Angel, I do not want to party."

He sat up and got up from the couch walking over to me, "Well, we could have our own party," He suggested, oh no, if he so much as touches me in that way I'll kill him. "No Angel, why don't you go have your own party by yourself, in your bedroom, with your door closed, and bolted. I'll just wait here." He shook his head clumsily, "No! I want to party with *you*." He smirked, I have a feeling he was sobering up very fast.

Angel grabbed my backend and pulled me to him roughly, he so did not go there. Using all my strength I pushed him away slapping him hard across the face. I started to make my way hurriedly to the door. I wasn't fast enough as Angel grabbed my wrist pulling me back towards him, "Yo! Did I say you could do that? No! I don't think I did!" He screamed in slur near my ear, I flinched trying to get out of his grasp. "Get off of me Chris!" Chris kissed my neck biting it harshly, I screamed as I felt my skin break, "GET OFF! *NO!* GET *OFF* OF ME!" I struggled against him, my red hair whipping around every which was as I struggled, his arms tightened around me. Spinning us around, he pinned me to the wall his body a hard barrier against mine. My head hit the cement wall as he did so and my vision blurred slightly. Talan was right, was all I could think as I felt Chris tugging at my clothes pulling at the overly sensitive skin at my neck again; I could feel small tickles of blood running red path down my neck as he worked open my blue and black checkered button shirt I had changed into once I got here.

    He finally managed to get it open sliding his hand across my stomach and up towards my chest as the other worked on my black skinny jeans. He managed to get them open and slide them just down enough to give him room to work. "Don't you dare try to escape," he growled in my ear as he turned me around, I felt disgusted with Chris and with myself for even letting myself get into this sort of position. He pulled my pants down lower, shoving them roughly to my knees, "Don't run." He growled harshly again rubbing his lower half against my skin, rubbing it red and raw. His member, obvious through his pants as it dug into me. He stepped back working on the belt of his own pants, seeing my opportunity I quickly reached for the cheap glass lamp that was on the small table next to the wall, my fingers brushed against it as it fell short, stretching my arm as far as possible I grabbed hold of the neck, bringing it towards me I raised it over Chris's bent head. As I brought it down, I heard the satisfying sound of the glass breaking and his body falling to the ground in a crumpled heap.

    Taking no time I pulled my pants up, my hands were shaking so bad I could hardly button them; finally doing them, I worked on my shirt, the tears in my eyes making it hard to see the buttons. I got half way before I gave up; Chris was starting to wake up, groaning. I walked quickly around him grabbing my leather jacket from the arm of the couch. Running into Chris bedroom, I grabbed my purple duffle bag from deep inside his closet; I kept it there whenever I came over here keeping my personal clothes in it that my parents have never seen.

I rushed from his room and looked once more over the dingy space; Chris was already trying to sit up. Taking in a deep breath, I opened the front door and ran out not stopping until I was on the street. I inhaled sharply before letting it out and looked both ways before I started walking down the side walk, duffle bag thrown over my shoulder, my hands deep in my pockets. I hated this part of the city, but this was the part I came to since I was thirteen, and just like my smoking... I didn't know why.

I was about four blocks away when I walked into a liquor store and asked the guy behind the desk if I could use his phone. He stared at me up and down, I was thankful I had buttoned the rest of my shirt up, the jacket making a good cover for the small lines of dried blood down the side of my neck. He nodded and handed me his cell phone from his pocket, "make it quick, I only have a few minutes left on my card." I nodded, promising him I would make the call short. Taking Talan's number out of my pocket I quickly dialed the number waiting for him to pick up, he answered on the third ring.

"*Hello?*" I nearly started crying again once I heard his voice, "Ta-Talan," I said into the phone my voice breaking; I have never felt so weak, so vulnerable, and so *stupid* in my life. For once, I was actually scared. "I n-n-need you to pick m-me up, I'm four blocks from Chris's place." I could hear the screech of ties and the blare of several horns, "Talan?"

"*I'm here Alex; I'm coming to get you. What happened, who's Chris?*" I could hear the question in his voice along with the urgency.

"You where right Talan I shouldn't have gone, Chris *is* Angel he h-he... I'll tell you when you get here alright?" I heard him sigh, "*Alright, but you better tell me everything.*" I said promised and hung up, handing over the phone back to the guy he was looking at me with curiosity, "are you alright? Do you need anything?" I gave him a small smile grateful for his concern, "no I'm fine, or I will be. A friend of mine is picking me up. Thank you for letting me use you phone." He gave me a smile and nodded. I walked out of the shop and waited against the front wall of the store in plain sight for Talan to see me.

I waited forty minutes in front of the liquor store before I finally saw Talan's car pull up in front of the store, stopping the small flow of traffic on the street, cars honking in protest. He got out of the car and ran over to me. "Alex? Oh my God, are you alright?" I felt his hands rest on my arms as he knelt down next to me, I didn't say anything and buried my head into his chest heaving out a sob, "Shh, it's alright. Come on let's get you out of here," He said helping me to my feet; my head was still buried in his chest as he walked me to his car. Opening the passenger side, I got in resting my head against the glass of the window when he shut the door. He came around to the driver side and got in, starting the car back up he pulled back into the street driving me away from this place, and away from my biggest mistake.

It was dark when Talan pulled off the highway ramp and onto Mulberry Street a few blocks away from the high school. "Where do you want to go?" He questioned looking at me briefly, I didn't know, I don't know. Making a quick dissection I asked him, "can I stay at your place tonight?" He nodded so I took that for a yes, "won't you parents be worried though?" He asked a moment later. I shook my head looking out the window, "I highly doubt it."

It was half-an-hour later when Talan finally pulled into his driveway. His house didn't look all that different from mine except my house was white with blue shutters while his was white with a red door.
    I got out wincing a bit when I turned my neck, feeling the lightly scabbed over bite open a bit. Shutting the door I walked up the walkway with Talan; waiting for him to open the door. When he did I walked in looking around his house, it was simple, yet homey and warm. I instantly loved it. "Come, on I'll show you the guest room." He took my hand in his and led me up the stairs, pulling me lightly over to the

second door on the right. "The bathroom is next door," he pointed to the door next to mine on the left, "if you need anything my room is across from yours and I'll put some sweats and a t-shirt on the bed for you." I nodded silently, I wanted to say something but I couldn't. I turned to the bathroom and opened the door, "Alex." I looked at him, "you promised." I know I did; now I just need to find my voice to tell him what happened.

Without another word, he walked into his own room while I turned back to the bathroom and shut the door behind me. I sighed closing my eyes, after I went to stand in front of the mirror looking at my reflection, I was a mess. My hair was a tangled mess around my face, dried tears streaked down my cheek my clothes where rumpled, and when I took my jacket off I had blood tracking down the side of my neck to my collarbone from an ugly looking cut with indents. How did I become so off track? It's as if the railroad was at one point and I was a million mile south at another point.

Peeling my clothes off I left them in a heap on the floor. I walked over to the shower and turned it on adjusting it for a moment to get it to the right temperature, once satisfied I stepped in, goose-bumps rising shortly on my flesh before my body adjusted to the water and I relaxed.

I picked up the bar of soap that rested on its holder and started to scrub my body vigorously trying to wash the feeling of his hands on my body, off. Feeling them crawling up my skin towards my chest, the feeling of him rubbing against me. I felt disgusted. After a vicious rub down of my body I worked some sweet smelling shampoo into my hair rinsing it out after. The dye in my hair washing out from using a different shampoo then my own, red water flowing down the drain leaving what I was sure was blonde hair in its wake.

I lost count of how long I had stayed in the shower for; having just stood there under the spray letting the water works its way down my skin. Finally with a sigh I got out turning the water off, grabbing a towel that was hanging on the rack and dried my body with it wrapping it around myself.

Peeking into the hallway I made sure no one was around before

I slipped out and walked into my room, my dirty clothes in hand. Making sure the door was locked before I pulled the towel off I laid the towel across the bed, and just as Talan had said, there was a pair of grey sweat pants and a black tank top. I smiled grabbing the sweats and pulling them on, the fabric soft against my naked skin, along with the tank top. I rubbed my hair dry with the towel before I set it back on the bed.

I hesitated before opening my door once more and walking over to Talan's room, I knocked, waiting for a reply, "come in," I opened his door and slipped in shutting it behind me with a click. "Hi," I said in a small voice, "hey. Do you feel any better?" I shrugged and went to sit next to him on his bed. "A bit, I still can't believe I would let myself get into a position like that, how stupid could I be?" I mean I go to a guy's house five days a week, while I tell my parent's I'm staying late at school for extra credit, I hardly knew Chris when I was twelve but still I let him talk me into smoking, and I let him talk me into coming to his place when I was thirteen, and I just don't know how I could be so stupid. "It's how we learn, Alex- what happened to your neck?!" He exclaimed reaching over to turn my head to get a better view of the bite. "It's nothing," I muttered haven completely forgotten about it by the time I had gotten out of the shower, even though this isn't the right moment I loved the way his touch shot little shivers down my spine. "It's not anything Alex; did Chris do this to you?" I didn't say anything and he got it. Shaking his head he stood up from the bed, "I'll be right back." And he left.

I took the time to get comfortable on the bed sitting cross legged and leaning against his pillow. I looked around his room; he had posters of various bands on his walls along with a few rappers I had never heard of. A silver desk was pushed into the corner along with a desk chair; a silver nightstand was next to the bed along with a lamp and a clock. The room it's self looked every bit of a boy's room but it also looked like Talan's room. It suited him.

He came back holding a white first aid kit, he sat in front of me opening it, silently he got out the alcohol out and a cotton swab dripping some of the liquid onto it, "this is going to sting a bit," I readied myself, at first all it felt like was water but then the sting kicked in, I bit my lip sucking in a breath. When he said it would hurt, dammit, he wasn't joking, it hurt like hell! Talan gently leaned in and blew lightly on the stinging skin cooling it instantly, I felt my heart skip having him so close to me. "Sorry for hurting you," He muttered. I just shook my head giving him a small smile, "you didn't hurt me you helped me." And I meant that, he was helping me in more ways than just cleaning my cut.

He looked up from my neck and stared at me lifting his hand to my face touching my cheek with the pads of his fingers; he just stayed like that looking at me, before he applied Neosporin on my neck and put a large gauze cover over it. "There, all better," He said putting the used cotton swab on his night stand along with the first aid kit.

I leant over and gave him a hug letting my head rest in the crook of his neck; he hugged me back maneuvering us so we were laying on the bed his head on the pillow. "You know," he started, "you never told me what happened at Chris's place." I breathed in his sent before I spoke, "all you need to know is he tried to rape me," I felt him jolt with a start and I held him firmly in place, which wasn't the easiest task in the world but I felt him relax somewhat and tighten his arms around me, I went on, "before he could get all the way I hit him over the head with something... a lamp I think. He fell, I grabbed my stuff and ran, than I called you and you know the rest." I wasn't going to go into details, I didn't want to and Talan knew I didn't want to, "you have to go to the police Alex," I shook my head sharply pulling back so I could stare down at him, "no I can't, I don't want to. If I go to the police than I'm going to have to testify and in this sort of situation I have a fifty chance of winning the trial, whereas Chris has the other fifty chance.

I've gone to his house since I was thirteen Talan making it so that he would be able to convince the court that I was a willing participant, and it would seem as if I'm just doing this to get money or some such. I can't Talan, though I do know he won't try to report me either because he knows I could do the same thing as I just explained. So, all in all, this is my chance to just walk away with a fresh start." After I finished my little rant he was quiet for a bit, just staring up at me; he finally said something after a moment, "it's not a fresh start, not yet Alex, not until...." He trailed off, and I knew what he was getting at: My parents. I sighed and nodded, "I know... will you come with me?" He smiled at me, my heart melted, "of course."

I stayed there just looking down at him; I brought my hand up to his dreads, brushing across them, letting my hand slide down the side of his face cupping his cheek gently. I leant down slowly, giving him time to turn away, when he didn't, I let my lips touch his in a soft kiss, it was my first kiss, technically my second, and it was everything I never expected. I always thought your first kiss would be awkward and wet, but this was soft, dry and sweet sending shivers to course through my body reaching my toes.

I pulled back looking at him, he lifted his hand to cup my jaw line bring me back down into a kiss. My eyes fluttered shut as I let my mind turn off, this kiss was more, oh, so much more than the first kiss, though it was still slow there was a passion to it, a need, a something I can't truly explain. I don't know how long we kissed, and I wasn't counting on pulling back anytime soon, but Talan eventually pulled back his breathing off slightly, his eyes dark though gentle as he looked at me. I gave him one last kiss before I scooted down a bit and snuggled into his side, he reached over and flicked off his lamp, I felt his arms wrap around me as I lay my head on his chest, the beats of his heart lulling me to sleep.

I smiled secretly as one last thought crossing my mind for the boy next to me, before completely falling: Talan you have no idea how much you have changed me; you've made my world a completely different universe....

Three

I swear I'm going to murder the person who is poking me. All I could feel was this finger poking at my forehead as I tried to sleep, not only was I not sleeping anymore but I was seriously starting to get annoyed. I opened my eyes, blinking away the sleep, fully prepared to yell at the person who was poking me… I so did not expect to come face to face with the cutest kid in the world.

Sitting up I stretched my hands over my head and yawned in the process, after, I looked at the kid with confusion. Who the hell was he? Just as I was about to ask him a sudden bang came from the hallway, I cringed at the noise, my head pounding with the start of a headache. Boy did I hate waking up, but that's what comes with not sleeping in, I am scowling right now if you couldn't get the picture.

"Well, I can tell you're not a morning person," said a voice form the door way with a chuckle. I turned to it, my scowl deepening. "I hate mornings," I muttered looking at Talan as he came to sit next to me on the bed, "Who was that kid?" I asked watching as Talan looked confused for a moment before realizing who I was talking about. "Oh, did he have blonde hair about yea high with a red balloon in hand?" He asked holding his hand about half a foot above the mattress. Uhh. Can we say forgetting what the kid looks like a stupid moment? "Uhh… I guess." I gave a small laugh. Talan just shook his head smiling, "It was my kid brother Jake, he turned six yesterday, that's why I was in the city, we were celebrating his birthday." Oh. "Well, are you going to get up any time soon?" I raised my eyebrows, "What, do you want to get rid of me already?" I asked in a teasing voice, he just rolled his eyes, "Reason being is breakfast is ready." He said giving me a smile. "What's on the menu?" I asked pulling the covers back so I could stand up. He smiled, "do pancakes and eggs sound good?"

"It sounds delicious, though, I have to ask one very important question...." He looked at me funny, "....Do you have strawberry jam?" He gave me a very sad face, eh what just happened? "The strawberry was attacked yesterday by my little brother's fingers during breakfast... we only have the nasty grape jelly left." He said cracking a smile. I scoffed, "Grape just won't do... innless of course you try it first and tell me how it is."

"Not likely, I'm a maple syrup type of guy all the way," I cringed making a face, "Ew." He just laughed as he started walk out of his room. Hey, he's forgetting something! "Talan?" He turned, "Can I have a morning kiss?" I know what everyone is thinking but hey! I am still a teenage girl; I am entitled to being all "lovey dovey"... or at least I think I am... am I right? "You know I gave you a kiss just before I got up." He stated going to stand in front of me, wrapping an arm around my waist. "But, I wasn't conscious so it doesn't count," He raised a brow, "Doesn't count? Then I guess I should never kiss you again while you're sleeping then, right?" Well... now that he puts it that way.... "OK maybe it does count, but, I still would like a morning kiss. Though hey, if you don't want to that's fine I'll just go get my breakfast instead...." I looked away slowly making my way around Talan's bodily wall before I felt him grab my upper arm and spin me around to face him, "I never said I wasn't going to kiss you." He stated before bring his lips down to mine. It was just like the first time, my toes curled and my breath vanished as I clung to the front of his shirt, my fingers fisting the fabric in my hands.

Just as it started to get heated a small giggle erupted behind us. We both pulled apart, our breathing was off as we turned to the small fits of giggles that had started up. There, standing behind us, who I supposed, was Talan's little brother Jake. He was seriously the cutest little kid in the world! He had slightly long blonde hair that fell to his shoulders and big brown eyes; he had a SpongeBob shirt on and a pair of black pants. "Jake, jeez, go 'way." I gave Talan a look, "Don't talk to your little brother like that." I said going over to crouch in front of Jake, "Hi, I like your shirt." He giggled looking away then back up at me. "Aw, Hello. Why are you in my brother's clothes? Did you sleep here?" He asked in a curious voice. I could just hug him, he's just so cute! "Something happened and I needed a place to stay, your brother was very nice about letting me sleep at your house."

"Do you like my brother?"

I grinned looking at Talan from over my shoulder, "Yeah... I like him a lot." I turned back to Jake, kneeling down to whisper in his ear, "though just between you and me I think he's a silly head at times." Jake giggled nodding his head in agreement. "Hey! What did you guys just say about me?" Talan questioned. Jake and I turned to look at him, "Do you think we should tell him?" I asked, whispered, to Jake. He shook his head. Playing along I looked at Talan while standing up, "Who said we were talking about you?" And with that, I took Jake's small hand in mine and walked out of the room, following the scent of freshly brewed coffee and pancakes.

"Have you had breakfast?" I asked Jake as we entered the kitchen, pulling out his chair so he could sit down. Jake shook his head eyeing the syrup. "Let me guess, you want lots of sugar with your pancakes?" He nodded his head licking his lips. I just shook my head taking a pancake from the large stack with my fork, placing it on the kid's plate, "Syrup?"

"Yes!"

"Yes what?"

He made a face, "Yes please."

Chuckling I grabbed the syrup pouring it over the pancake, "That's better, "

Talan entered looking at the two of us in turn, "I can't believe my little brother has stolen my girlfriend away from me," he said shaking his head while taking two cups from the cupboard, "Coffee?" I nodded going over to him. Wrapping my arms around his waist I laid my cheek against his back, "Sugar and cream?"

"Two, and yes please." I mumbled against his shirt.

I felt Talan turn around wrapping his arms around my waist, "Are you feeling better?"He asked brushing his hand across the bandage at my neck. Sighing I nodded slowly. Getting on my tips tops I brought my hand to rest on his cheek as I gave him, what was supposed to be a small kiss, before he deepened it, sliding his hand around the back of my neck, bring me closer-

"Ahem?"

Once again, we pulled apart only this time blushing when we saw, who I defiantly knew to be his father. Jake on the other had both his hands over his mouth, his body shaking from the suppressed laughter. "Hello," I said breaking the awkward silence, "I'm Alex. I'm sorry we didn't tell you I was staying the night. Nothing happened or anything, I just need a place to stay." I explained in a slight rush, I didn't exactly want him to get the wrong impression when he just met me. I mean jeez, that would be really bad since Talan and I are now a couple... I think. I'll have to ask him later. He just chuckled, "Talan already explained everything Alex, including what happened." I looked at Talan, "Now don't judge him, he just needed a little advice. I told him what you said was very reasonable and most likely true." He pulled a chair out from the kitchen table and sat down looking at the teens, "Now, though, enough of that, I would like to introduce myself. My name is Jacett and I'm the father of that moron and this trouble maker," He said pointing to the two boys in turn. Talan gave his father a look while Jake just went on eating his pancakes adding more syrup in the process. "That's enough Jake," Jake pouted while giving his father a scowl, putting the syrup down, "Never enough," He said with his mouth full.

Grabbing my mug from behind Talan I took a sip of the almost bitter drink, "Mmm, much better." Talan grabbed my free hand just as I was about to take another sip, and pulled me out of the room and into the living room, "Talan?" He looked at me, "Why did you pull me out of the kitchen." I asked shaking some of the spilt coffee off of my hand. He shrugged, "I just wanted to be alone with you, you know?"

I gave him a look, "Ok, well, I wanted to ask you a question... I know I haven't known you for very long, two weeks, and well... I, it's just that I was wondering," He's stuttering, what could he possibly want to ask me that that makes him stutter? "I was wondering... if you would like to be my girlfriend?" Ah, ok. "I thought I was already considered your girlfriend, I mean by the way you said it in the kitchen," So sue me for beating around the bush. A light blush covered Talan's cheeks as he scratched his neck, "Yeah well, I just realized you might not have liked that. I just sort of jumped to the conclusion that you where my girlfriend." I smiled leaning over and quickly pecking his lips, "I would love to be your girlfriend so long as you stop stuttering like a moron." He grinned, "Deal."

We started to talk about random things: cheese and our favorite birthdays when we were little, when I felt my tank top being tugged at, "Do you want to see my balloon?" I looked over at Jake than at Talan, winking I got up from the couch we were sitting at and followed as Jake dragged me by my hand up the stairs. "What's your name?" He asked as we entered his room; LEGOS where scattered on the floor along with toy cars and dinosaurs. A small messy twin bed with star bed sheets was pushed against the corner. "My name is Alex."

"Alex," He said trying the name out, "Alex, this is my balloon, it's my favorite color." He said holding out a red balloon for me to see. Happy Birthday was printed in the middle in big shiny silver letters. "It's very nice; did you get this for your birthday?" He nodded, "who got it for you?"

"Talan, he gave it to me this morning. He said that he was sorry he couldn't make it to my birthday party, but I saved him some cake... then I ate it." He said making a happy face while rubbing his stomach. I laughed, "Is that right? Well I have to say, I'm sorry for having to pull your brother away from your birthday party." Jake shook his head, "Talan said it was important, like when daddy needs to go to work at bedtime." I made an 'oh' sound, looking down at Jake, "Well then thank you for understanding, and Happy Birthday, I hear you turned six." Jake nodded his head vigorously, "I'm a big boy now." I gasped in shock, "No way! But if you're a big boy then you don't get to have any fun. Like you won't get to get away with stuff and blame it on Talan, you can't live in Never Never Land, and-"

"Hey, don't go giving him ideas." Jacett said as he walked into the room. I smiled sheepishly, "Sorry, I couldn't help myself." Jacett chuckled, "Well if he gets into trouble I'll know who to ground." I just stuck out my tongue. "Talan is looking for you, and this monkey here needs a bath." I stood up looking momentarily at Jake and laughed out loud. The boy had a twisted look on his face as if taking a bath was the worst kind of torture. "Awe it's ok Jake, baths our fun." His face twisted even more, "no their not." He said stubbornly crossing his arms, crouching down I stood Jake up and looked up at him, "I'll make you a promise Jake," He looked at me curiously his face going back to normal, "if you can take bath for me, I promise I'll buy you a lollipop, a red lollipop." His eyes lit up as he started to squeal. Grinning I stood up, moving out of the way as the little boy ran out of the room. Jacett looked amazed, "How did you-?" He shook his head, "never mind, you have a very special way with kids Alex, I hope you know that," he said, walking out of the room towards the sound of the bathtub filling and a high pitch squeal of child's laughter.

I smiled to myself as I walked out of Alex's room in search of Talan. I soon found him in his room, his clothes having been changed to street clothes, my own clothes folded neatly in his hands. "Hey," I said coming up behind him. He turned and looked at me, my clothes still in his hands, "hey," he whispered in a low voice. I gave him a meek smile and took the clothes from his hands. "It's over, okay?" He nodded though gave me a look, "home. You have to go home now," he said in all seriousness. I let out a puff of air and nodded my head slowly. With all honesty, I didn't want to confront my parents just now, but if I didn't do it then when would I? "Ok. Yeah you're right. We should go now then; my nerves may be shot if we wait too long."

My house stood in front of me like an unavoidable doom. The white paint of the house and the blue shutters were all too familiar to me, reminding me of the years I've spent in this house and hated it.

"Alex," Talen said catching my attention as he took his hand in mine, "come on." With a half smile, I let him lead me up the pathway and to the door that loomed in front of us. I let Talen knock; as we waited outside in the summer air I breathed in deep and I felt a hand squeeze my shoulder, smiling at the touch from my boyfriend. The door opened and there stood my mother in the doorway, all primped and plucked as usual, though her eyes seemed tired and that's when I noticed the little smudges of makeup under her eyes. She had been crying. "Annie?" She asked in a worn voice. I nodded, pursing my lips into a smile. "Come in," she said stepping aside. I hesitated for a second, Talen nudged me forward and I walked past my mother into the familiar house. The place was lit from the sun streaming in from the windows, but, still, it held a gloom for me. "Jordon! Come here please," my mother called. "Sit, please," she said gesturing to the couch. Both Talen and I sat, but not before Talen introduced himself. "Ma'am, my name is Talen Mayett, I'm a friend of your daughter's." Mother just looked at him, giving him a polite smile, "It's a pleasure Talen. I am Katrina Joans," Just then my dad walked in, "My husband, Jordon." Talen nodded in respect, "Talen Mayett, Sir." Jordon all but grunted and sat opposite of two teens.

I was nervous yes but I needed to do this. With a supporting smile from Talen as he sat down, I took his place to stand and started to speak. "Ok, so before you ask question I need to tell you guys a few things," I paused. "When I was twelve I met a guy name Ang— Chris, and...," I shook my head, I can't blame people for what I made myself do. "Let me start over. When I was twelve I started to smoke, when I was thirteen I started going over to a guy name Chris's place, I've been going there since yesterday, five days a week after school. I told you I was staying late at school for extra credit… I wasn't. I'm sorry for lying to you," I took a breath before turning to my mother and continuing. "Ma, *I* dyed my hair the red color, the salon didn't do it, and it wasn't an accident. Also, I hate the clothes you make me wear. I hate, *hate* them with a passion. When I was at Chris's I would have a bag with the clothes I bought myself, and every time I would change into them when I got to his place." My dad opened his mouth to speak but I cut him off. "Listen, please dad? I don't smoke anymore, I have never drank alcohol before... well only once but I never did it again," I said with shrug. "I made a terrible mistake though. I shouldn't have gone to Chris's place, ever. Yesterday Chris tried to... do things to me," I cringed at how the words sounded. "Though I somehow got out of there before anything could *really* happen," I sighed, this wasn't coming out how I wanted it to. Instead of standing, I sat and closed my eyes momentarily. "Look. I'm not the type of daughter that loves to be perfect, I am too damn far from the truth. I like colors, all these pastels make me sick. I don't want a mother who is perfect in every way, I rather you have a few flaws," I said to her, rounding on my dad next. "Dad, you are a hard working person I will give you that, but as truthful as that is you are so lazy sometimes and *so* self righteous that its sick, to me and to yourself. Why don't you try coming home and being *with* your family rather than with the quarterback for the Colts. I think it would help you some. You know what's really funny? It's the fact that even if you can't accept what I'm saying to you, or who I am, really. I won't care because how I'm living now isn't healthy, at all. Oh, and another thing, I loathe the name Annie, I go by Alex and I would appreciate it if you would call me by that too. " Whoa, who knew telling the truth felt so good?

The living room was silent as my father worked his jaw and my mother stared at Talen and me in turn with a passive stare. I could feel Talen shift besides me as the two of us become awkward in the silence that surrounded us.

My father cleared his voice and in a harsh tone he said, "I don't accept it."

I nodded already knowing he would say that, turning to my mother who was gnawing at the corner of her mouth, "I... I accept it only because I knew something was up."

I gapped, "then why didn't you do anything to stop me?"

She shrugged, "because I didn't have any evidence to prove anything. Though I can say you're grounded until further notice," I also saw that coming too.

I could feel the conversation coming to an end as I felt Talen stand up, taking me with him, "Mr. and Mrs. Joans, I'm sorry for saying this at this time, but I don't think a better time will be around. I'm not just friends with your daughter, I'm her boyfriend," He said with a smile. You know, I may just start to love this boy.

I couldn't believe it when my mother actually just rolled her eyes and ushered us out of the room and towards the stairs, "Alex, upstairs now, go change. Talen, are her things with you?" Talen nodded, and all I could do was stare. "Well, go get them; I honestly don't want her walking around in sweatpants all day." Talen smiled in understanding and turned away from us. I couldn't help but hug my mother when he left; caught off guard I could feel her smile warmly and hug me back. Maybe I finally got my wish for normal parents... or *a* normal parent.

My room was the same but unlike before, it wasn't just a place I lived, it sort of felt like it was *mine*. I stripped my clothes, changed into some underwear and waited for Talen or my mother to bring me my clothes Talen had placed in his car before we had left his place that morning. A knock sounded and I opened it a crack, peaking from behind the door. It was my mother. I let her in and she followed with my purple duffle close at hand.

"Why didn't you tell us before?"

I gave her a sidelong glance as I riffled through the bag, pulling from it a short black pleated skirt with a large belt to company it, a pair of long pink leggings and two tank tops, one white the other black. A pair of black flats followed next. "You weren't really my mom until now, if you want my opinion. You were more of a robot than anything else. Dad is... I don't know about him, he's selfish and yeah I don't really understand why you married him. Though again, my opinion." I pulled the items of clothing on, waiting for my mother's reply as I sat next to her on the bed, moving the duffle to the floor.

"I know... I know I haven't been the best parent in the world. I guess I got too consumed by a certain lifestyle that it took away me from my own child," she said with a sigh, casting her head down.

"Well, we'll work on it, ok? Both of us."

She smiled at me, "well then, we can start with you telling me about your boyfriend," she smirked raising an eyebrow with a teasing glint in her eyes.

I just shook my head with a laugh; she fell into this roll rather quickly didn't she? "Later, right now Talen and I have to go somewhere," I said standing up and walking to my vanity mirror. I was right, my hair was once again it natural light blonde shade, my brows just the same.

"Where are you two going?" She questioned, coming to stand behind me, looking at our reflection.

"School," I said simply, "there's something we have to take care of."

She nodded in understanding, "yes, well come home this time. Please," she said with a chuckle.

I nodded, "right, again, sorry about that." With that, I left. Though I couldn't wait for tonight, I think this is going to be a good change.

Talen met me outside by the car, opening my door for me as I neared. "So how did it go up there?" He asked as I got in. I smiled, waiting for him to get in before I continued, "it went well. I think my mom and I are going to be allot better. My dad and I? I honestly don't know, but hey, at least I still have my mom now. We'll see how it plays out, though I think things will be changing for the better," I said with a grin. Talen held my hand in his as he pulled away from the curb. "I'm glad things are changing. Now why do I have this feeling that you want to go to the school?" I laughed, "We have a few things to take care of, and besides I left my wallet in my locker."

The school was as crowded as always, it was 12 and everyone was milling around the grass lawn in front, while others were most likely in the cafeteria. Talen parked and I hoped out, slamming the door behind me. Talen came up beside me and put his hand around my waist and walking beside me as we went up the school steps, entering the semi crowded hall.

"She's in the cafeteria," I muttered mostly to myself as I scanned the hall for signs of Courtney, and coming up short.

Talen didn't say anything but walked alongside me, letting me concentrate for a moment. I stopped by my locker; undoing the lock and pulling it open so I could retrieve my wallet. A chain hung from it, so I could clip it to my belt and tuck it under the waistband of my skirt, I shut it just as I pulled it out and turned back towards the way we had been walking.

"What do you think you will say?"

I shrugged, "I have no idea. I think winging it will be my best option."

The cafeteria was just as crowded as the lawn, and the sound of talking students over powered all other sound. Though when we walked in everything went quiet, and those who hadn't noticed soon stopped to stare as we walked up to Courtney's table, the group of cheerleaders in their own little world as they gossiped about a girl only a few tables away.

"Ahem?" I cleared my throat, my success in capturing their attention succeeding.

"Well, well, well, look who it is," snickered one of the bitch posse.

Courtney turned, eyebrow raised unnaturally high, and with a laugh, she spoke. "Wow, Annie, look who's trying to be cool now," she said with a smirk.

I rolled my eyes and crossed my arms, "I only came here to tell you one thing."

"Oh? And what's that?" She asked, her smirk never slipping away.

"Get over yourself, no one likes you and I have a rather strong word choice for you but I think I may restrain myself, instead here are four words and one meaning: Long walk, short pier." With that, I gave her my best smile and grabbed Talen's hand in mine once more, having dropped it, and made our way through the silent cafeteria.

"*Bitch!*" Courtney screeched loudly. I could almost see her stop her foot.

With a look behind my shoulder, I stated "No, actually, it's Alex; though I think *you* should try out 'Bitch' then again 'Slut' may be a better name." The room laughed as we got to the door, with one last look I smiled back at the teens looking at me. "Guys, girls, grow a pair why don't you? Courtney is just one person; her little clones are nothing but puppets." I didn't have to stay to know that everyone was agreeing.

The air outside was warm and delicious as I stepped outside, a smile on my face as the wind started to blow. I had learned a few things from the past month or so… hells maybe a few years, give or take my past mistakes. One: that life sucks. Two: life sucks. Three: life only sucks if you let it suck. I let people push me in different directions and I *let* them screw up *my* life. I let it become screwed up, and truthfully, I was done with it.

"We have to make a stop before we go home."

Talen looked at me, stopping in front of the car, "oh? Where?"

"The drug store, I promised Jake a red lollipop… I think I might get myself one too," I said, the last past more of a thought really.

My boyfriend smiled, "sounds good to me. Why don't we all get one?"

I hummed in agreement, "Can we walk? I feel like walking."

He gave me a heartwarming grin, and I could feel myself start to grin in response. "Whatever you want." Hmm, I liked the sound of that.

Things were definitely going to be different now…. I had a feeling I was going to love it.

Crash

One

Everyone crashes. It's sort of slipped into our immune system. To feel something, anything, just to be able to feel a *touch*. We crash our cars– most likely not on purpose, but then you do have your rather crazy ex-wives; we crash because we can't seem to stay awake for another minute, we crash planes, boats, love and any other human emotion. And sometimes, just sometimes, we crash into each othe, just so we can have a sense of being with another person, to feel them, when we ourselves feel alone.

Love, what a weird word, they say it's suppose to make you happy and sentimental. They never said it was supposed to make you feel like crap, feel put down... scared and in the dark.

Janise Wane, 31 years old, watched in a slow haze as her husband screamed at her. Her arms wrapped around her waist and head down, she watched him slam cupboards and throw the dirty dishes from their just concluded dinner party, to the floor and walls. She flinched as he advanced on her, taking a hold of her upper arm in a firm iron vice grip. She coward, shrinking noticeably in size, as he drags her out of the kitchen and into the living room.

"Who do you think you are?!" Her husband yelled at her in a rage, "Acting that way in front of my friends!"

Janice fingered the hem of her simple black dress while shaking her head, "I'm sorry," she whispered in a small voice. Tears threaten to spill over as she sat there, head bent low, her hair obscuring her face from her husband's enraged sight.

She didn't know what she had done; she had laughed at the jokes and served the diner while making polite conversation with their company—co-workers from his job. His temper always got out of hand but she had never seen him this angry.

"You're *sorry*? Sorry for having flirted with my co-workers!" He stepped in front of her and leaned in close, the smell of alcohol clear on his breath, "You slut." And with that, he brought his hand down upon her cheek, leaving a bruising mark as her head whipped sharply and her body fell to the ground. The side of her head nicking the corner of the class coffee table.

With blurred vision and a hazy mind, she tried to pick herself off the ground, her arms giving out under her in her attempt. The last thing she remembered was the terrifying touch of her husband's grip on her hair as he pulled her off the ground, and then everything went black.

The Corner Market

The sound of the nonstop city traffic of Chicago could be heard through the brick walls of the small natural food market. The smell of fresh garlic and spices wafted from the back deli and tickled 28 year old Dave Jonathan's senses as he stared out the window and at the twilight air, watching the cars pass by, speeding away.

A plump woman with a bright face came up to his check stand. "Hi," she greeted.

Dave acknowledged her slightly, his mind too tired to register an equally cheerful reply. The scanner beeped every time he past the food over it. "24.20," he muttered not looking up at the woman as she slid her credit card through and entered her pin. Dave handed her, her receipt without a word and she left, the door's bell chiming felt like a hammer to his foggy mind.

Scrubbing his face, he moaned loudly as twilight become night and the traffic outside never dimmed. Thoughts of money, rent, and bills that needed to be paid creased through his mind not letting his thoughts go.

An hour or so after twilight, his boss called him to his office.

"Jonathan, have a seat," he said, calling him by his last name, gesturing to the hard looking chair in front of the desk that was cramped into a 6 by 6 room. Dave felt claustrophobic as he sat down, the wood as cold and hard as it looked.

"Sir...." He said in a low tone.

His boss nodded subconsciously and pulled out a thin white envelope, "here is two weeks pay. I'm sorry but this is just not working out."

Dave took the envelope, stood and walked out. His feet like cement on the floor, he pushed himself out of the market and turned right, walking down the street missing people just barely as they past him.

The night was humid and dry. City lights lighting up the night like day. Dave reached his grey and old dodgy apartment building, walking up the cracked cement stairs and up to his apartment house 3B. As he walked up to his faded door he noted the white note taped to the middle of his door and a lock chained to the door.

"Shit," he muttered bringing his fist down on the door, his head hung low as he pulled the piece of paper off. "*2 months' rent due, one week to come up with money or I rent the place to someone else.*" As he read the note, he crumpled the paper in his hands and threw it to the ground. "Shit...," he muttered again while pushing himself to the railing and taking a deep breath.

The hinges of a door creaked from down the hall; Dave didn't have to look up to know it was his landlord.

"You got my note?" The landlord questioned coming to stand by him. Dave peeked a look at him and turned away, his landlord's greasy hair was slicked back from his oily face. A large stomach showing skin form under his sweat stained grey shirt.

Dave nodded.

"I mean it. One week or I'm handing the space over to someone else," he said. "Your junk can stay but only for a *week*! Then I'm getting the garbage guys to pick your stuff up."

"Here," he said taking the white envelope with his paycheck in it.

"I didn't check to see how much it was, but it should cover a quarter of it."

"Give me the rest you come up with or I'll have the locks changed," he warned poking Dave's arm with one beefy finger.

Again, the landlord nodded, footsteps were heard, and the door down the hallway sounded shut. Dave scrubbed his face with his hands and turned back the way he came. His skin scraped against the peeling paint of the staircase railing as he slid his palm against it and turned on the street once again that night.

The Red Light

26 year old Alyssa Jonathan was leaned against the brick wall of what the girls called, *The Red Light*. To accompany the name red lights were placed outside and inside the club while the girls were dressed in little to nothing at all, out on the street to bring the business to the joint.

A hand rolled joint hung loosely between her lips, the end glowing bright as she took a drag from the addictive drug. This wasn't a life she had wanted for herself, given that most of the girl didn't want a life as a low class, dirt poor whore, but being as weak as she was and desperate for money....

This wasn't life; it was hell– her purgatory. Cheap drugs, sex with fat greasy men who have nothing better to do with their time then spend money on girls who most likely have AIDs or Herpes and any other disease you could catch.

A blank look crossed Alyssa's face as a memory crossed over her mind like a comforting blanket. As a little girl, she had always been a dreamer. Wanting to explore new places, and be taken on exciting adventures. She loved frilly dresses with lace and had a passion about flowers... it was a perfect childhood. Dreams of a husband and a house in the country with children, is what she wanted the most though as a child.... But as the year progressed and she grew older, her dreams vanished and all she longed to do was get out of the house she grew up in.

Her heart was dead; her soul was ice, her feelings numb and touch dull; it's the feelings of a slut... a person in hell.

"Hey baby." Alyssa looked up at the street and saw a man, in a beat up old mustang, pull up to the curb.

"I'm off," she said stubbing the joint out on the wall behind her before she pushed away and started toward the entrance of the building.

"Aw sweetheart, don't be like that," the guy cooed following slowly with his car.

Alyssa just shook her head, "go find one of the working girls. I'm sure they could help you with your *tiny* problem." She could hear him mutter a 'bitch' as he stepped on the gas and pulled away from the corner.

Just as she was to enter, she heard her name being called out.

"Alyssa!"

She squinted through the red lights and the black of the night, the shape of her older brother came into view as he approached her. "Dave?!" She questioned as he stopped in front of her, "What are you doing here? I mean, why are you here? How did you find me?"

Dave shook his head, "I had nowhere else to go," he said truthfully, looking her in the eyes and then down at her attire, his eyebrows pulling together. "I... I heard you worked in this area. Don't live far from here, but I've never actually seen this place. Aly, don't tell me you- you sell yourself?"

Alyssa crossed her arms over her scarcely clad chest, "yes I do. It's not something I enjoy but I needed the money." She couldn't look at him as she spoke, disgusted by her appearance in front of him.

"Aly...?"

"*Don't*! I don't need your pity or sympathy! Just... don't," she sobbed out.

Dave made a cooing noise and tugged her into his arms, "Shh, it's alright, Aly, it's alright." A feeling of dread crashed through him as he held his sobbing baby sister. "I'm sorry," he whispered.

She nodded into his chest, "me too...."

They stayed like that for a few minutes, just standing there wrapped in each other's embrace. When the moment ended, they pulled apart and just stood there, arms hanging to their sides limply.

"Let's get you out of here," Dave said breaking the silence. Alyssa nodded absently while pulling twenty from the waistband of her skin tight skirt, "we can take a cab instead of walking," she muttered.

"Thanks." With the twenty in hand he hailed a passing cab and helped his sister get in before sliding in next to her.

"Inner city," Dave said to the driver.

The driver looked back at Dave, "where?"

"I'll tell you once we get there."

Inner City

Janise stared out the window of her living space, fingering the bruise on the side of her cheek lightly, her emotions a whirl wind of emotion that felt like a tidal wave knocking her over.

She had a wealthy life, nice shoes, lovely clothes and a flat that cost a fortune. Was it what she wanted? No, not even as a child did she want to be completely afraid of being left alone with the man she chose to marry. It wasn't even a thought that crossed her mind.

The door bell rang and Janise rushed over to the door quickly before the person could ring again and wake her husband– who was currently asleep down the hall. When she opened the door, she found her two younger siblings standing there. Her sister clad in dark, ripped, skin tight clothing that showed more then covered. Her brother though dressed in jeans and a blue t-shirt, looked tired and in much need of some rest.

"You guys, what are you doing here?" She whispered stepping into the hall and shutting the door behind her with a silent click.

Dave started first. "I... I lost my job and my landlord kicked me out of my apartment, I found Aly... well she'll explain the rest."

Alyssa hung her head shortly before looking at her sister, noticing the bruise on her cheek, "Jan, your cheek," she said in a mellow tone brushing her finger tips against the marked skin. Janise shrugged, "It's nothing. What about you, Aly?" She gestured to her clothes. "What's with the street clothes?"

"I work at the Red Light," she muttered as Janise gasped.

"How? You were always the one who wanted the husband and kids. How did you end up working as a whore?"

Aly shrugged, "who knows anymore, I can't remember. I've gone over it so many times that I've actually forgotten it... I know I'm a slut, not even a good one."

Janise put her hand on Alyssa's face, cupping her cheek gently, "I would have helped if you needed it."

The other sister just shook her head, "no, I think you're the one who needs the help. What happened to your face Jan? Please tell us."

"They say in a perfect marriage everything goes right... I've had three miscarriages and my husband beats me," she said tucking a stay hair behind her ear. "Welcome to a perfect world."

Dave stepped in and brought his sister into his arms, "You should have told me," he mumbled into her hair. "I would have done something."

Janise laughed stepping back and crossing her arms, "What? What would you have done? James is a lawyer; he's got the law behind him if you so much as touch him in the wrong way."

"Your right.... But I still wish you had told us."

Alyssa nodded in agreement.

"Yeah, we live a few miles apart, I should have called."

A thud sounded through the door as footsteps approached and suddenly the door swung open, James blank face staring at them. "Who are you?" He asked in a clipped voice. "Janise? Who are these people?"

Janise coward slightly at the brief look he gave her, "um my family. James, my brother Dave and my sister, Alyssa," she said pointing to them in turn.

The brother and sister looked at the man before them in an angry light, though with subconscious actions, a mask fell into place and they both gave a small meek wave.

"Hmm, well say goodbye now. You can see them some other time," with those final words, he turned and left.

"You married him?" Alyssa asked bewildered as Janise stepped into the entryway.

The elder just shrugged helplessly, "I'll be right back."

Dave and Alyssa turned to each other when their sister disappeared behind the door.

"I can't believe…." Alyssa started.

Dave just shook his head running his fingers through his hair, "she should have told us," he muttered multiple times to himself, halting when Janise reappeared.

"Come on," she said walking between them and towards the elevator.

Both followed her, running to keep up with her fast strides.

"Jan? Where are we going? I thought you had to go back inside?"

Janise looked at Dave and smiled, "I haven't seen my brother and sister in years, the one thing he can't take form me is my family," she said pushing the ground floor button, "even if it is only for a few hours."

Both, Dave and Alyssa, stood on either side of sisters, smiling to themselves, knowing what she meant.

When they reached the ground level, cars were lining the walls of all shapes and sizes. A beep followed from a black BMW to their left. "Come on, get in," Janise said getting in the driver's seat.

Alyssa got the front while Dave took the back, and just as they shut the doors Janise started the car and sped out of the basement, joining the city that waited for them.

It didn't take long for Janise to reach the edge of the city, dawn just starting to peek at the horizon, the sky turning the softest shade of blue as she parked the car in front of an abandoned building; the windows all broken in from kids throwing rocks at them, the paint on the stone grey and dead.

The trio stood in front of the building, looking up at was once their home while growing up. So much having changed since they were little, they could hardly recognize it. But their own little touches on the place hadn't faded from the years, such as their hand prints on the side of the stone steps leading up to the door.

"The roof," Was all Janise said in a clear voice, she didn't wait for them as she walked into the building, not having to wait long for the younger two to follow her in.

The walls inside were peeling and bare of any pictures. There were cobwebs in the corners and the sound of mice in the walls could be heard over their footsteps as they climbed to the very top of the building, where Janise shoved open the metal vault that lead up to the roof.

The weather had changed and a cool wind now blew in the morning air before the humid heat took over once again. Dave took a deep breath as he climbed up and onto the hard top that looked over the city. A view like no other met their sight as they went to the ledge and sat down, their feet dangling over the side.

"Who knew...," Alyssa started. Janise and Dave looked at each other in turn before watching Alyssa, "Who knew," she started again. "That one screwed up night could bring us together."

"Who knows how long it will last, too," Dave said as the sun started to peek through and a light burst of orange crossed the sky.

Janise shook her head lightly, "I know when I go back to the flat that James will hit me and I honestly cannot do anything to stop it."

"Have you tried?" Dave asked watching his sister who sat beside him.

She chuckled giving him a sidelong glance, "of course I have. I've tried everything I can think of."

Alyssa touched her hand that lay beside her and stroked the skin with the pad of her thumb, "if you ever need help, I will be there for you," she said.

"Both of us," Dave interjected.

Janise took both her brother and sister's hands in her own, "thank you," she said, "really, thank you. What about you guys? Dave you need money, Aly, you can't keep working as a whore."

"I'll get a new job," he shrugged, "everything will play out how it chooses to."

"And I, I will quit... but I need your help, I don't have a place to live. I usually just live in the back of the Red Light." Janise gave her shoulder a squeeze and said, "We'll help you. Don't worry."

After, their voices quieted and they just sat there watching as the sun rose higher and higher in the sky until, like a burst of color, the sun rose to its peak and stood casting oranges and reds across the world of Chicago.

The noise below grew and the city awakened. And just like that, reality crashed in on them and the night world in which they had found each other, disappeared.

Janise returned to her apartment flat and to a very pissed off husband, who in turn was not satisfied when he found her.

Alyssa went back to the Red Light, working the streets and taking in what little cash she could from clients.

Dave... Dave went to find work.

A month later Janise Wane was found beaten to death in the living room of her home, when her friends had come to take her to brunch.

Alyssa Jonathan was shot from a bullet not meant for her in a drive by, and was reported dead when the paramedics arrived. The shooter was never found.

Dave Jonathan was unable to find work with a high enough pay, and the job he did find fired him two days later. He ended up losing his apartment space and moving onto the street, where he currently resides.

Life, reality in general, is a bitch. Not everything good comes out of life, and half the time we end up getting slapped. It hurts, it really does. Life isn't perfect, God didn't make life perfect, and he never meant too. It's a hard truth to come to terms with but in the end when we do come to fully understand what it means to live, to be a slave to a bitch... we crash into it just to say: "Fuck you."

Wake Up

One

Why? Addie Johnson thought to herself as she stared in the mirror of her bathroom. She lightly traced the bruise that was forming on her cheek.

Grabbing a washcloth from the towel cabinet, she turned the warm water on, wetting the cloth, she dabbed at the bruise and at the blood at the corner of her mouth; wiping away the evidence of today events. When she was finished Addie limped into her room shutting the door behind her; she went home early from school that day thankful her parents weren't home to ask questions, because she knew that if they where, she would end up spilling everything to them. She dropped her school bag near the door and walked over to desk sitting down she took out a piece of paper and a pen, she just couldn't take it anymore the bullying and name calling, it just wasn't fair, all she wanted now was to close her eyes and sleep life away, sleep the pain away and never wake up.

Pulling her black hair to the side, she took the cap off the pen and started to add the black ink to the paper.

"Hey freak where you going!"

Addie turned to the voice, coming face to face with Jake Riddle, captain on the football team and the one person Addie feared the most. "What Jake?" she wouldn't let him know she was afraid, no, she would stand her ground, what little she had left of it.

Andrew, Jake's second in command, came to stand by his side, "don't talk back! He asked you a question."

All of a sudden, Addie felt a pain in her stomach; Andrew had punched her right below her ribs. She doubled over, not being able to breathe, and even as she tried she felt a sharp pain erupt causing her to clutch at her stomach, "I didn't." she rasped out.

"Aw, look, she's bowing down, but you know Drew, I just don't think that's low enough, she should be on the ground." With that, he kicked her feet from underneath her, making Addie fall to the cold tile of the school hallway, her hands under her; she lay on her side, the pain from her stomach still throbbing.

Pushing up with her hands, she looked up at the two guys looming over her with smirks, tears threatening to spillover here blue eyes, "poor little baby is going to cry." They taunted while laughing.

"Why...are you doing this— AH!" she gasped in pain as she fell onto her back; Jake had kicked her in the ribs, this time shoving the toe of his shoe into her skin.

"Because I'm bored," Was the last thing they said before they started on her.

All Addie could feel was numbness as hands and feet came at her, bruising every spot possible. Tears streaming down her face she curled in a ball trying to protect whatever she could.

She didn't know why this happened; it had started the first day back in her sophomore year. She hadn't been expecting it, Jake and Andrew had asked if she needed help finding her new homeroom and instead of taking her to her class they had drug her to the out of use girls bathroom on the second floor, beating her in till her skin was broken and raw. She remembered skipping school that day hiding out in the jungle-Jim tubs not knowing what to do, or what had happened for that matter.

"Hey!" a voice came from down the hall, Addie new it wasn't a teacher so it had to be a student...a male student by the deepness of the voice. "What do you think you're doing?" Addie could hear him rush over, urgency in his voice.

The two jocks stopped when they heard the voice, turning to look at the person, Addie couldn't see her 'savior' the tears clouding her vision the pain making her blind.

"Mind your own business if you know what's good for you," Andrew warned, he turned back to the girl on the ground kicking her in the stomach watching as she withered in pain.

"If you don't get out of here I'll call for a teacher." He threatened the warning clear in his voice.

Jake leaned down with one more swift punch to her face he whispered "you're lucky this time, but next time we'll get you harder and there will be no one around to stop us." She flinched as he flicked her forehead before walking away with Andrew close at his heels.

Addie could hear them retreating down the hall, struggling to get up she winced at the pain that coursed through her body like daggers, using a locker for support she slowly pushed herself into standing position she staggered a bit tripping over her feet.

"Hey, are you alright?" the boy asked grabbing Addie's shoulders gently letting her regain her balance. "You should see the nurse. I'll take you." He started to pull her towards the nurse's office.

Addie ripped out if his hold, regretting as she did so, the pain increasing "ngh, no I'm just going to go home. Thank you though... for stopping them." She didn't bother waiting for a reply as she walked, limped, down the hall, school bag in hand Addie could feel a set of eyes on her, watching her back as she retreated out of the building.

Addie shook her head clearing it of the unpleasant memory of the previous hours before, and stared at the paper in front of her, re-reading what she had written:

'Today I see that tomorrow is nothing but perfect... a perfect hell. Capturing me in its fiery breath I fight and fight, struggle and struggle against its pull; its pull to bring me down. Holding my breath, I hold it for as long as I can until I can't hold it any longer, clawing for the surface I fight for air to no avail. Sinking lower and lower, I die with every pull of fire, I go, leaving behind the person I am and sinking into the person everyone thinks I am. So watch as I fight for my life and die as I try....'

Putting her pen down, Addie walked slowly over to her bed. She, as gentle as possible, removed her shoes and socks. Pulling her legs onto the bed she laid down staring up at the ceiling, her hair fanned out beneath her.

"What have I ever done God?" she questioned "I'm so confused... so alone. This is happening and I don't know why... why?" She asked out loud to the silence, that one word holding a thousand questions. Her eyelids fluttered shut against her bruised face as she drifted off to sleep a silent tear escaping down her cheek.

"Addie...Addie...Addie Johnson, wake up. You need to open your eyes."

Addie opened her eyes as she felt someone shake her lightly on the shoulder; bright green eyes stared down at her into her blue ones, "AHHHH-" the person over her covered her mouth.

"Will you stop yelling, I'm not going to hurt you, I want to help you."

Addie looked at the person; she was still laying on her bed, the other body hovering over hers. "Who are you?" She asked cautiously.

"Well that's hard to say, am I your conscious or an angel? I am neither... well that wouldn't be right now would it, hmm. I am human but also an angel in a sense. You could say I am your guardian angel sent here to earth to help you regain your faith, and make sure you don't get into any trouble." The person said.

By the voice, Addie now knew it was a male; it was definitely deeper than a girl's voice, but also pleasant.

Peering closely she tried to see his face, all she could see was his green eyes nothing more so sitting up she pushed away from the person and turned on her bedside light. Addie gasped, because there sitting next to her was a beautiful teenage boy, his hair was light blonde, almost a shade of white. He had a small hoop looping around his lip for a piercing; he wore a pair of light stonewash jeans and a light weight, soft looking baby blue v-neck shirt, the color of the fabric making his eyes seem aqua instead of green.

"Uh could you stop staring?" he asked clearing his throat.

Addie hadn't realized she had been ogling the poor guy, snapping her mouth shut, she blushed, "sorry" she muttered looking away slightly.

"It's alright."

Looking around her room for a minute, she then turned her gaze back on to the handsome stranger, "what's your name?"

"James."

Addie nodded thoughtfully for a moment, "Why are you here James?"

He shrugged, "to help you, like I said, I'm your guardian in a sense." He said smiling.

She scowled, "I don't need your help." She said stubbornly crossing her arms.

"You do."

"No I don't." Addie said turning away from him.

James lost his smile though his eyes were still gentle, he grabbed her chin and made her look him in the eyes, "You do Addie, you've lost faith in yourself you've lost faith in life and in everything else."

Addie cast her eyes down "no one cares."

"That is what I am going to show you."

Addie hit him on the side of the head. "What are you trying to do? Out do Jake and Andrew? Some angel you are." She scoffed.

James rubbed the side of his head "uh, ow. I'm sorry that came out wrong, what I meant was that I am going to show you that some people do care,"

"Oh, and how are you going to do that?" She asked raising an eyebrow.

"You know for a girl who is suffering you sure do have an attitude," he said before he placed a hand over Addie's eyes; removing his hand a second later Addie opened her eyes blinking she looked at her surroundings.

Mouth agape she stared in awe, "where are we?"

"Paradise, every human is allowed one glimpse of Heaven. Paradise, whether it's before they die or like you, those who need to regain their faith."

Addie couldn't even begin to describe what it was like, it was like nothing she had seen, or felt, before. It was light, that was all she could do to try an explain it, It was as if the whole place was filled with everlasting light, the peacefulness settling in on them as a warm breeze went by kissing their skin. Addie breathed in deep the scent of roses and lavender feeling what she hasn't felt in what felt like a long time... joy. She smiled taking in a deep breath.

James watched the emotions play of the girl's face, awe, wonder, peace. It was amazing for him to see her like this finally again. The last time he had seen her smile like that was when she had come home from a trip with her family. Smiling himself, he grabbed her hand, "it's time to go," she looked at him.

"But we just got here." She protested.

James shook his head, "yes and we have already exceeded are stay, like I said; only a glimpse is aloud. For all of this," he gestured out in front of him, "is supposed to remain a mystery until it is our time."

Addie looked once more at her surroundings, "do we have to?" he nodded, with a sigh she gave in; "close your eyes." Addie shut her eyes feeling the warmth vanish, "open."

Upon opening her eyes, she was met with a damp smell of beer, vomit and cigarettes. "James...?" she asked worried she didn't like this place.

James laid a hand on her should letting her know it was ok, "watch," he whispered pointing to a grey door at the end of the room.

"You stupid little shit!"

Addie winced at the harsh words, the door at the end of the hall slammed open hitting the wall with a crash, causing her to watch with wide eyes as a boy was shoved roughly into the room, his hair was dark brown and long, and his body was tall and thin. Addie inhaled sharply when he turned towards her.

"Don't worry he can't see us." James reassured, thinking she thought the boy could see them.

Addie shook her head no, what made her gasp was the fact that the boy was beautiful. His skin was a pale shade of ivory, with dark brown eyes lined with black minus that of the black eye and blood running down from his hair line, Addie couldn't think of a more beautiful creature, well, except for James, upon which she turned to him, "why am I here? I thought you were showing me that some people do care."

James didn't turn to the girl as he spoke, "showing you that people care about you has several different meanings, I am simply showing you the one that people usually turn away from." He said frowning as the man who had shoved the boy, hit him in the throat causing the boy to clutch at his neck, his beautiful brown eyes bugging as he tried to breath."Worthless piece of shit," he spat.

"JAMES!" James gripped her shoulder even harder as he stared on, a sad and almost frightful look on his face.

Turning back to the scene she watched as, who she assumed to be the boy's father, beat him kicking and hitting every inch of his body until the boy was nearly unconscious. "...James." He whispered before falling into darkness.

Addie whipped her head around staring at the light haired boy, "he can see you?" He shook his head, "then is it a different James?" Still he shook his head. She saw a silent tear slid down his face dropping to the floor, James stared at the passed out body before them whispering so quietly that Addie could barely hear him, "He's my brother," her jaw dropped, eyes going wide, "I died when I was seven, a car accident... drunk driver, the whole cliché. And after our mom died, dad lost it, getting drunk every night, and taking everything out on Chris.

The reason I am this age and not younger or yet, not alive, is because I was sent here for a reason... to help you Addie. I don't think you would have listened if a five year old little boy came up to you saying that he is your guardian angel, no, so I was sent as you see me, to fit in with the rest of you, to blend in so well that you wouldn't see me when I helped, as if I were invisible. I was a ghost in plain sight."

She closed her mouth looking at James with sad eyes, "I'm so sorry James... I-I've been so selfish can-can't we do something to help him?" she said stuttering through tears that threatened to spill over.

"We already have...."

The girl blinked, realizing the scene had changed from the dark room to what Addie thought looked like a... cemetery? "Wha-what...

why are we at a cemetery James?" She looked around at the all the grave stones. James pointed to the one in front of them; Addie stared down at it and began to read:

> *Here lies Chris Valitor*
> *Son of Kevin and Christy,*
> *and younger brother of James Valitor.*
> *September 3, 1991 – February 15, 2010*
> *May angels always watch over him*

"Hey, hey, don't cry." James said gently as he wiped away her tears from her face.

Lifting her fingers to her face she felt the wet tears on her cheeks, "oh, I'm sorry."

"No it's all right to cry, I just don't want you to be sad, it's a good thing to let your emotions out once in awhile."

She didn't know why but an unknown anger started bubbling to the surface in a rush, and with a rage, she rounded on the boy. "Why did he have to die? Why couldn't you save him? He's your brother!" She scream at James hitting his chest as hard as she could, her slight frame shaking with a mixture of sobs and anger, she didn't want the beautiful boy to be gone from the world, something as pure as he didn't deserve to die. "Can't you bring him back? Do anything, just don't let him die," She sobbed, finally creasing her blows to James and just rested her head against his chest, her tears wracking her body.

"I cannot bring the dead back Addie, no one can. Only God, he, and he alone, can stop death. And only he can bring someone back from its dark grasp."

"It's not fair." She whispered into his chest her words muffled.

James rubbed her back soothingly before pulling her back to look at him. "Life is not fair, nothing in it ever is, but you just have to deal with it taking everything that it throws at you. Don't let others bullshit you around," she raised a brow at his language "I think God will let it slide this time."

"He shouldn't have died," she looked back at the grave with a sad heart. Kneeling down, she traced the tombstone with her fingertips.

"Think of it this way," he said kneeling down beside her, "there is no more suffering, he can finally be at ease with himself and with the life he had lived, just as you will be when you find your way to heaven."

Addie brushed her hands over the beautiful boy's name whispering, "I'm glad you're not suffering anymore. I hope you're happy." The wind picked up brushing her hair and skin with a light caress, Addie knew; she didn't know how, that he had heard her. Standing up she looked at James, "now what?"

He smiled and gently cupped her cheek in one warm hand, "now you wake up."

"James wait," she stood no her tip toes and kissed his cheek, "thank you," she whispered in his ear.

Grinning he whispered covering her eyes once more, "Wake up... Addie wake up..."

Addie jolted up in bed with a start, glancing around her bedroom, light was streaming in from the window, she had slept all through the rest of the day and the night. Getting up she realized that her body didn't hurt anymore as she stretched her limbs cautiously. Walking over to her full length mirror she glanced at her reflection, the bruise was gone from her face along with the cut, lifting up her shirt she touched the unmarked skin, they were all gone. Addie rushed over to her desk and looked down at the poem she had written crumbling it up in her hands, she tossed it into the small garbage bin on the floor next to her desk, "It's time to start over. This... can't go on."

Changing from her old clothes, she threw on some new ones along with a pair of converse shoes before grabbing her bag and running out of the house, she didn't stop until she was standing in front of the school.

Running through the school doors, the halls where empty save the janitor and a few early students, walking, almost running to the principal's office she knocked timidly. A voice called from inside, "come in."

Opening the door slowly she stepped in closing the door behind her, "Sir, there's something you should know...."

Feeling lighter than air Addie grabbed her books from her locker, Jake Riddle and Andrew Green had been expelled from the high school when the principle had learned of what they had done, what they had been doing. Not wanting anything like this to happen again, he had taken it to the authorities. They had enough proof to send them to juvenile hall, because even though the bruises where gone the scars were not and that was enough evidence along with numerous others coming forward.

"Man, James, wait up dude!"

Addie turned quickly to see a guy with long brown hair, race up to his friend, a boy with light blonde hair and a lip piercing who had turned around, waiting for his friend to catch up to him.

No it couldn't be...could it? Addie thought to herself. She watched as the boy with the piercing start walking away with the guy with the long hair, as she turned back to her locker she saw the boy with the blonde hair look back at her and wink.

Smiling to herself, she got the rest of her books out, slamming the locker door shut she started towards her first class. She wasn't as alone as she had thought.

Welcome to My Silly Life

One

JESSICA STARR DISSAPEARS FROM CONCERT?
The singer, Jessica Starr, 27, suddenly disappeared from her own concert in Tokyo, Japan. Critics, fans, and worried personal have been searching desperately to find the singer who was to hit off her nationwide tour in Tokyo. Though no one knows what happened, a few angry fans from the concert suspect the worst from the singer and think the disappearance was a staged event. If it's the truth or not we will never know. Jessica, wherever you are, your fans are....

"Worried about me," Jessica Starr finished as she put the week old newspaper aside, and leaned her elbows against the iron railing of her balcony view from her parents loft apartment in Malibu California. She had been here for a week now, trying to figure things out; to take a step back, and look at a few things.

She just shook her head against the warm salt water air of the beach; the concert, it wasn't supposed to happen like that. The lights were suppose to hit the center, the crowd was suppose to cheer, and Jessica Starr was suppose to sing loud and clear; but some things that night weren't suppose to happen....

Jessica stood in her ten-by-ten dressing room, the lights lit up her face as she stared into the mirror before her; her reflection staring back. Her makeup was perfect, lashes were long and fake while her cheek bones looked feverish and her lips looked swollen with how much red lipstick she had on. The outfit was sparkly and girly and black and purple, the shine of her hair was brilliant with curls set down her back. It was perfect, yet she felt as if she were playing dress up; the kind that felt like you had just gotten into your mom's make up bag and wanted to be pretty like mommy but ended up looking like a clown. When you were little, it made people laugh and coo, when your twenty-seven people just don't understand how you could mess it up. Problem is, is that people didn't think she messed up, and yet to her it seemed like the clown was staring back at her and it wasn't funny this time.

"Jessica it time."

The singer looked over to the door and gave her bodyguard, Mike, a small nod and a smile to accompany it. The door closed and she turned back to her reflection, with a sigh she stood and walked back a few paces giving herself a onceover in the mirror. The black of her pants and bright purple of her glittered top was enough to make her roll her eyes, "Where's TLC when you need it," she muttered chuckling to herself as she made her way to the door and flicked the lights off as she walked out.

The walk to the stage wasn't rushed; it was slow and paced as she took her time to collect her thoughts. These were the questions she asked herself before every concert: *Why did I choose this life? Why do I sing? Why am I dressed in such a ridiculous get up? It was always the same.*

"Jessica?" The singer gave Mike a smile and let him lead her to the platform that would raise her to the stage. "You ok Miss?" He asked giving her a concerned look as she stared at the platform.

She just shook her head, "no," she said with a smile, "I'm fine.... Mike?"

"Yeah?" He asked, his brown brows rising.

"I need you to do me a favor?"

"And what's that Miss?"

Jessica sighed putting her hair behind her ears. "You know the trapped door where my mic stand is on stage?" He nodded. "Well I need you to open it when I tell you to; and please make sure the mat is under there," she add with a chuckle.

"Miss I'm not allowed to let you do that. Though If you don't mind me asking, but why?"

"I need to answer a few unanswered questions I've been putting off for awhile now... that and I really want a pepperoni and sausage pizza right now; I haven't eaten for months!" She said with a wide eye expression. But when it came down to it she just touched his beefy shoulder in a desperate manner. "I need your help Mike, please?"

With a pause and a registered sigh, he agreed. "What do I need to do?"

Jessica stepped up onto the platform. "When I give you my mark, open the door. From there I'll give you further instructions." With that, she felt the platform jolt and begin to lift her. "Remember: on. My. Mark." Soon after Mike's head vanished as she entered the arena, the cheers were definite against her ears as she waved and gave the crowd a smile, her face lighting up on the two huge screens on either side of the stage. Her bass player handed her, her mic. "Hello Tokyo!" The screams grew in volume. Her tall black boots clicked silently against the floor as the roar of the crowd over took her.

She made her way down the long stage, waving to the sea of people. "How is everyone tonight?" She gave a grin as the crowd cheered. Jessica walked up to her mic stand and put her mic through it; resting her head momentarily against the twisted metal of the mic's head.

The cords of the guitar and the thump of the drums began to play to the beat of her heart as Jessica covered the head of the mic with her hand. "Watch world, I'm about to make Houdini proud," she said with a bow of her head. With a small secret smile, she stomped down hard with her left foot and the trapped door gave way under her. The crowds were still cheering and the band was still playing as she disappeared from the stage, but moments later after Mike had drawn the door back up to its place the music stopped and the crowds were suddenly besides themselves; in which Jessica couldn't really blame them.

"Ok Mike, this is what's going to happen, I need you to go get your car—yes your car; I need you to pull it up to the door I came through this morning. Do you remember? Ok good, I'll meet you there in ten minutes, alright?"

Mike nodded, "got it. Though what are you going to do once you leave?"

"I need you to take me to an ATM machine; there should be one in this city.

After that, the airport; now go!" Mike didn't need to be told twice as he reeled around and took off down the corridor that was soon going to be over crowded with press, her manager and others like them.

Looking both ways, the place was clear with no sign on people, she made a right and ran as fast as she could in her three-an-a-half-inch heel boots. "Oh I feel ridiculous running like this," she mumbled to herself and paused taking the time to unzip her boots and leave them neatly next to the wall; she scrunched her toes getting the feeling back into them before taking down the hall way at a swifter pace.

Her dressing room lights flipped on as she entered, slamming the door behind her. The purple glitter top came off first, and then came the black skinny jeans that looked like they were painted on. The fake eyelashes the blush and then the lipstick; it all came off and reappearing onto the cotton ball she had coated in makeup remover.

Pair of light wash old worn jeans with naturally made holes in them were folded on her small couch, along with a grey jacket paired with a light pink shirt. Jessica went to the cloths and slipped them on, loving the soft feel of the worn material, with a few minutes left to spare she slipped her socked feet in a pair of tan Uggs and grabbed a well used jean jacket, slipping the hood her grey jacket over head in the process. Just as she was about to leave she stole her wallet from the side table, stuffing it into the back pocket of her jeans.

It didn't take her long to make her way into the corridor again, reaching the metal door and slipping through unnoticed. Mike's old black BWM was pulled up to the door and she ran around the side and got in.

"Right on time," he said as she shut the passenger door.

Jessica shrugged, "I've learned that being late helps no one."

The streets of Tokyo....

The lights were bright and wild as people crowded the area, Jessica stare out the window as Mike maneuvered his car carefully through the streets. When the car jolted to a stop he turned to the singer who was currently watching the huge screen in the square hat showed a picture of the previous advents of the concert. A smirk lifted her lips, "Houdini would be proud," was what she whispered and Mike couldn't help but smile.

"Miss, there's the ATM."

Jessica stepped out of the car, mindful of the traffic, and walked over to the closed bank; taking her wallet from her pocket and entering her pin number as she pushed her debit card into the slot.

She took nine-hundred from her debit and visa card, storing the cash in her wallet and shoving it back into her pocket.

Mike pulled away from the curb when she shut the door, pulling back into Tokyo's night life.

Narita International Airport....

Just like the city, the airport was packed with people of all races. Jessica made her way through the airport, maneuvering through the mobs of people and waiting in line before her, she came up to the desk.

An Asian lady with curled reddish brown hair smiled at her, "Hullo, may I help you?"

The singer pulled her wallet from jeans for second time that night, "I need two first class tickets to Los Angeles International for the first flight leaving Tokyo right now."

"I'm sorry ma'am but it looks like the only flight leaving right now is in fifteen minutes and there are only a couple of seats left in economy."

Jessica shook her head, "that's fine, two please."

"And how will you be paying for this?"

"Do you take cash?"

"I'm sorry ma'am but you would have to go to the airport's office."

"I guess with debit," she said handing over her credit card.

The process went through and she was soon handed two tickets. "Loading bank is C3." She waved the next person up, "Next please?"

Jessica stepped aside and walked with Mike close behind her and arriving at gate C3 with a few minutes to spare.

"Ticket please?" She handed hers and Mike's ticket to the guy at the booth; he looked them over, tore off the edge and handed them back. "Enjoy your flight."

"Miss?" Mike asked as they continued their walk, "what are you planning to do once you get to California? You're apartment is in New York."

Jessica turned to Mike and giving him a smile, "I'll let you know when we get there. For now, we just need to find our seats. I have a feeling this is going to be a very uncomfortable flight."

Jessica shook her head, breathing out a sigh as she leaned away from the balcony. "Where did it change?" She had lost track. The clothes had become tighter then glitter had become mountain high and the makeup heavier than ever; heels higher and secludes longer and the times for herself were shorter and fewer and farer apart.

Taking one last look at the beach she turned around and walked back in to her old childhood bedroom. The bedroom looked like any beachside bedroom; brightly painted walls, mosquito netting draped around her full bed and fell to the hard wood floor. The walls were painted bright sea green while everything else resembled the sea; something that she loved when she was younger.

Jessica made her way to her small closet and opened the white folding doors. Standing on her tip toes she reached up to the far back corner on her closet and pulled from the shelve an old purple box with stickers from past years covering the skin.

With a smile, she took the box gently in her hands, went over to her bed, and scooted into the middle; crossing her legs and setting the box down in front of her. Hesitating hands whispered over the lid, but with no other thoughts she popped the top off and set it aside.

Memories of her childhood from age six to sixteen stared back at her. Collected stickers, photos, nick-knacks from her past friends; prom ticket, old friendship bracelets... it was all here.

"Why did I start singing?" She muttered to herself in the silence of her room. She picked up an old photo of her and her two childhood friends, Rebecca and Catalina, dressed in feather boas and a ton of bright makeup on. Jessica laughed at the picture in her hands; they were thirteen by the looks of it. She moved onto another one of them when they were fifteen, pajamas on makeup off and hair tied back, and of course fuzzy animal slippers, monkeys for Cat, Frogs for Rebecca, and tigers for Jessica. They were a trio, the three of them, the three musketeers. "Why did I choose this career?"

"We're going to be bigger than the... erm... Becca give me a couple bands to work with!" Cat exclaimed as they sat around the living room, a bowl of popcorn in the middle of their circle and papers scattered everywhere with scribbled lyrics on them.

Becca rolled her eyes, "Cat we can't automatically become the world's most famous pop group over night," she said, giving her friend a look.

"I know that!" Cat said, "I'm just saying we're going to be bigger than the two combined."

Jessica looked between her two friends as they bickered back and forth, enjoying it though praying they wouldn't drag her into it.

"Jess will be our head man... or woman I guess." Cat said turning to Jess.

And there was the drag. "I will?"

"Of course," Becca said cutting in. "You're the best singer out of all of us, it's only natural that you would be."

Jess shrugged, "I don't know, I guess I never thought about it before."

"Well it's already settled."

"And to think I have no say in this matter and yet I'm ok with it," Jess said laughing.

Jessica put the photos back, pulling out the prom ticket; prom night of 2000.

"So how do I look? Hmm?" Becca asked as she twirled in her dark blue gown, her dirty blonde hair curled and pinned up. The three of them were backstage at the prom, the curtain hiding them from view for the moment.

Cat and Jess looked her over, "Purfect darling, perfect," Jess commented a moment later.

"Agreed," Cat said.

Becca beamed and surveyed her friends attire, "you two look fabulous!" She said, giving Cat's black two piece skirt and shirt a once over and Jess's silver off the shoulder gown a peek. "I love them."

Her two friends smiled and gave her a quick hug just as the curtain started to rise. As it rose, Cat and Becca went to their mics' on either side of Jess as she went to stand in the middle.

"Good Evening, Malibu Coast High School!" Jess said with excitement clear in her voice. The prom crowd cheered, exhilaration pumped through the three girls as the music started to play. "We're The Trio and we're going to kick things off with a slower tune."

"Oh boy," Jessica said with a smile, remembering prom night. That was a night, she swore, she would never forget, that night everything was perfect for the three of them. She placed the fading prom ticket back in the box, but as she did so, the corner of a piece of paper slipped up and with curiosity, she slid it form under the bottom of the box. It was folded neatly into a square and had the words: Song for remembering scrolled across it. With gentle fingers, she unfolded the piece of paper and was met with her old song: Welcome to My Silly Life. It was a song she had written when she was eighteen; having just graduated high school and on her own at that time, with moving out and all that, she had been in a bind for money, and for friends who had moved far away after graduation to attend their separate universities; she had felt this was her last resort for comfort, and unknowingly the big step for her future.

The cheap one bedroom one bathroom apartment was small and cramped; but with small touches Jessica had soon made the walls pale yellow and furniture wasn't the prettiest but it was something she had worked hard to pay for. It was a place she hadn't known existed until a few months ago, she didn't think most people who lived in Malibu knew of this place; the whole of the kitchen space was connected to the living room slash bedroom, with the bathroom being the only private room.

"Starr you owe me two months' rent!" Yelled the landlady; pounding on her door in the process.

Jessica looked at the door and sighed walking over to the door, "I'm sorry Mrs. Chen, just give me two more weeks," she said leaning her head against the doorframe. She heard the grumbling of the elder lady and then a grunt.

"Fine, I give you two more weeks! Two! Then I want my money!"

"Yes, yes ok whatever you want."

Footsteps sounded away from her door and Jessica let out a breath she had been holding, "what am I doing?" She asked herself as she pushed away from the door and walked into the kitchen, opening one of the three drawers that resided in the small area she pulled out a stack of paper and a pen. With items in hand, she went over to her couch and sat down, setting the paper on the cushion next to her.

The past years of her childhood flashed in front of her eyes; singing with Cat and Becca, playing dress up, first dates, first break ups; prom, graduation and learning to grow up.

With pen in hand, she grabbed a piece of paper and began to write.

Jessica smiled as she read over the lyrics, and as she read them a small chip from her heart that had been lost was suddenly back in its rightful place. With one last look at the collected items in the box, she shut the lid—keeping the lyrics with her—and walked back over to her closet, setting the box where it had been previously. With that done, she took her cell phone out of her pocket and slid the screens lock off. **37 Missed Calls** was flashed across the screen and Jessica rolled her eyes, they were all from her agent. With a sigh, she pressed the call button and waited patiently for her agent to pick up.

"Jessica!" Shouted the voice of her agent Rick Gale, Jessica opened her mouth to speak but was cut off by Rick's voice again. "Where have you been? I've been thinking the worst! Dead body, ditch, rape, cut up body pieces! The whole shebang! You have alot of explaining to do Jessica Starr!" He shouted.

The singer pulled the phone away from her ear as he ranted on, when he finally came to a stop she held the phone back to her ear and spoke, "Rick, I want you and everybody else, at your father's recording studio in an hour."

"Bu-but why, you disappear for a week and now you want to record a song! Care to tell me why?!"

"Yes, if you stop yelling," she said while rolling her eyes and walking over to her bed and sitting down.

"Well? Why?"

"It's simple: I had to figure out something."

"*You had to figure out something?*" He asked in a deadpan voice. "*You're not learning your multiplication tables anymore, Jessica!*"

"I know Rick! And stop yelling! Jeez. I just, I didn't know why I had started singing, I lost—I guess, to put it in the most dramatic way possible—I lost my will to sing... I came home to find it," she said shrugging her shoulders, knowing Rick couldn't see the movement.

Rick sighed on the other end of the line, "*Ok, fine. I'll see you in an hour, Jess.*"

Jessica nodded unconsciously and ended the call. She sat there for a minute before picking up the lyrics and folding the paper neatly and putting it into the pocket of her pants; taking another piece of paper from her nightstand drawer, along with a pencil she scribbled a note to her parents before she left.

One Month Later....

JESSICA STARR RETURNS TO THE STAGE!

Jessica Starr, 27, returns to the stage after a month of absents. Though still no one knows what happened to the singer on that night of the concert in Tokyo, Japan. We are glad to have her back. She will be starting her nationwide tour again in Tokyo, and let's just pray that she stays on the stage this time....

Jessica chuckled and set her iPhone aside, closing the newspaper article that it was opened up to. After a month of being gone, she was happy to say that it felt good to be back. And though it still felt the same, it was completely different. Rick had agreed to her terms of changes if she would agree never to disappear again for some unscheduled R&R, without telling him first. Her stage outfits were now hers to choose, her makeup was lighter, a softer natural edge and her hair wasn't the harsh dark color the stylist had insisted she have, it was now set into her natural waves of honey brown hair, parted to the side and placed down her back. Her outfit was comfortable yet chic; Rick approved of it and didn't complain; which Jessica was grateful for.

Her small heeled pointed toed boots clicked lightly against the dressing room floor as she opened the door and made her way to the stage. She felt good about herself after so many years; her outfit made her feel girly with its cream colored ruffled blouse and tan leather vest, soft worn distressed jeans and its brown boots. Her music sounded like heavens music to her ears, and the steady rhyme of her pulse comforted her as she calmly made her way to the stage.

Instead of taking the platform up, she took the stairs and took the mic her lead guitarist handed her. The crowd was silent this time, no cheers, no screaming, nothing. It was just silent, waiting for her to say or do something.

Jessica cleared her throat, her pulse, though never betraying her, stayed calm as nervous feelings came over her. "Hi…." The sound of her voice seemed to echo forever in the arena, she sighed. "Look, I'm sorry for what happened last month… things happened, I realized a few things that I didn't exactly have answers for. I know some of you can understand, and I know most of you can't. I didn't stage the disappearance, as some have said; it was purely a spontaneous action. I got to the stage that night and I realized I needed to figure a few things out… and I did; and in that process I came across something I had forgotten, something that I want to share with you guys tonight." She took a breath, "this is a song written by a silly girl who was only eighteen at the time, and this is my song for remembering. This is, Welcome to My Silly Life."

When she finished speaking, the sound of the piano and the soft cords of the acoustic guitar played through the amps. Jessica closed her eyes, breathing in deep… this was it, she was all right. This is her silly life.

The Perfect Match

One

A heart is a heart; it can be loved, cherished, broken and ripped apart into tiny pieces that cut through your skin like the sharpest of knives. No one can change that, even the strongest of people… no matter how hard they try.

A heart though, only has one match. A perfect fit to its broken corners, nooks and crannies. That perfect match fills in the blanks to things you didn't even know you had forgotten, to things you didn't even know you knew.

The perfect match teaches you the meaning of *Love*.

Carissa Kayles ran her fingers through her tangled mass of dark blonde hair and let out a puff of air as she bent over, hands on her knees as she took deep breaths. Her white tank top and jacket were soaked through and as were her leggings as beads of sweat rolled down her neck and back, even though it was the middle of winter.

Central Park wasn't overly crowded today– an oddity on Valentine's Day. A few elder couples walked here and there with young couples in love thrown in between; even a few single people walked by themselves, through the park, enjoying the twisting paths. A stroll through Central Park– in a New Yorker's life– was a tradition on Valentine's Day– or any other day for that matter.

As Carissa straightened herself she took note of all the couples that passed by her and with a sigh, she walked over to one of the numerous water fountains, choosing to ignore the couples rather than feeling sorry for her lack of a relationship on the most romantic day of the year.

That feeling of self pity started to gnaw at her stomach again as she remembered her rather recent break up with her fiancée just a week ago. The water cool her flushed body as it washed through her, she straightened and leaned against the cement fountain, remembering the past week with a certain distaste.

The days were spent in bed with two mountains of tissues on either side of her, a half gallon of Cherry Garcia and black and white movies of Fred Astaire and Ginger Rogers. If you asked her how she had felt, she would have replied by either mumbling some incoherency or bursting out crying, it was usually the latter. Her friend Stacy had finally pulled her growing ass out of her tiny one bedroom apartment in Brooklyn, and forced her back into the real world of chaos and reality. What a loving best friend.

Carissa shook her head and chuckled while rolling her eyes at the memory of Stacy shaking her white tip French manicure at her and yelling at her to get her lazy, sorry for herself, ass out of bed in her oh so nice New Jersey accent.

A large crash came from the street and jolted Carissa out of her thoughts and away from her week of self depressions and heartbreak. With one last intake of water from the fountain she was leaning against she started to jog away. The rhythm of her feet on the pavement made like a steady hypnosis lull. Her thoughts once again wandered as did her eyes and all to soon she felt herself being jolted, once again, back down to reality by a solid object and the bruising contact of the slightly slushy pathway concrete.

"Oh God, are you alright? I am so sorry," said a deep masculine voice.

A large hand met her arm and helped pull her up from the cold ground. Carissa made a sound of disgust as she felt the back of her leggings, feeling them soaked through.

"Are you alright?" Asked the voice again.

Carissa looked up from her wet pants and into a set of caramel eyes. She smiled, "Yeah I'm fine; I'll have to go home now," she said. "But other than that, I'm good."

The stranger nodded, straightening the oversized black beanie he was wearing, and giving her a friendly smile. "Well, if there's been no bodily damage then I guess I should go."

"Yeah, thanks for helping me up."

He smiled again, "not a problem." He went to walk passed her getting only a few feet before he stopped. "Hey, out of curiosity: what's a girl like you doing alone on Valentine's Day?"

Carissa raised a blonde brow, "A girl like me? What's that suppose to mean?"

"Nothing, just that you don't seem like the type to be alone on a day like this," he said gesturing to the couples in the park.

"Well I could ask you the same thing." She said putting her hands on her hips and giving him a look. "I mean it is after all 7 am, wouldn't you rather be spending this time with your wife?"

"I'm not married."

"Girlfriend?"

"Nope."

"Ok then, I guess that answers that," she muttered.

The male shrugged, "and you? Husband? Boyfriend? Single?"

"Fiancée." He made an 'oh' sound. "Or rather, lack of. He broke it off a week ago."

"I'm sorry to hear that."

Carissa gave a soft snort, "yeah me too."

"I'm Jessie Calister by the way." Jessie said coming closer to her and holding out his hand.

"Carissa Kayles."

Jessie smiled, "Well Carissa, do you mind telling me how far away your home is, your clothes are pretty soaked, sorry."

Carissa shook her head, "I live in Downtown Brooklyn but I stayed at a friend's place last night, she lives a few blocks from here."

"You'll catch a cold if you walk, or jog, from here in your clothes. My friend's café is one block from here, actually, if we can cut across this grass it's just around the corner. His sister works there and always keeps spare clothes around, I'm sure she can lend you something."

Carissa thought about it for a moment but the numbness that started to creep into her legs made her final decision for her. "Yeah, alright, sounds good to me."

The two started across the sodden wet grass, the water seeping into their sneakers as they made their way through the grounds.

Coming upon the sidewalk five minutes later, the crowds, already dense with mobs of people, they walked to their destination.

Jessie hadn't lied when he said it was just around the corner, The Stop café was more of a laidback lounge style stop rather than a café. The walls were burnt red and the countertops were dark stone, it was dimly lit though held a comforting feel of having been lived in. Carissa grinned as she walked into The Stop and immediately fell in love with the small café.

A warm hand fell to the middle of her back as Jessie guided her to the counter. "Stay here, I'll be right back." He said.

She shrugged. Where was she going to go?

Jessie disappeared behind the counter and into the back of the store. The girl stood there glancing here and there at the many abstracted paintings that lined the walls along with black and white fashion photos.

Magazines were stacked on whicker coffee tables and dark cream colored chairs and couches were strewn all around the spacious area.

"Oh, you poor thing!"

Carissa turned around, bewildered, as a female voice from behind her made a tsking sound. She came face to face with a petit girl with bright green eyes and a wild mass of blondish brown curls. "You're soaked!" She exclaimed turning Carissa in a circle, the poor girl looking around wildly for Jessie, or anyone who could help her get the girl off of her.

"Uh yes, I have noted that. Who are you?" She asked trying to step back but the counter limiting her.

"I told you I would find her," came a voice from behind Carissa. The hostage girl turned her head to find Jessie and another next to him who was a couple inches shorter with a muscular build though not overly stocky, his light brown hair hanging unnaturally straight, slightly past his shoulders.

"Fee, your scaring Carissa," Jessie said walking around the counter again, prying the smaller of the two off. Fee rolled her and let Jessie pull Carissa away from her touchy fingers.

"Actually," Jessie started. "We were wondering if you could lend her some clothes."

"Yeah, Jessie pushed the girl, now look were its landed her: in a room full of losers," said the guy with the long hair as he leaned over the counter to flick Fee's face.

"Says the long haired freak who *wishes* he could be like us, you have to be *cool* to be a loser."

"I can't believe we're related." He muttered.

Jessie rolled his eyes, "Carissa this is Alex and Fee, they are related, not that they tell anyone that," he said with a chuckle. "And don't worry, this is normal."

Carissa smiled at the pair; the girl wasn't so bad once she realized that she wasn't in fact crazy. "It's nice to meet you guys."

Fee smiled brightly, "Carissa, come with me. You and I look to be the same size, though you might be a bit taller but that doesn't matter, dry clothes are better than wet ones. Agreed?" Carissa nodded her head obligingly, and let Fee drag her by her hand, behind the counter and into the back.

"Strip for me my darling." Fee said in her best French madam accent while she walked over to a trunk that had been shoved against a wall. Carissa laughed and stripped as she had been told to do, taking everything off but her undergarments.

"Here these should fit," Fee said tossing Carissa a pair of jeans and a pink sweater. "I have some boots you can wear. What size are you?"

Carissa pulled on the jeans, buttoning them and pulling the fuzzy warm pink sweater over her head. "6 and a half."

"Perfect, here." Her curly hair bounced every which way as she danced over to the blonde's side. "I'm a 7, because I sadly inherited Big Foot's feet, so these will fit you perfectly since yours are tiny."

Carissa laughed taking the black boots Fee handed her, "Thank you."

Jessie and Alex were talking amongst themselves when the two girls walked out of the back room. They both turned when Fee announced that they had arrived. Alex just rolled his eyes at his sister and smiled at Carissa. "I'm glad my sister's clothes fit you. They look better on you then her anyways."

Fee scowled swatting at her brother's arm. "Shut up you idiot."

"Not until you murder me will I be as silent as the grave."

"Moron."

Carissa shook her head turning to Jessie who was gesturing for her to follow him. He led her to a window seat in the corner, two cups of coffee sat on either side with a two scones. "I didn't know how you liked your coffee so I just guessed. You seemed like a cream and two sugars type of girl."

"Well you guessed right, except you left out a sugar," she said with a smile as she sat down, Jessie pulling her chair out for her before he took his own seat.

Jessie grinned and produced a small packet from out of thin air. "Your sugar, miss."

"Why thank you, Mr. Calister."

They sat there for a little while, sipping their caffeinated drink slowly. Carissa was the first to break the silence. "So, coffee...?"

"I thought I owed you that much."

"You have already done so much that this is sort of a bonus for me," she said with a small smile, taking another sip of the perfectly made coffee.

Jessie watched her slowly, taking his time to look at her. Her long blonde hair that curled and hung loosely down her back, light skin and long lashes that complemented green eyes that stared back at him from time to time.

Carissa caught Jessie's eye and she tilted her head. "What?" She asked.

"I can't fathom why a guy would break off his engagement to a girl as beautiful as you." He stated in a confused manner.

Carissa blushed lightly looking down at her cup, "I can't either…," she murmured. "Not the beautiful part but the breaking it off, I don't know why. All he said was that is wasn't working out."

"Well he's an idiot," Jessie said. "He doesn't know what he just missed out on."

"Exactly," she said nodding in agreement. "He had his chance. It's over now, time to move on."

The two peeked at one another from above their coffee and grinned. A silence once again hung in the air, but contentment hung with it, creating an easy atmosphere.

"So, Carissa," Jessie started. "Tell me little about yourself."

One year later….

"Omigosh!" Stacy said in a rush as she bustled around Carissa's one bedroom apartment with a hand full of tall thin champagne glasses. "They're going to be here any minute! Rissa, what are you doing standing around by the windows? Get over here!"

Carissa sighed, smiling at the thought of her friends arriving; she peered out of her large living room windows and smiled. The night lights were everywhere, creating a wonderful glow that illuminated through her home. White Christmas lights were intertwined here and there throughout her apartment, creating an almost fairy like appearance to her simple living areas.

"Coming," She called from over her shoulder, taking once last look at the busy city that lay out her window covered in snow, before joining her rushed friend at the dining room table.

Carissa set the dishes, which lay stacked neatly in the middle of the rectangular dark oak table, placing the five plates on their assigned place mats. Stacy had gone all out this Valentine's Day, bringing her red cloth place settings – which were currently in use now– and all of her lights. Though leaving the dishes and cooking to, of course, Carissa since she couldn't cook a decent meal even if it was to save her soul from the devil.

Champagne glasses were placed primly in front of the plate and silverware in their correct order. The doorbell rand just as Stacy sat the last food dish on the table, along with an uncorked bottle of *Veuve Clicquot Ponsardin's* brand of champagne.

Carissa went to the door, opening it to reveal the smiling faces of Fee, Alex, and Jessie– who was holding his own bottle of red wine. Carissa smiled at them and step to the side to let them in, "come on in you guys." She said shutting the door as Jessie passed her.

The two went into the dining area to see Stacy to say hello. Carissa smiled as she remembered just last year when they had all met for the first time, and now a year later here they were on Valentine's Day, altogether.

"Carissa?"

She turned at her name. Jessie was standing behind her a look of nervousness washed across his face as his brows pulled together and he chewed on his bottom lip.

"What's wrong?" She questioned, stepping closer to him in the empty hallway. "Jessie?"

Jessie nodded taking a moment to gather his thoughts before speaking. "I, Carissa, I want to ask you something." Carissa nodded encouragingly. He groaned, "You know this was so much easier in my head."

"You make that sound like a good thing," she laughed.

He just rolled his eyes and continued. "I wanted to ask if you could... would you be my Valentine?" The last words were soft and questioning, though the look in his eyes was intense and bright with hope.

The two didn't notice when a set of three eyes peaked around the corner to eavesdrop on them.

Carissa raised her eyebrows, surprised by his words, but not entirely. He had always been her friend, but always more so to her. He was, to her, her Jessie. With a smile and a tilt of her head, she said yes.

The grin on Jessie's face was wider then possible and with a flick of his wrist, he produced a single red rose from thin air. "A rose for a rose," He whispered bending down to kiss her cheek.

"Oh, what a sap!" Alex cried dramatically, breaking the moment. Carissa and Jessie turned to their friends with a look of lack of interest.

"Shut up you git!" Fee scowled, straightening herself along with Alex and Stacy.

"Both of you shut it! Don't you see their trying to have a romantic moment?"

Fee rolled her bright green eyes, "the freak ruined it obviously."

"Says the girl who said we should eavesdrop on them."

"I didn't," she said facing her two friends in the entry way.

Stacy spoke up, her New Jersey accent becoming thicker as she spoke, "now since we have all witnessed our two best friends confess their love for one another, after a year of putting it off." Jessie and Carissa shared a confused look while Alex and Fee snickered behind her hands. "We have to complete this lovely memorable moment with a Valentine's kiss! So shall I do the honors of kissing your oh so yummy Valentine, Rissa? Or would you?"

Jessie shook his head, "I'll be kissing her thank you very much, Stacy." With that being said, or stated, he turned Carissa in his arms and without so much as a hesitation, he kissed her. A slow and sweet one, a perfect one that made Carissa's heart leap from her chest.

A chores of "ahh's" echoed through the tiny space as Stacy and Fee smiled at the sweet moment, Alex making a gagging motion with his finger though secretly smiling at the couple.

When the two broke apart after a moment, they turned to everyone with a smile on lit on their faces.

"Ok now that that's over with, it's time to eat!" Stacy all but shouted.

Fee snorted in disagreement, "Yeah and while you're doing that, I on the other hand will be getting to know that nice bottle of bubbly that has been calling my name since I stepped out of the cab," she said striding into the dining room.

Georg and Stacy followed behind her, rolling their eyes at each other as she spoke. Jessie and Carissa followed behind their friends, linking their hands in the process.

As the dinner progressed, everyone at the table at one point or another, took the time to look around at the smiling, laughing, faces that surrounded him or her. This was it; the thing people talked about most in life: Love. It didn't have to be romantic or about being sentimental with the one you love. It was about *this*. The love of spending time with the *people* you love, not just one, but *all*. And at one point or another, through the dinner, they had all realized it. They had, indeed, found their perfect matches.

Goodbye

One

Two years ago

I was happy, I was beyond ecstatic to say the least, it was perfect. The night before last, my best friend Jacob, who has been my best friend since we were young enough to take baths together, asked me out. It was something surreal, something I didn't think would ever happen.

"Hey."

My heart skipped a beat when I heard his warm voice and felt familiar arms wrap around my waist from behind me. I turned in Jacob's arms facing him.

"Hey," I said back smiling up at him; his brown eyes warm as they stared down at me.

"Hey," he whispered again before leaning down and sweetly kissing my lips, I smiled into the kiss. He pulled back after a moment, pulling me close to him; he hugged me gently in his arms. "You have no idea how much I've wanted to kiss you," he said laughing slightly.

"So you've told me." And he has, numerous times since our first date last night, I told him if he didn't stop I would slap him… he agreed to stop.

He raised an eyebrow, "have I now?"

I laughed, "Yes you have, Mr. Allen."

Jacob leaned in closer to me, leaning his forehead against mine, "well, Miss Brown, may I ask you now? Can I kiss you?" I rolled my eyes but nodded, and he leant down the rest of the way, kissing me.

One year ago

Today was the day I had asked Sara to be my girlfriend and I couldn't be happier, we were supposed to celebrate our anniversary, but now everything looked grey. Sara has finally graduated, its summer, and were spending as much time together as possible before she leaves for college. But, now, I was left alone, Sara was at the beach alone, and even then, no one was there; the sky was the color grey. A hurricane warning had been sounded on the news a few hours ago and it looks like it's finally starting to kick in.

Her mom called her from the hospital; her dad had a stroke and was now under critical observation. Her mom had heard the warning on the news and told Sara to stay at home until it passes, of course Sara refused but in the end, she gave in and stayed. Her house was only a block away from the beach, the one place she comes to think, so naturally, this is where she came.

I stood at the edge where the sand kissed the sidewalk watching her silently; she was a few yards away from the water, her knees to her chest. After a moment of watching, I finally started walking over to her, coming up behind her. I knelt down, situating myself behind her, she leaned back into my chest and sighed, "It's going to be alright." She relaxed even farther and I wrapped my arms around her.

Present

"Jacob! Come on it's time to cut the cake!" Sara called up the stairs; a second later Jacob came into view, a grim look on his face.

"I'm here," he said, the look vanishing when he came to stand in front of his girlfriend of two years. Sara gave his lips a quick but loving peck before she grabbed his hand and guided him to the dining room.

Sara's mother and father were there along with Jacob's family, all of whom were standing around the dining room table, smiling as he and Sara walked in, hand in hand, "About time, I was about to take Jacob's place and cut the cake myself." Andreas said chuckling as Jacob went to stand in front of the large round dessert, Sara by his side.

Jacob rolled his eyes good heartedly, "Mom, slap Andreas for me."

"I'll do it," Ronny said reaching around their parents to hit Andreas on the back of the head.

"OW! Watch it Ronny, that hurt." He growled rubbing the back of his now throbbing skull.

Jacob shook his head grinning, "So are you guys going to sing Happy Birthday or what?" And they did, rather obnoxiously. After Jacob cut the cake, he served everyone first saving himself for last, raking his finger across the icing and licking it off.

After, the family enjoined to the living room, their cake in hand, as they talked to one another. Jacob pulled Sara onto his lap as she passed by him on her way to the kitchen, empty plate in hand. "Jacob!" She squealed grinning as he gave her neck a quick kiss licking the patch of skin in a teasing manner, "happy birthday, birthday boy."

"I'm not a boy; I'm a man of twenty-two."

She just gave him a smile, "you're a man when I say you're a man Jacob Allen, until then you're still a boy." He stuck his tongue out at her, "my point proven, peter pan."

"Aw, but I thought you liked my tongue." He said faking a pout as he smirked.

Sara blushed to her roots, "shut up Jake, not around the family." She hissed lightly, slapping his shoulder gently. He muttered a 'fine' with a roll of his eyes and let her go.

After that, everything went smoothly, though something was still nagging at the back of Jacob's mind. He knew he had to tell Sara soon, his family already knew, now he just need to get Sara alone to tell her…. to explain.

An hour later

Everyone had taken to the backyard with their drinks leaving the house empty except for Jacob and Sara who where in the kitchen finishing the last of the dishes.

Jacob set aside the dish towel he had been drying with and turned to his girlfriend. "Sara," She stopped washing and looked at Jacob, raising her eyebrows in question. "I need to tell you something... can you stop washing for a second." He asked pointing to the dish in her hand. She looked confused as she put the plate down and dried her hands on the dish towel.

Knowing he now had her full attention, he started, "About a week ago my boss gave me a big promotion, one that people as young as me don't get. Usually it takes years to get this sort of offer but he said my work ethic has really surpassed the older employees of the company.; and for me that is a really big deal, even you know I want to be successful in this career, being an architect is what I've always wanted. This is my chance Sara and... " He took a deep breath, "the job is in New York... I have to leave tomorrow at five in the morning."

Sara didn't speak for a long time having taken up the dish towel, ringing it in her hands in silence. Then finally, she broke the agitating silence, "why are you telling me this now?" She asked in a whisper.

Jacob swallowed, "I didn't want you to try and stop me."

"*Stop* you?" she said in disbelief. "I would never try and stop you, Jacob, if this is something you want to do then I'll let you do it. Besides, a few miles won't mess up what we have," she said smiling a bit, brushing her fingers over his cheek.

Jacob hung his head, "that's just it, I can't think about my work and about missing you. It would be too much for me to handle."

Sara blinked, what was he getting at? "It's called multi-tasking, Jacob, it's something the human race has been doing since time began."

"No, jSara... I think we should take a break."

At that moment Sara felt her heart shatter into a million pieces, hoping she had heard wrong but she knew she hadn't. Tears welled up in her eyes as she looked at the man before her. "You can't mean that Jake... please say you can't mean that," she pleaded, her voice breaking.

Jacob could feel his heart become lodged in his throat as he stared at the only girl he's ever truly loved. It killed him to say this, but it need to be done. "Yes." Was all he could manage to croak out. With that, he leaned forward and placed a small chaste kiss to her soft forehead, feeling her body shake with silent, repressed sobs, before turning and leaving; leaving the one thing he understood the most behind.

One year later

Sara could still recall that day as clearly as if it had just happen a moment ago. She had been miserable since Jacob had left; sure, she hid it from her friends, because after six months they finally told her she had to move on. Though she couldn't inside, she could still pretend on the outside.

She had started her second year in collage that fall; having dated a few guys to pass the time, the relationships only lasting a few weeks to a month at the longest. Her studies the only thing keeping her reasonably sane— and from breaking down, but even then a few tears would slip down her face causing her to push her homework aside for a moment, taking her time to cry silently while she remembered.

"I'll see you later, 'okay?"

Sara nodded to Selena, her roommate, as she headed towards her next class. Sara continued down the campus sidewalk alone, heading towards her car in the campus parking lot, pulling her scarf tighter around her neck. The October air was starting to become cold, the falls where chillier in Rhode Island than in California; her once loose single layers became heavy and warm sweaters and scarf's.

She was almost to the parking lot— the orange and brown leaves crunching under her feet as she walked, the brightly colored trees lifting her spirits— when she stopped suddenly; her heart clenching. He was here, Jacob was here, and he was standing a few feet away from her, looking down at a piece of paper in his hands, a look of confusion on his face. Sara smiled at the face knowing it well, before frowning. *Why is he here?* The thought whispered through her mind as she made her way closer.

"Jacob?" She asked in a questioning voice, her voice got his attention.

He turned to her, a grin appearing on his face, "Sara."

She walked closer, "what are you doing here?" She asked folding her arms around her stomach.

He licked his lips nervously, "I... quit." He said simply, "I, realized I couldn't be there while you're here. I couldn't...." His words trailed off as he looked at her, then to the leaf scattered ground.

"Why now? Why not then?" she questioned in a demanding voice. "You just said you were going; you didn't even try to make it work between us. You just gave up like a coward, Jake," she said in a rush, she needed to know why, and she needed to know now. "I loved you… I…," she smiled, "I *loved* you. You left the next day, I went over to your apartment before the sun was up to try and convince you to, somehow, keep *us* together. Your landlord said I had just missed you." She didn't care if she was hurting him, and by the look on his face, she was. But he had hurt her too. "I tried to call your cell phone, but you never answered because you changed your number. I asked your brothers, I practically got on my knees and begged… you have some damn loyal brother's, Jake, they wouldn't give it up."

Jacob gave her an apologetic look, "Sara… I am so sorry. I-I thought it was for the best." By now, he had tears threatening to spill; he couldn't even explain how sorry he was. "I have a new job, it's here actually, and there are some site plans that need to be looked over for an office building here. I did quit the one in New York, but they said they didn't want to lose me as an employee so they offered me a job anywhere else so long as it's in the states. Next thing I know I'm packing my bags, your mom is on the phone with me, and I'm— in your own words, practically on my knees begging for your address." He finished giving her a look that told her he was telling the truth.

Sara stared at the man before her, emotions a whirlwind of doubt, confusion, want, and hurt. Her mind told her two things; one side told her to take him back, but the other was telling her to leave, to move on. She swallowed thickly, "I don't know," she said, confliction clear on her face.

Jake stepped closer to the conflicted girl, "Sara, I love you."

The young woman looked away for a moment, taking her bottom lip between her teeth as she controlled her thoughts, before she looked at Jacob's face, and with realization she smiled, "I know you do, but here's the thing, I *loved* you—"

"I know and—"

"No. Jake. You don't know."

He gave her a confused looked, "You love me right?"

She shook her head, smiling, "past tense. Lov*ed*." She lifted her hand in a goodbye, giving him a brilliant smile, "Goodbye, Jacob, enjoy your life," with that she brushed past him and left him standing in the middle of the sidewalk. She laughed at the happy feeling that crashed into her as the weight lifted from her heart; it was the feeling of being free, it was the feeling of saying goodbye.

I Will Follow You Into The Dark

"I will never let you go from my life, even if Death itself comes at my door."
"If Death comes knocking at your door, I'll be there to greet him, before he takes you."

One

Ever had such a strong connection with someone that it almost hurt? Ever love someone so much that you would do anything for them? I bet you wouldn't die for them. I bet you wouldn't look Death in the eye and say, "back off." I bet you wouldn't sell your soul to save theirs.... Well I did. On July 27th 2012, I sold my soul to Death to save my friend. In the year 2012, on July 27th, I died.

"Wake up...wake up!"

18 year old Saige Alison groaned as her best friend, 19 year old Gracie Davis, shook her from her sleep.

"Do you know what time it is?" She grumbled out as she stretched before sitting up.

Gracie rolled her eyes, "it's eleven in the morning—nearly twelve, and your dad is throwing a fit downstairs; I suggest you get your lazy ass out of bed and go down there to see what's up."

Saige peered at her small friend, her light brown eyes and dirty blonde hair familiar to her, "Something is always up with him," she said with a casual smirk as she drew back her covers and stood up, her own height towering over Gracie's.

"Yeah, well, this time he's flipping," Gracie said sitting cross legged on her bed.

"Fine," she said straightening her t-shirt and shorts that had found themselves wrapped around her body. "I'll go fix whatever it is this time, just give me a few minutes to get myself together."

Gracie sighed, "I know you're tired of doing everything around here, but your dad does everything out there. You know what they would do to you if they saw you weren't marked." The smaller girl stood and walked over to her friend, putting a hand on her arm.

Saige nodded slightly, "I know," she swiveled her body around to look at her friend, "why do you get to roam free while I have to hide like a prisoner?"

"Because you father works for the government, while mine is just a shop keeper."

"I know," she said repeated.

"Look, one day, we're going to leave this place, and find some remote area where they will never find us."

Saige smiled, holding out her pinky, "promise?"

Gracie nodded, linking her pinky finger with Saige's, "pinky promise."

"Ok, now shoo! I need to get ready."

"Ok fine," Gracie sighed and leisurely walked out of the room, shutting the door behind her.

We had to live a life of secrecy, filled with the truth hidden behind a mountain of lies. It weighed down on us from time to time, making us crack, but we held firm, we couldn't give in; if we gave in, it would mean to give up our free will, giving into their control, and merciless power. We dreamed of a time where we could be free, just as we had been as children… but no, now all we can dream of is escaping the, "free world".

"Hey," Saige said as she came up from behind Gracie in the kitchen.

Gracie smiled at her friend, "you finally awake?"

"Eh," she shrugged, getting a mug from the cupboard and pouring herself a lukewarm cup of coffee with two sugars. She took a sip and her gray eyes held a pained expression in them as she tasted the coffee, "This will do the trick."

Gracie grimaced, knowing full well that the coffee must have been made in the early hours of the morning.

"That's disgusting."

Saige took another large sip, "yeah well, it's this or me going to bed again. Now, where's my dad?" She asked looking around the room as if expecting him to suddenly jump out from behind the counter.

"Living room."

Saige gave her a 'let's get this over with' look, and the two girls made their way into the living room. Saige twisted her dark red hair over her shoulder and made her way over to her father, who was bent over his briefcase muttering under his breath. "Dad?"

55 year old Carl Alison, looked up at his daughter with a straight face, "what?"

"You needed me?"

"Oh, right," he straightened, and shut his briefcase, "I already found it. Listen I have to go to work now, stay off the main roads."

Saige glanced down at her father's wrist as a small black rectangular shape flashed before her eyes, the letter and numbers A11 on it in white. The verichip, as they called it. "Why do you work for them?" She asked confused, shaking her head.

Carl smirked, "because, The Boss, knows what he's doing; he's going to make this country a better place with his order system. The whole world could be affected, now that, would be the overall win."

"So, because this guy takes control of the people's power of speech, this makes him king over everything?"

"Not yet, but today that's going to change," he said this as he left, and just as he got to the front door, he called behind him, "stay away from the main roads!"

"I know the drill!" She called back to her dad, but he was already out the door and didn't hear her.

Gracie had taken to the leather couch in the meanwhile, "you know he really wants you to get it."

"I know," Saige said, plopping herself next to her friend. "If I weren't me, I would probably get it."

Gracie gave her a look, "if you weren't you, I would ask you, who you were."

"I don't think I would know how to reply."

My father was just a lowly politician at the time when The Boss came into power; when someone would talk to him, that person would forget his name the minute they had walked away. But times changed, and my father was power hungry, he wanted it all: money, reputation, the title, he wanted all of it. The Boss gave him an easy way out of what he called his miserable life, all he had to do was sign himself over to him, and he would receive a chip that would surgically be placed in his wrist. It would give The Boss every access to my father's personal life, my personal life. My father, for the sake of greed, handed over his life.

Gracie and Saige had grabbed their coats from the hook by the front door; just minutes after her father left, and took to the outside world, though making their way through the back alleyways, away from the main road. The Seattle air was crisp and cool as the air misted over and a grey overhang stood over them. The girls pulled their coats tighter around themselves and stuffed their hands into their pockets.

"Where do you want to go?"

Gracie thought for a moment, "the coast," she said, making her mind up.

Saige turned to look at her, "do you know how hard it is to get to the coast via back ways?"

She just brushed it off, "we'll put our hoods up and take to the main roads, stay off the transportation systems, and we should be fine."

"Alright munchkin, let's go."

"Hey! I am not a munchkin!"

Saige chuckled, "your right, your fun sized."

Gracie pursed her lips, "that's better."

"Come on, we better go now before it hits noon," Saige said taking Gracie's hand in her own.

The girl's got to the edge of the alley, and peered into the main street; it was as if glimpsing into another world. They took a deep breath, and grasped tightly with their hands.

"We'll make this easy." Gracie nodded, and the two girls's stepped out into the open.

If only it was that easy.

The girl's walked hand in hand, for what seemed like forever, having to keep their heads low and stay within each other reaching distance. Cameras were everywhere, and they couldn't risk being caught.

They didn't take their time getting to the coast; their steps were hurried with quick strides. Finally, they broke free of the dense crowd of the city, reaching the edge of what was the main road that led onto two roads, one leading on from the main road, and another that led them to the beach.

The girls took the route down to the beach, the cold hand kicking up behind their heels as they walked down a small hill. The beach wasn't crowed, there were two people walking but no one else could be seen. Gracie and Saige took a seat on the sand, their knees to their chest as they curled into themselves, shielding away from the wind; Gracie lent on Saige, laying her head on her shoulder.

The sea was angry, the waves tossed back and forth in hate as a storm raged forward, he wind started to blow harder and the rain began, a down pour. The girl's readjusted their hoods and snuggled in closer.

"Do you think," Gracie started, "if we were to perish in the sea right now, would anybody care?"

Saige hummed in thought, "No," she said with a shake of her head. "I don't think anyone would be the differ."

Gracie looked up at her, "Do you want to drown?"

Saige looked out to sea, watching as the waves tore at each other, "I think it would be the easiest way to escape... but I don't think it would be the right way."

Gracie nodded in agreement, "I was hoping you would say that."

"Well you know me, I always like a good challenge," she said with a short laugh.

"Hmm," she acknowledged. "Crap! That's cold!"

"What is?"

"The rain, it's soaking through my jacket."

"'Kay, that's our signal to leave."

Helping each other to stand, they made their way back the way they came, the wind pulsing in their face as they climbed back up to the road.

The main roads were even more crowded than before when they returned. "What's going on?" Saige questioned as they stopped by a wall, resting against it, tried to figure out what was going on. It was unusual for it to be this crowded.

Both looked around, taking in their surroundings, something though caught Saige's eye, "what's the date today?"

Gracie shrugged, "I don't know, the third of July?"

"No," Saige said, shaking her head, staring across the street, "I don't think it's the third."

"Then what?"

"I think it's the fourth of July," she said pointing to a banner they had missed. It screamed **"Our New Independence, Make a Difference in Yourself!"**

"Shit," Gracie muttered.

"What?"

"That's what your dad meant," she said looking at Saige with wide eyes.

She was starting to get impatient, "What did he mean?"

Gracie looked around before taking Saige's hand and dragging her to an alley, "a couple weeks ago my parents were watching the ten o'clock news, I was getting some water, they were saying that they had perfected the ultimate cure to everything: diseases, cancers, even the incurable could be cured is what they were saying. They said they were going to release it on Independence Day at two o'clock, everyone has to get it, make a difference in yourself."

"So really it's like a Venus Fly Trap, innocent to look at, in this case hear, but on the inside, really you're just setting yourself up to be eaten," she said, realization dawning on her.

"They make it sound so good, but really it's a vaccine...."

"They could be setting it up so the verichip would be inserted through the process...," she trailed off.

"A cure to cure even the incurable; everyone will want it."

Saige peered out of the alleyway, "that's why there are so many people."

"Makes sense, looks like it's more than just the whole city."

"More like the whole state."

Saige took a deep breath and let it out, "we need to get out of here." Just as she said that, a clock somewhere chimed. It chimed twice. "Now!"

Each girl took each other's hand and held fast as they counted to three before pushing out into the crowd. A loud banging sounded through the area as police officers started to enter the area out of nowhere with thick plastic shields, hitting the front of it with their batons.

"Their surrounding the area," Gracie said in a state of shock.

Saige shook her head, "city is going into lockdown, and we won't be able to get out if we don't go now."

Gracie stopped Saige as she tried to push past the people on the sidewalk. "We'll never make it on time going through there, we have to take to the streets; it's not as crowded, we'll make it in better time."

"We'll be seen," the other pointed out.

"Better than being dead."

Saige nodded, knowing they had no other choice but that one. "Don't lose me."

"Never." Gracie grasped her hand tight and they ran onto the street, swerving past people in a blur. The shrill sound of a whistle blew from behind them; they didn't slow down even as the shouting people began to receive the vaccination.

They ran as hard as they could, and as fast as they could. They were nearing the edge of where the police line started, they were nearly there.

"Ngh!" Gracie groaned.

Saige whipped her head around when she heard her, "what happened?!"

"No!" She cried, her vision blurring slightly from the pain, "Just go!"

The officers had surrounded the area, their only hope was to go up and then down. They dashed to the nearest apartment building, and climbed the stairs up to fourth floor. A window was at the very end of the fourth floor hall, and a ladder going down the side of the building was just barely peeking above the ledge of the sill.

Saige shoved the window open and climbed out carefully, helping Gracie out. The two girls looked down below and noticed the guards a few yards away.

"Shh," Saige said as they began the decent down.

They tried to keep quiet as much as possible, though the rust on the old metal stairway mad it near impossible. Finally after five minutes of creeping down the stairway, they jumped to ground level, and with no hesitation, they ran, they ran until their breath was ragged and shallow, with sides throbbing from the stitch in it, they ran until they reached an old forgotten area in secluded grounds surrounded by trees and the wilderness of forgotten land. Coming down from their run was easy enough; they slowed to a walk, still on alert for any sounds or movement.

"Crap," Gracie muttered, clenching at her side, under her ribcage.

Saige quickly went to her side and gently lowered her to the ground, sitting her against a tree. "Let me see it." Too weak to move, Gracie let Saige remove her jacket and lift up her shirt, exposing her ruined skin.

Her fair skin was stained with blood from a puncture wound, "it's bleeding heavily," the girl murmured, stripping her own jacket and removing her dark long sleeved shirt from her body. "Can you sit forward?" She did and Saige wrapped the shirt securely around the wound, causing the bleeding to stop, for now.

"Long johns?" Gracie said with a slight amusement to her voice, as she watched her friend pulled her coat back on, and helping her with her own.

"In Seattle, when it rains, it's usually cold. Besides I only wore the shirt, the pants kind of gross me out," she said explaining herself.

Gracie chuckled, "I should have figured as much. Here, help me up." Saige grabbed her arm and took most of her body weight as she helped Gracie to her feet. "We need to find some shelter."

Saige looked around, and for a long time she didn't say anything, "I think I may know this place," she said aloud.

"How? It's a jungle?"

She just shook her head in thought, "I think this is the area where that old man use to live, do you remember him? He used to scare the crap out of us?"

"Oh yeah; later on we realized he wasn't really going to eat us."

"Wow," Saige muttered, "what happened?"

"Seems to me that he died."

"Well, if we come across his remains then we'll know for sure."

"Let's just find the house for now; I'm starting to lose energy."

They treaded through the thick green land, Saige helping Gracie carry some of her weight, holding an arm under her as to help her stay up. They walked for thirty minutes, fighting their way through the overgrowth, before they finally stumbled upon a small wood hunting cabin that looked like it hadn't been used in a century. A few of the windows were smashed, while the roof had missing pieces to it, the door was worn though sturdy enough, along with the walls. It was cold but dry and away from the crowds, and that is all they cared about.

"I need to sit down, set me down," Gracie said. Saige obliged and carefully helped lower her to the ground.

Saige did a quick check through of everything, the water didn't work, the kitchen was grey and bare, no bed save one with a spring sticking up through the mattress. The girl slid down the way next to her injured friend. "Well there's nothing here, no food or water, no blankets and there's only one bed and it has a spring sticking up from it. Also it looks like mice like to camp out here too."

"Why does the mice thing appear worse to me than the lack of food?"

"I still don't get why you don't like them, they're so cute."

"Gross buggers."

Saige glanced down at the makeshift bandage, "do you know what did it?" Gracie looked away. "Gracie?"

"Needle…."

"Vaccine?" She nodded. "Crap, what are we going to do now?" She asked running her hands through her hair.

"Pray for a miracle?"

"I can't lose you," she said, leaning her head on top of Gracie's.

"I'm not dead yet," she said with a small smile.

Saige smile back slightly, and pulled the hood of her jacket up, doing the same for her friend, "we should get some sleep, and tomorrow I'll find a way to get us food." Gracie could feel her eyes getting sleepy and she nodded her head slowly. Saige helped her to lie down, making sure she was bundled up before laying down herself, wrapping her arms around herself; she watched as Gracie fell asleep, though she herself didn't close her eyes, she didn't dare to sleep.

It was a vaccine to cure the incurable, a miracle, a death sentence to all. It would only get worse.

The hours past, soon the afternoon past, and the darkness crept in. Saige's eyes scanned the darkening room as the creaks and moans of the cabin started to cry out. Gracie stirred slightly, having only woken up once for Saige to check her wound. The bleeding had stopped fortunately, but the wound itself was still an angry red with dried blood surrounding it.

Gracie stirred again, she groaned as she opened her eyes, "What time is it?" She asked holding her side as she sat up.

"I don't know, assuming it's around seven right now," Saige said, watching her. "Question."

"Hmm?"

"Why do you think it bled so much?"

"I don't know," the girl said with a slight shrug of her shoulder. "It could have possibly hit a vein or something larger; it definitely did not feel small. Though I think I only got half of the vaccine shot."

Saige looked around the room before turning to her friend once again, "how do you feel?"

"Well I have had better days," she joked. Saige gave her a look. "We'll see what happens." Saige turned away to stare at the peeling wallpaper. "Will we be able to go back? Home I mean."

"No," Saige sighed. "I don't think we'll ever be able to go back. We were seen running away from them; obviously they know we're not marked."

"Our parents...."

"My dad won't care; he never did like the fact that I didn't want the chip."

"I don't know how mine will react."

"Well it's too risky to find out now," Saige covered her mouth as she yawned suddenly, blinking back sleep that threatened to take over.

Gracie gave her friend a small smile and placed a hand on her shoulder, "go to sleep, I'll take watch for a little while."

"But—" She tried to argue.

"No buts," Gracie said stopping her complaint. "I'm fine, for now at least. If their looking for us then they'll wait until morning, it would be stupid to come out here at night."

Saige stared at her for a minute before exhaustion finally swept over her and she realized she would be useless if she didn't get some rest. "Only for a few hours," she mumbled, settling herself on the ground, pulling her hood up once again, wrapping her arms around herself.

"Just sleep," Gracie muttered, laying a hand on her covered head in a comforting manner, in seconds she could feel the girl's body go lax as she fell into the hands of an untouchable world.

The dawn broke and Gracie watched as the sky slowly filled with light. She gently shook Saige awake and the girl sat up, blinking away the sleep and stretching. The whole of the cabin filled with new light as it streamed in through the windows.

"It's beautiful," Gracie murmured.

Saige looked at the dawn's morning light and with sudden thought, she glanced at Gracie. "We live for this, new beginnings," she said looking back to the windows. "We won't give up."

Gracie looked to the outside world, beyond the windows, "never."

An hour or so had passed since dawn and Saige had taken the time to walk around outside, getting a feel for the land, to see if anything had been left behind that was useful. She walked around to the back of the cabin to find a cellar door that led down; she pulled at the large heavy wood door, grunting at the weight, the door moved slowly until she got it to a certain point where she could swing it open.

The stale smell of rust and dust filled her senses. A set of cement stairs led the way down and she took them one by one, ducking her head under the ceiling before straightening and coming to the last stair. It wasn't a large room, yet it wasn't a small one either. Metal shelves lined the walls on either side, the sides were rusted with age and a thick layer of dust coated everything. Forgotten nails were strewn here and there; an empty box lay in the corner, on the wood counter that rested against the back wall, a small box laid on top of it, two more small boxes half the other's size laid next to it. Saige glanced curiously at the boxes and neared the table, peeling back the flaps of the small box she glanced inside and found a tiny hand gun; the length was so small that it measured half way to her fingertips from her palm. The boxes next to the one she opened were bullets; she took one out and studied it before opening cartridge and placing one into it; it was a perfect fit. She took the bullet out and placed it back in the box, closing the lid and gathering both boxes in her hands. She took one more glance around the room, making sure there was nothing left worth taking, and left. She used her foot to push the heavy wood door shut, it banged loudly once before everything was quiet again.

Saige entered the cabin with the gun and bullets in hand.

"Where did you find that?" Gracie asked as she watched the girl come in and crouch in front of her.

"Storage area I think, sort of cellar I guess," she said. "I don't think the old man died here, by the way. I think he left."

Gracie gave her a bewildered look, "why would he leave?"

Saige looked up from the gun, "why do you and I want to leave?"

"Ah, ok. So what are you going to do with that?" She asked, gesturing to the weapon.

The girl took six bullets from the box and filled each slot, before locking the cartridge back in place. She took another six and stood up so she could stuff them into her front pant pocket. "I'm going into town, I don't know what to expect," she said, pulling up her undershirt and tucking the small firearm into the waistband of her jeans, pulling her shirt down to cover it.

"I'll come with you!" Gracie exclaimed, going to stand up.

'No," Saige said, touching her shoulder, pushing her gently to the ground. "I need you here, with the vaccine in your system we don't know what will happen, or when. We can't take the chance. I'll be back in a couple of hours. I'll try and get another weapon, some new clothes, and food."

"How are you going to do that? If they are looking for us, then they aren't going to let you just waltz into the city and take things."

"I'll figure something out."

There was no point in arguing with her, Gracie saw that. "Fine," she said, giving in. "Just, be careful!"

"I will be. I'll be back soon."

The trek through the brush was easy enough in the daylight, if you weren't running. Saige made it to the edge of the city in just a little over fifteen minutes, marking her way as she went so she could find the path again. The buildings and homes loomed over her and she felt an eerie silence creep over her. With a puzzled mind, she walked forward, stepping into the threshold of the enemy. It wasn't crowded, there weren't allot of people around… there wasn't anyone around. The streets were empty and all the stores were closed up.

She paced herself, walking through the supposed empty town. Her footfalls were quiet on the concrete. She tried one of the doors on a café; it was locked though it was opening hours.

"What happened here?" She questioned aloud to no one. A small wheezing cough sounded from the other side of the building, the sound like an echo. With brows pulled together, Saige followed the wheezing to find a man with a balding head, and thin wire framed glasses in a white coat, lying against the side of the brick wall of the café. "Sir?" She questioned, nudging his leather shoe with the toe of her own sneaker.

The man, who looked to be in his early fifties, looked up at her. The white of his eyes were yellowed and his skin looked shallow and pasty. The man laughed sarcastically, "You haven't gotten it," he said in a rasped voice.

Confused she answered, "Haven't gotten what?"

"Infected," he said with a cough. "Some die and some, lose their minds…," he started to crackle.

Saige scoffed, "so everything you guys said was bullshit, not surprising."

The man glared, "no! We perfected the vaccine, but sometimes testing on animals doesn't quite show the same affect that it would have on a human. Oops," he gave a sadistic laugh.

Anger welled up in the girl and she took several steps forward and bent forward, taking the man's lab coat lapels in her hands, fisting the material and bring his face close hers, "you son of a bitch, you screwed and messed with peoples' lives; possibly killing half of the state, just for the sake of wanting to have God like power. That's sick."

"Yes, well this is a sick world, girly, we don't always get what we want now do we?" He said grinning at her.

"You tested on animals; they wouldn't have the same effect as we do. You should have know that!"

"We do…."

Realization dawned on her.

"Now do you understand?"

"We were the guinea pigs… you didn't perfect it at all did you?!"

"You could say that last bit was a lie."

Saige shoved the man to the ground roughly in disgust, "sick bastard."

"Don't think it hasn't been done before," he said with a small grin, his eyes squinted at her, "I recognize you… your that girl they want, the one who ran yesterday." Saige stepped back suddenly. "Yeah… where's your little friend you were with?" He chuckled under his breath, "doesn't matter, they'll find you. They always do. You can't hide forever."

"They can try, but they will never find us."

The man shook his head from side to side unsteadily, "whatever helps you sleep at night."

Saige had enough of this man, with a racing heart she stepped away from the man as he started to wheeze again. She continued down the street, looking every which way for people who may have been lingering outside, but she saw no one.

She picked up her pace and turned right down the street that led to her house. She arrived at the large condo building and walked up the stairs leading to the door, she tested the door it was open. She stepped carefully into her home; it looked the same, though something felt out of place, as if someone had been through it who wasn't supposed to be. She took a steady look around, making her way towards the laundry area.

Laundry baskets lined the wall with dirt clothes; Saige checked the dryer, and much to her relief there was her clean clothes. She pulled from it two pairs of jeans, new socks and two shirts, with sweaters. She looked around the room, spotting a cloth laundry bag; she opened it and stuffed the clothes into it before making her way to the kitchen. She raided the cupboards for any dry foods, coming upon a bag of chips and trail mix, along with bags of dried pineapple and bottles of water. She took it all.

A thud sounded from upstairs and she stilled, glancing up. It came again, and she carefully opened the silverware drawer pulling out the large butcher's knife. She carried the bag out of the kitchen and placed it carefully on the floor near the door, taking to the stairs. There was another thud and her blood rushed through her ears as her heart pounded. She entered the top floor hallway, taking slow quiet steps as she pushed onward towards her room. The door was open; she laid her body flat against the wall, peeking her head around the corner to see what was causing the noise. It was a person, they weren't alone, there was two others going through her things as well. She looked away and swallowed. Her heart pounded and she gripped the knife tightly in her hands.

The noise stopped and she turned her head towards her room again, she couldn't see them, they had disappeared. She stepped away from the wall and cautiously walked into her room. The window was opened, her drapes fluttering *from the breeze that came through. She walked to the window and looked out, no one could be seen. A crunch was heard from behind her and she whirled around, her face coming inches away from one of the people who were in her room. It was a woman with brown hair, her skin was pale and blotchy, and the white of her eyes were yellow and diseased looking. She screamed and swung her arms upward, they came crashing down upon Saige, her whole right side jerking as she was tossed against her dresser. The knife flew from her hands, and she saw stars as her head was hit against one of the knobs on the drawers.*

"Ugh," she groaned out, she put a hand to her head and tried to clear it. The woman cam nearer to her, her companions behind her, easing in from the back; Saige spotted the knife and tried reaching for it, coming up short. The woman and her friends were closing in, desperately Saige searched for any form of a weapon and then she remembered the gun tucked in the waistband of her jeans. The lady launched herself at the girl just as she pulled the gun out, a shot was fired out and then other and then other, blood splayed across her face, painting the walls too. She shot the gun until the three bodies were strewn on the ground.

Saige took a shuttering breath, her nerves oddly calm. She stood and reloaded the cartridge with the last of her bullets she had. One of the bodies moved, a man with shaggy blonde hair, no more than a year older than Gracie; started to get up. Saige aimed the gun at his head, shot once, the body jerked forward, and fell silent. She swallowed and collected the butcher knife, both weapons in hand, as she walked to the bathroom; she took a revealed breath, looked at herself, and washed her hands and then her face, ridding her skin of the red stain. Though for her clothes, it was hopeless, there were stains on her shirt and jacket.

She stared at her reflection, taking the time to examine her actions. Her survival instincts had kicked in, she couldn't justify what she had done, it was kill or be killed, and she wasn't going to die, she had to look after Gracie. There was a new type of strength to her; she could see it in her eyes. Saige pushed away from the mirror and hurriedly ran down the stairs, wasting no time to see if anyone else was in the house, she had everything she needed; now she needed to get back to Gracie. Just as she grabbed her bag, something caught her eye; she straightened, leaving the bag where it was as she made her way around the side of the leather couch. "Oh God," she gasped out looking away. Her father was sprawled on the floor, his skin was just as white as the woman's had been upstairs, his eyes were open and his mouth gapped open as if he had tired taking in a breath just before he died. "I'm sorry dad," she whispered. The girl scrubbed her face and turned away, "there's nothing I can do now." She stuck the knife through her belt loop and grabbed her bag in one hand while the other held the gun.

She opened the door and looked both ways to make sure the way was clear; it was just as deserted as before. She stepped out, and without bothering to close the door, she made a run for it; not caring how much noise she made, she just had to escape the area, she couldn't take them all on her own. The bag slowed her but not completely. She pushed herself to the limit, her lungs burned as she breathed heavily. That was all that could be heard, the voice of her breath and the heavy footfalls of her steps; somewhere a door opened and that only caused her to run faster, she ran until she reached the cities edge, not stopping until she was hidden from view.

She watched as more doors opened and normal looking people stepped out, though they weren't normal, they were different, they weren't human anymore; they walked around as if they were possessed. That's what they were, they were possessed by their greed for money and fortune, of immortality; they were possessed by demons of want. They most definitely were not human anymore.

And in that moment, I had realized that this wasn't just a fight, or a war between us as humans; this was a war between God and the Devil.

Saige stumbled through the front door, having tripped over a stray branch that had broken away. The door creaked on its hinges as she pushed it open. The cabin was quiet, the space in which Gracie and she had been staying in, was empty. "Grace?" Saige called, the sound dying instantly. Saige stepped forward, gently setting her bag down; she walked past the kitchen, glancing in doing a quick body check, she did the bathroom next and then the bedroom. She pushed the door open and stepped in. "Shit, Gracie," she breathed out rushing to her friend's side. She was passed out on the floor, her face visibly coated in a sheen of sweat. Gracie's usually fair skin was a deathly white; her eyelids were closed though Saige could see her eyes moving underneath them in a rapid back and forth motion.

The girl got onto one knee and lifted Gracie's head up so she could get her arm under her, and did the same to her legs, with both arms under her she went *into a crouching position and grunted under the weight as she used all her strength to lift her friend up. She took small unsteady steps towards bed, making sure not to place her anywhere near the spring that stood up from the mattress. She straightened her legs only for Gracie to curl into herself. She shivered and Saige felt her cheek and then her neck and forehead, she was normal. Gracie moaned and tossed her head, becoming quiet a moment later.*

Saige ran into the front room, and grabbed her bag, running back into the bedroom; she undid the string that kept the bag together and pulled out one of the water bottles. Unscrewing it, she lifted it to Gracie's head, pouring some of the contents into her exposed mouth. She could see her throat work as she unconsciously swallowed. Saige felt her friend's clothes and realized they were soaked through. "Damn," she muttered, sliding her friend's coat off; it wasn't easy to undress her friend, the material of the clothing sticking to her skin. She managed to pull off her jeans and shirt, untying her own shirt that was wrapped around her waist, she then wet the ends of Gracie's shirt to wipe away the sweat from her body and face, lightly racking away the perspiration on her skin.

She then dressed her in a clean pair of jeans she had taken and a new shirt, pulling the sweater over her head. She then did the same for herself, taking the knife from her belt loop and placing it on the window sill of the single window; wishing for nothing more than to strip out of her bloodied clothes, she washed the grime from her face and hands, and then changed into her own clean clothes. She tied the bag again and set it in the corner with hers and Gracie's dirty clothes.

With no thoughts she just glanced down at the girl that lay before her, curled into herself once again, Saige didn't utter a sound as she went to the wall and slid down, staring quietly at the form on the old bed.

A week had passed with no disturbance, Gracie hadn't woken from her sleep and it worried Saige, she gave her water daily, though without food she wouldn't last long; the girl, to pass the time, had gone to her house many more times, taking the rest of the dried and packaged food. The trip to her old home had become difficult, the streets were now crowded again causing her to hide her face from the people, and take to the back streets again; though she had managed it. She would sit at the edge of the city, hidden from view, and watch the day's progress, observing the people and their daily activities. Nothing was strange; people went about their days, nothing unusual; but Saige couldn't help but feel like something didn't fit. One day her curiosity got the better of her, she left the confinements of her hide out and took to the corner of the street, her hood pulled up, obscuring her face from wandering eyes. She casually leaned against the building wall and watched the pedestrians go about their daily chores.

A hand grasped at her hood from behind and pulled it away from her face, nearly every pair of eyes on the street went to her; Saige's whipped her body around, coming in contact with a solid form. Hands came out and grabbed her by the shoulders, "let go!" She screamed pushing with all her strength at the hard chest of the man who held her. His skin, just like the others before him, was a pasty white, the person, up close, looked dead, but his body moved and Saige could see he was very much alive.

She swallowed, glancing at every face that stared at her, taking note of the white paper that was taped to a store window with hers and Gracie's face on it. Her eyes widened as the man took another step closer to her, her heart raced and she did the only sensible thing she could think of, she fled.

She ran, her feet pounding against the pavement, it turned into dirt and rock. She didn't stop, she never glanced behind, concentrating on the path ahead of her, her breath came easy as she flew past trees and overgrowth; she cut through tall grass like a knife adrenalin pulsing through her veins, her feet carried her to the cabin, only then did she slow to a stop.

It was quiet, nothing could be heard, her body was tense and alert for any movement. She pulled the gun from her pants and cocked it, holding it by her side, ready to kill if necessary.

She turned around, he was there, behind her; his face held a sadist smirk, Saige pulled her fist back and hit him square in the jaw, his head whipped back, and she took the time to put a few yards between them. The man cracked his neck and looked at her, a snarl erupted from him and he ran towards her; Saige felt her heart hammer as she aimed the gun at the oncoming man and shot him twice in the chest, he dropped just a foot away from her, landing at her feet.

The shot from the gun still rung in her ears s she lowered the gun and stepped away from the body, turning away from it. A crunch could be heard and her breath caught in her throat as she slowly turned around, watching as the previously dead body, rise from the ground, and turn to face her.

"What the...," she trailed off, stepping back.

He came closer, blood soaking through his shirt, staining it, "He wants you, and your friend," he said in a cold voice.

Her eyes went wide as she tried to move, but couldn't, she had cornered herself into a tree.

"Stupid girl," he said, coming up to her and breathing into her face. With a force that knocked the breath from her, he swung her body around and threw her into the air, throwing her body like a rag doll.

She landed on the ground with a thud, her body convulsing in pain. The man neared her and lifted her by the neck of her sweater, "you should stop running," he hissed in her face, his breath like rotting eggs.

She winced form the smell, "and become like you?" She scoffed, looking him in his dead eyes.

"Such a stupid decision."

Saige felt her body being lifted higher and her body dropped so he held her neck now, he was choking her. Her legs kicked out and her face turned red as her neck bulged in resistance. He just looked at her with cold dead eyes. Saige struggled, feeling her blood pound through her head, her lungs fighting for air she couldn't obtain; she thought of Gracie just a few yards from her in the cabin, and new found determination and strength filled her. With reaching fingers, she pulled the knife from her belt loop, the man's concentration on her face, and twisted her body, as she turned, her hand shot out and the steel embedded itself in the flesh of the man's neck.

He dropped her and she crumbled to the dirt, holding her neck as she drew in large amounts of oxygen. She glared at the man as he stumbled back holding the knife between his hands. "Bitch," he rasped out, blood oozing from his mouth.

Saige stood, keeping her distance. He glared at her and pulled the knife from his throat. She stared in shock as he threw the knife to the ground, sitting out a wad of blood.

"You can't kill something that is already dead."

Fury burned in Saige and she lunged forward, dropping her shoulder as she rammed her body mass into the man's stomach, catching him off guard, he flew to the ground. She dropped the gun and grabbed the knife he had tossed to the ground and hacked at his throat. His eyes were wide and hallow as she decapitated him. He didn't move, not an inch, he was just there, blood covering the grass and dirt in a red stain.

The girl swallowed and hurriedly scooted off the man's now limp body. She brought her legs up and dropped the knife, her hands shaking, the adrenaline wearing off. Blood once again covered her hands and she tried to wipe it off only to leave a red residue on her skin. She didn't move for a while, just staring at the body, it took her a long time to figure out what the man had meant by someone who was already dead, she remembered the people, their skin, what they had become, they weren't alive, they were dead, though their bodies were possessed by something much larger than the human soul. It soon became twilight and the girl shoved herself off the ground. She picked up the feet of the man and dragged his body to the tall brush and trees, hiding it from view. She turned to the head, and with disgust, she picked the heavy limb by the hair and walked over to the body, throwing it to the ground next to it.

Saige picked up the knife from the ground, sticking it into the earth and pulling it out, the blood whipped away by the soil. She took the gun and walked to the cabin, a wave of exhaustion crashing over her like a storm, she made her way sluggishly to the bedroom, only to find Gracie sitting up slightly against the wall. "Gracie!" Saige exclaimed, wide awake now; she rushed to her friend's side on the bed and sat down, placing the weapons she had in her hand on the window sill.

"Your hands!?" Gracie said looking at the blood stained skin.

Saige fisted her hands together, "not mind."

Gracie looked up at her face, "whose is it?"

"Things," Saige sighed, glancing away, "things, aren't good right now. When you went into that coma I had to keep you hydrated, but to do that I had to go into the city," she said, looking back to her friend. "The first day I went, I killed three people and found my father dead; though I managed to bring back food and water along with a change of clothes."

Gracie glanced down at herself and finally noticed her change of attire, "thanks."

Saige waved it off, "I came back here to find you passed out on the floor in a sweat, your body was covered so I couldn't just let you stay that way."

"Where did the blood on your hands come from? I woke up from a loud sound that sounded allot like a gun."

"Just another one of the locals," she joked. Gracie stared at her. "The vaccine changed allot of people, some go insane while others die, those who died...." She didn't know how to say it without sounding completely nuts.

"What?"

"This is going to sound insane but, I think—I know the people who've died, they've been possessed." Gracie gave her a look. "I know how it sounds, but the man I just killed, I shot him twice in the chest, one just near his heart, he should have been dead, and he wasn't; he got right back up again and threw me through the air as if I was merely a pebble."

"How is that possible?"

"I don't know," she said exasperated.

"Then, how did you kill him?"

"...I cut off his head with that," she said pointing to the butcher's knife.

Gracie raised an eyebrow, "that's disgusting, yet its survival." Saige nodded in agreement. Gracie glanced behind her friend's shoulder and gave a short scream.

Saige automatically went into a lunge position, ready to spring at any moment as she turned to face the person, thinking it was another who had followed her and the man; but the person who was behind her didn't look like the others. His hair was pitch black, his skin was pale though healthy, and his suit and tie were all black along with his shoes, his eyes a bright unnerving blue.

"Well, look who we have here," he said in a cool voice. "The two girls' who have caused me so much trouble."

"How did you find us?!" Saige snarled, it wasn't a question, but a demand.

The man tsk-ed, smiling, "now is that any way to treat a guest?"

"Who are you?!" She demeaned.

He lost his smile, "enough. My... pets, as you would say, informed me of your little detour into our city."

Saige looked at him, "you're the Boss aren't you."

"So slow to figure it out?"

"What do you want?" Saige questioned, clenching her jaw together.

The Boss's smile came back and he stepped up to her; lifting a hand, his first finger twitched and she was once again cut off from her air supply. "I want you and your friend dead, mostly you though, you two have the power to change what I want to happen; I can't let it come to that." A bang sounded and his face changed to one of annoyance as he looked down at his chest to find a bullet hole in it. "You'll regret that," he hissed before vanishing.

Saige dropped to the floor and Gracie dropped the gun, rushing to her friend's side, "Are you alright? Let's get you to the bed."

Saige obliged and let Gracie steer her to the bed so she could sit down, "I have to take watch," she rasped out.

"You've done enough tonight. You said you got some water and food?"

Saige nodded, "it's in that laundry bag, there should be a lighter and candle in there too; eat some of the pineapple, it will be good for you."

Gracie pulled out a bottle of water and handed it to Saige, the girl took a sip and laid on the old mattress as she watched her friend as she rifled through the bag, coming up with the lighter and candle, the dried pineapple in her hands. The candle burned bright enough for them to have a steady orange glow in the room. Gracie ate the bag of pineapple and tossed the trash to the floor.

"Thank you for stopping him," Saige muttered.

"Well you were right about things not being good right now," Gracie scooted her body down so she was eye level with here, "I can't let you die," she said. "Who would I be if you weren't here?"

"I don't know... who would you be?" Saige asked.

"Someone who isn't myself; I think I would become a shell of who I am... but not me entirely. I can't ever let you go from my life, even if Death itself comes at my door."

Saige's eyes drooped and she yawned lightly, "If Death comes knocking at your door, I'll be there to greet him, before he takes you."

Gracie smiled, "get some sleep."

That's just what she did, she and Gracie both fell into a deep sleep; both hoping that maybe when they wake up, it would all be a dream.

We were only human, we couldn't know, we didn't know, we didn't want to know, but the truth hurts. On that night, in that little bedroom, Death made its self present, watching over Gracie as her days of a slow death began.

Over the next few of weeks Saige had tired numerous times to get into the city, but everyway had been blocked; The Boss had held up his threat, he had made it impossible for them to get anymore supplies, and they were nearing the last of their food supply.

Gracie had been up and walking about for a few days after she woke up from her coma, her strength increasing, but after the first week had past, her strength dwindled down to nothing and she felt herself become increasingly weak from daily chores such as walking. She hid her weakened state from Saige, her friend, having done so much for her already; she pushed forward every coming day, though everyday her body felt close to the edge.

They were down to their last water bottle; their rations having all ran out the day before. Saige threw the laundry bag aside with a sigh; she stood and walked to the living area where Gracie was leaning against the window sill.

"So?" She asked, shifting her weight on the worn wood.

Saige shook her head, "I have to go."

"You can't!" Gracie said pushing away from the window, her body swayed from the sudden movement and her weakened limbs shook.

"Whoa there," Saige said, coming forward and stilling her friend as she swayed. "You ok?" She asked looking at her pale face and the dark half moons under her eyes.

Gracie just stepped back, leaning on the window again for support, "I'm fine; but you won't be."

"Ye of little faith," she said with a small smirk.

"Not little faith, just allot of doubt. You said yourself that The Boss has every section blocked off, how are you going to get into the city?"

Saige shrugged, "I have the gun and knife."

Gracie's eyes went white, and she shouted, "You're going to kill again!"

"It's the only thing I can do!" Saige yelled back at her. She shut her eyes and calmed her nerves, "it's the only thing I can do... I can't take care of you if I'm dead."

"But I'm—"

"Oh save it, Grace. Don't think I can't see it, I've been your friend long enough to know when something is wrong. Its offensive that you think I know so little."

Gracie turned her eyes to the floor, "I'm sorry."

"It's alright," she muttered, coming forward and wrapping her arms around her friend, "I love you, I can't not know everything about you. You're my sister."

Gracie turned her head up to Saige and gave her a small smile, "I love you too, I just worry… you know?"

"Hmm, I know. Look I'll be fine," she said, pulling away.

"Do you promise you'll come back?" Gracie asked, holding out her small pinky finger.

Saige smiled, "Pinky promise," she said, entwining her pinky with Gracie's. She walked away into the bedroom and grabbed the now empty laundry bag along with six more bullets from their slowly dwindling down supply; she stuffed the bullets into her pant pocket and checked to make sure the gun was still in her waistband along with the knife in her belt loop. She entered the living area again and stepped in front of the smaller girl. "I'm going now."

"Be careful."

"You too, if you hear anything hide, or see anyone, don't let them take you." Gracie nodded. "Good, take this," Saige said handing her the knife.

Gracie glanced down at the knife she was being handed, "what, no, I can't take this."

"You can and you will. I have the gun, I can't leave you here unprotected; I would never forgive myself if something happened to you," she said. "Now take the knife."

Gracie glanced down at the knife and slid her hand over the handle, "I'll do my best."

Saige let go of the blade and nodded, "I'll try and be back in a couple of hours, if not then I left you the last water, it's not much but it should hold you until morning."

"What happens if you don't return at all?"

"Then you leave this place; get far away from here, if they have me they'll come after you."

Gracie looked at her, "you promised."

"I know," Saige sighed, "And I can promise you I will come back— for you; though, I can't promise that it will be right away."

Gracie swallowed, "Ok, I can live with that," she said, giving her friend a small smile.

"You're brave Gracie, I know that and you know that; now it's time to show the world that." With those words, she left her friend's side and strode out of the cabin.

Gracie turned to watch out the window, her friend disappearing from view. The girl turned away and slid down the wall, her strength finally giving in. Her body shook from its weakened state and she tilted her head back against the wall, her eyes closed to the world. Knife held weakly in her hand. Her body, from the inside, burst into flame and a hot flash of fire washed over her skin as she broke out into a cold sweat.

A floorboard creaked from somewhere in the room and Gracie's head shot up. A man in a black suit stepped from out of the shadows of the room. Gracie quickly tightened her grip on the knife and pushed past her weakened state to stand, facing the man with the knife pointed at him. "Who are you!" She demanded.

The man didn't say anything, only stepping closer until the tip of the knife was touching his chest.

Gracie's wall wavered and her hand began to shake, "Who are you?" She asked, not giving in.

The man lifted a cold death white hand, and gently lowered it onto her shaking hand that held the weapon, pushing it down. The knife fell from her hand and clattered to the floor. He then placed a hand to her forehead and watched as her eyes rolled to the back of her head as she fainted, her body dropping; he caught her limp form and quietly kneeled to the ground, lowering her down. "You can't kill Death, Gracie Davis," he whispered, brushing her hair away from her face, "Nor can you escape me...."

Saige crept silently to the city edge; The Boss had set up guards around the perimeter, making it nearly impossible for her to get in.... nearly being the main objective. The girl crept around the edge, hiding in the brush until she got an opening guarded by only one officer; it was one of opening for the back door of a drug store. "This makes it so much easier," she chuckled silently to herself.

Fortunately for her the officer was turned away, so taking the gun from her waist band she flipped it so she was holding the barrel, and with as little sound as possible she made her way behind him and struck the butt of the gun to his temple as forcefully as possible. The guard's body jerked forward but didn't fall. "Shit," she muttered as he turned around to stare at her. She cocked the weapon and fired once to his head before turning and fleeing. She knew it wouldn't kill him, he wasn't human, the body was just a vessel; it didn't matter to the one occupying it how damaged it got, so long as it had all its body parts attached.

Saige tripped over an uplifted root, her face meeting the ground, the side of her temple smashed against the side of a rock and she saw stars; she shook off the feeling of severe pain and got to her feet, pushing forward. She could hear the mass of bodies coming after her, it was a chase, a hunt, and she was the animal. Her breath was ragged as the pain pulsed through her, her head pounded and she could feel the small trickle of blood making its way down the side of her face from the wound at her temple. Eyes blurring she shook her head and they cleared just in time for her to miss the oncoming tree trunk. They closed in on her, she could feel them breathing down her neck, their breath creating chills down her spin.

"No," she whispered, as she saw the cabin come into view. Her body had unconsciously carried her to the one place she didn't want them to come to. "So stupid," she muttered, as she stopped in the clearing in front of the cabin. She stopped as she listened to the pounding bodies that neared her.

"Well, well, well, look what we have here," said a cool voice form behind Saige.

Saige recognized the voice and turned to face the Boss, her chest heaved as she glared at him.

"I knew you couldn't stay away for long," he said with a smile. "How's your head? Does it hurt?"

Saige dropped to the ground as intense pain shot through her skull, wrapping its sharp tendrils around her mind. She looked up at the man and glared. "What…." Her words got lost as the pain continued and she wrapped her hands around her head.

"What ,what? What am I doing here? Well I'll tell you," he said circling the girl, smiling all the while. "I'm here to kill your friend, have you watch, and then I'm going to watch as every limb on your body is torn from its socket."

Saige's head shot up past the pain and she got to her knees, "you won't touch her!" She screamed, getting to her feet.

The Boss raised an eyebrow at her, "is that so?" Saige's nostrils flared. "Let me tell you something my dear girl, I do what I please, not even my perfect father could stop me."

Large amounts of rustling came from behind Saige as the Boss's guards came from behind her and blocked her entrance and exit.

Saige pushed past the Boss and ran into the cabin, the door slammed open, hitting against the wall. Saige's eyes scanned through the room, stopping at Gracie's body that lay out on the floor. "Get away from her!" She cried at the white figure in black that kneeled over her friend's body.

"Looks like Death is already here," said the smirking voice of the Boss from behind Saige.

Saige dropped to her friend's side and looked down at her pale features, her lips had lost their color, her eyes were sunken in and you could see the veins entwine in patterns across her cheek. Saige's eyes filled with tears, she looked to the figure who had kneeled over Gracie, "your death?" She choked out. The figure nodded, "please don't take her from me." The figure didn't say anything.

The Boss came over and kneeled next to the two girls, he stroked Gracie's hair away from her sweaty face, "such a sweet looking girl," he cooed.

Saige's eyes flared and she slapped his hand away, "don't touch her," she snarled.

The Boss looked up at her, with a smile he said, "God doesn't want her anymore, so if she dies, she'll be mine anyways," he said with a smile.

"What! No, that's not true!"

"Oh, but it is. You see, your friend Gracie here, has fallen from grace; she's been tainted... by me. She has my mark in her skin, it's not visible, but it's there. So you see... God doesn't want something that's such a...disgrace."

"No...no," she whispered, turning to Death. "He's lying, right?"

"I don't lie... I mislead, but never lie."

"That's the same thing! Please," she begged Death, "He's lying right? God wants her... right!" Death didn't say anything. "You can't have her!" She said through clenched teeth at The Boss.

The Boss tsk-ed, "Her soul, is already mine."

Saige looked down at Gracie's small features; she could see what she use to look like, her dirty blonde hair like sunlight in the summer, her skin a light tan... she could never be unhappy when she smiled at her; she couldn't let that go.... Saige turned to Death and looked him in his black eyes, "this is going to sound selfish, it's a selfish request; I can't live in this world knowing she's in a place where she would be hurt, I can't live without her," Saige swallowed heavily. "To save her, I'll give you me."

The Boss scoffed, "What you can't do that."

The two ignored him. "Please," Saige pleaded, "I'll give you my soul in place of hers, just please, please, please save her. I'm begging you."

A hand clamed onto her shoulder in a hard grasp, "hey," The Boss hissed, "it's impossible."

His hand left her shoulder and was replaced by several cold hands clamping around her arms, "no, let me go!" She screamed, "Please! Save her! Please! Just let me take her place, it's yours! My soul is yours, just... save her," She whimpered as her body went lax, her eyes never leaving Death's as the Boss guards dragged her out of the cabin and out into the open area in front of it.

An outraged scream erupted from inside the cabin, though that was the last thing Saige heard as she felt her limbs being pulled in every direction, her body crying out in protest. She closed her eyes and cried out a blood curdling cry as she felt her limbs being torn away from her body, and soon everything was black.

Sometimes, when you don't think you'll ever come out alive, you come out surviving.

Most people say they see a bright light at the end of the tunnel, sort of their passage way to heaven; but all Saige Alison and Gracie Davis saw when they opened their eyes was a white room, nothing more, just a room with white walls and white hardwood flooring. The two girls looked to one another and relief washed over them both, "Grace!" Saige exclaimed, embracing her friend.

"Oh, God, Saige, I thought."

"I know, I thought I had lost you."

"It was never God's intention for either of you to lose each other," said a calm voice in front of them.

The girls pulled away and looked at the face of Death, "where are we?" Gracie questioned.

Death glanced at both in turn, slowly sliding to each face carefully, "Some call it Purgatory, some call it the in-between stages, limbo, the nether world; there are many others but that is just a select few."

Saige peered at him, "what do you call it?"

"I do not call it anything, we just are; we are nowhere, we just are where we are, there is no place or name for it, we just are," he said coolly.

The girls looked at one another before looking back at Death, "what did you mean before? About God's intentions?"

"God needed you for something much greater than to live your days out on earth."

"What does he need?"

"He needs the both of you, to help build it up again."

"Doesn't he already have it? We were just there," Saige said, a small bite to her worlds.

"You've been dead for four months and four days, in that time the world has been completely wiped clean."

"So what? The rapture happened. You're talking apocalypse?"

"There is no such thing as the rapture, simply, just a false prediction created by a woman by the name of Margaret, in Scotland in the 1830s, leading people to believe that if they went to church they would be taken to heaven before the tribulation occurred."

Gracie looked away, thinking for a moment, "wouldn't that be the truth? If you go to church you can be saved."

Death nodded slightly, "yes that is true, to some extent. Not everyone who goes to church though will be saved; they take the grace of God with greed in their heart, wishing only to save themselves. Would they sacrifice every item they possessed in their life, to give it all up for God? No, they most likely wouldn't. Humans' lost their innocence a long time ago; they walked around the world perfectly possessed."

"So, no one was saved?" Saige asked bewildered.

"Some were, not all, but some. Some who thought they would be saved, were not; they took God's forgiveness for granted."

"What about us?" Gracie questioned.

"I can't say what you did personally, God chose you. That is all that matters."

Saige licked her lips, "now what happens?"

"You live." Death same closer and placed one hand over each girls' eyes, removing them minutes later. The scene changed, the white room was gone and they were placed in a world they didn't recognize. It wasn't one dull color but every color; bright green wilderness surrounded them, a blue cloudless sky hung over them while the sun hung bright and glorious, a mellow breeze blew to cool the heat from their faces.

"You once knew this place as Seattle," Death said.

Gracie and Saige looked at their surroundings, noticing they were standing in a large green field that sat at the top of a cliff. All of the land was laid out before them.

Gracie spoke up, "I thought the apocalypse was supposed to result in waste and destruction?"

Death looked away from the scene and turned to the girls, "apocalypse is simply a word, it is not written in stone; it destroyed the world you once knew, but it didn't destroy the one you have yet to know."

"So, what now?" Saige asked.

"Now you find the others, some didn't die; they simply went to sleep to awake to a new day. They're out there, now you need to find them. Lucifer is still out there, he's waiting, you won't find him, and he can't find you, but just know he is out there; make the best of this new beginning." Death turned to the girls. "You've been given a second chance, do with it as you will, but do so wisely." And then he was gone. The girls didn't blink or look away, he simply was gone.

Gracie swallowed and looked to Saige, "so what now?"

"What did Death say to do?"

"He said to find the others'."

"Exactly," Saige said looking to Gracie, "that's exactly what we'll do."

"First we have to get off this cliff," Gracie muttered.

Both girls took one last glance at their unexplored new home and turned away from it, treading through the long grass down the hill, their new life just beginning.

We didn't care about what would happen tomorrow or the next day, or if this was just a dream, we just lived for this moment, for this day. When tomorrow came, we would live for that time, but for now, we live just for today; because if there was one thing I learned in my previous life, is that peace doesn't last forever.

We Are Born Again

Wait for it. Time. It passes slowly.
You don't know, when this darkness will fade,
It's like your body is striving for it,
Yearning for the colors,
For the warmth,
For the touch of the sky.
Just wait for it,
You never know when it will come,
The time, it just ticks by and by,
And you just sit by and by and by.
And it's like forever is coming and going,
Never knowing, when it will arrive.
So just stay, by that window pane,
Watching as the day breaks,
Watching the moon die and the stars
Wash their mark from the sky,
Watch as the sun breaks, from its chains.
It's confined light burning so bright,
It shines! From its veiled light,
It breaks through,
Sunrise. Sunset will never come,
For today is a new day,
The light of hope, of glory, peace, of a new dawning,
It was once confined, but never again.
So watch as the war begins, because now we are born again!

Goodbye

Goodbye is like a sweet kiss, it only comes when it hurts the most.
The people you love disappear and you're left with tears,
A shadow of doubt in your soul,
Thinking it was you who told them to leave.
The pain is like a knife, digging in your spine,
Twisting and gouging in your flesh.
In the hardest time, in the hardest moment, you have to take
That steel from your back. Say goodbye to the pain
Say goodbye to the memories, pushed back into the black abyss
They stay, forever never seen, forever silent
they stay, and they lay, forgotten.
Painful memories are left alone, once the people of old pass.
Though when you don't notice, like a flash
They come back, tidal wave force.
It hurts like a burn, a cut; a tear in your heart.
With a silent prayer your begging, let it end, let it be the end.
Let me say goodbye.
To the past of us laughing, friends are screaming,
and the two of us just being.
I don't need this memory, make it stop, let it disappear.
Let me say goodbye to a once loved thought, word, and deed.
Let me let go of these feeling I hold so close
To a wounded heart, bruised and beaten it stays,
here in my chest it silently cracks.
Let me heal; let me start all over again.
Let me say Goodbye.
No more pain, labored breaths from unshed tears.
This is…Goodbye

Hello
(A child's thoughts)

You say Hello to me
I say Hello to you,
It like the whole world is stopping
But we just keep spinning,
Round, round, round
We go, I never want to stop.
I think its God that tells
Me I have to let go,
Its hard, but I drop my fingertips
I watch as you fly by,
Spinning around.
Round, round, round
You go, I watch you go by,
Waving my hand, saying farewell.
God told me I had
A gift to give:
A smile, a hug, a friend
These are my gifts,
I am here,
Just for you,
Giving away my presents,
Leaving them there for you.
I dance for so long,
A merry little twirl,
Until he tells me its time.
And then its stops.
And you go by,
I say farewell,
I have done my job.
It hurts, but that's all right,
Because here is you,

Another friend of mine.
I say Hello to you,
You say Hello to me,
And soon were dancing,
Round, round, round we go.

Surrender
(Never surrender... not in life)

Broken, inside, afraid to see yourself.
Emotions, inside you,
Conflicting,
A raging war inside your soul.
You're afraid, to see yourself,
Shattered pieces of the glass,
Broken beneath you.
Mirror, mirror on the wall,
Help to see the path that I may take.
It's hard to see
When your eyes are shut tight,
Creeping away
From the pain,
Shield away.
Your stupid thoughts, set scars,
Embedded in your bones.
The mirror on the wall,
Shows you the monster
You are becoming.
It cracks and fails, falling to shards,
No matter, it can't be helped,
Your soul is falling,
You are fighting,
It wishes to surrender,
I want to surrender.
I will surrender.
I will never surrender.

For You

Take me in all that I am,
Take me in as the child I am,
Take me in as the sad little girl.
Take me in as your child from blessing;
Take me in as the innocent.
Take me in as I am.
I was born for You,
From Your lips
Came a prayer,
And here I am,
Just for You.
This is I,
In all Your light
Kneeling for you
Take me in
As I am.
The gate of light won't
Open, just yet
I know.
I am not finished,
You have a prayer for me
A single last request,
I must complete:
To live in a world full
Of hate and strife,
That I may bring some joy,
Not to all, but one or two,
A few may I call,
To talk about You.
For You Are
That prayer,
That single last request,

For in Your name
I shall bring two
Kneeling souls,
That they may be
Children for You,
In Your kingdom,
For eternity.

Naked

I am naked,
I can't help it.
I am bare
As the day I was born,
Welcome to new feelings
I cannot explain this sensation.
This is me, whole,
Complete,
In my state of nudity.
I feel my emotions washing over me.
This is me, naked,
Bare,
In every morning color.
I am Adam's Eve,
This is who I am.
I feel changes,
In who I am
I can't explain it
This is me,
I feel the wind
Like a gentle caress,
It touches me and I touch it back.
My naked skin
Has become whole
I am not afraid
Of my nudity,
My feelings full force,
They are exposed,
I guess that's a good thing,
No matter how weird I may seem,
I am naked in this light,
And no one can stop me,
For I am free.

If I Die Today

If I die tomorrow
Would there be no more sorrow?
If I die in a year
Will there be no more tears?
If I die today
Would you even care?
I can't change how I've acted,
I can't change how I've been.
This path is not where I started
How did I get all the way over here?
My feelings are numb
My soul is still
The breath in my body
Has become no more
I have never been here before.
I don't know words to describe this
A feeling like wanting to drown
I'm being pulled under
The water is tugging
It wants my coral reef soul.
It was once beautiful and whole
Full of color and life
But over the years it's become
Damaged and shattered
Too many pieces
To put back together
So if I die today
Would you even care?

White

White.
A plain color,
Figment of light,
A Piece
Of something
Unfinished.
It stays unfinished,
not colored
Within the lines it stays,
Never going over
That boundary.
White just stays.
It stays and never goes.
Plain and simple, it is;
No red, orange, or yellow,
The green, blue, and purple
Has gone from it.
Is it proud?
To be alone.
No company it holds,
Just stands alone,
With nothing to comfort it
In its darkest of shades of creams,
So why does it stay?
Alone, all alone?
No gentle green,
No mellow orange,
No calming water,
No passionate fire,
They are gone,
Leaving white.
The plain sad color,

Told them to go,
It wanted no one,
It wanted to be alone.

Big FAT Thank Yous

OK, so as you can tell, this is the Thank You page. I personally think that every book should have this page, why? Because allot of people are involved in the process of getting a book ready for stores, it's a long road and the people who help you for no fee, or for a little one, or even a large one, deserve a public thank you.

Here is my big fat public thank you to all those who have helped me with this book.

For starters, I would like to thank all the people who read the first few chapters of **Loving Wildflowers** on the fan fiction site THF, along with the stories **The Perfect Match, Bury Me in the Frozen Ground, Bury Me in a Blanket of Rose Petals, Snow, Goodbye** (previously known as Silence), and **Finding Balance**. Once I realized I wanted everyone to read these stories and not just a select few, I took them off and began to make this collaboration. Also, the people on that site who made banners for those particular stories, thank you; the covers gave the story a finished feel to it when it was posted on that site.

My dad always gave me the best dreams at night about daring adventures and of course, he told me he was a pirate (which to me he still is!), so I loved having dreams of swashbuckling pirates and the raging sea. So I thank my dad for always supporting in my writing and for giving me that talent.

My Mum for being the best critique I know, she helped me allot with growing up and being the best possible mother I know.

My brother, well, he didn't help, but I love him anyways.

Finally, to the people at AuthorHouse Publishing and everyone who worked with them and myself to get this book published. Now, I don't exactly know their names because well, while writing this I haven't met them yet, reason, is because when you do self-publishing you usually end up sending in your book before you meet the team who works on your cover and printing etc…, well that's how its working out for me….

Heather Rivière for doing my French Translations.

Alyss Ann Callia for being a great friend and looking over my German translations.

Last but most certainly not least, the Whytock Scottish Scribes, thanks to them I have a last name that means writer; it must be fate.

I guess that's all; you know when I'm re-reading this page, to me it sounds like a speech I'm giving at a big event, how un-original….

What's an ending without the words, "The End"?
Not an ending at all.

THE END!

CPSIA information can be obtained at www.ICGtesting.com
Printed in the USA
LVOW122231230911

247645LV00002B/39/P